FLESHLY
ATTRACTIONS

FLESHLY
ATTRACTIONS

René Maizeroy

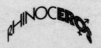

This is a complete translation of the novel, "La Peau," by René Maizeroy.

First Rhinoceros Edition 1995

First Printing July 1995

ISBN 1-56333-299-X

Cover Photograph © 1995 by Trevor Watson

Cover Design by Dayna Navaro

Manufactured in the United States of America
Published by Masquerade Books, Inc.
801 Second Avenue
New York, N.Y. 10017

PART THE FIRST

I

Was Lucien Hardanges the son of the Marquis d'Albevine? The old fogies of the Jockey Club said so, in those odd moments of small talk when they seemed as if turning over the pages of some bygone *Almanach de Gotha* of venal love; when they raked the cold ashes of memory and evoked remembrances of the Opera ballet, the Tuileries balls, the festivals of the Château de Compiègne and all the forgotten glories of the Second Empire.

Perhaps Lucien's father was Napoule, the tenor, who never slept two consecutive nights in the same boudoir and drove women crazy, thanks to his velvet voice and its supple tones, recalling the songbirds of his native Toulouse. He was too handsome for a man. His features resembled the head of a hermaphrodite as sometimes seen on cameos dug up in Pompeii. Now and again his fancy led him to grant the charity of a night of pleasure to some immature actress unknown to fame and let her have a small taste of the joys of that paradise in his arms which she had heard of and envied, causing her to cast begging glances at him as she found means to brush against the great singer in the wings. Mme. Baldieux, the oldest *ouvreuse* of the Bouffes Parisiens theatre, swore that the author of Lucien's being was the Count de Roccavecchia, of the Pope's bodyguard. At one time he had come to the Gay City, bringing the baretta to the Cardinal-Archbishop of Paris. The Italian nobleman had wandered from theatre to theatre, seeking for the youngest apprentice-courtesans; green fruit to be plucked without falling foul of the law; without having to pay those high prices which sweep away a fortune almost as quickly as a dog licks a platter clean. Maybe, all said and done, Lucien's sire was a passer-by whose name was never to be revealed, a client having no time to lose in flirtation, but who buys an actress's photograph in a shop on the Boulevards, shows it to a procuress, asks the price and gets his money's worth, standing on no ceremony and avoiding all sentimentality; footing the bill of half-a-night's voluptuousness exactly as if settling for a restaurant supper or a ride in a hired vehicle.

His mother was Marie-Rose Hardanges, the star of operetta who had caused the sly suggestiveness of Hortense Schneider to be forgotten. Saucy Marie-Rose, with her ringing, clear, fresh voice had galvanised the old-fashioned scores of Offenbach and was now the first among the footlight favourites of Paris. She would have been greatly puzzled to give a name to the father of her boy or even to try to guess who was responsible for his entry into the world. Had she wished to resent what was called during the XVIIIth century in France: "a lack of politeness," she would not have known whom to scold.

At first, she thought that there was nothing to fear. She

was only behindhand in her monthly reckoning, because through rehearsing by day, acting till midnight, and bending her loins in the gymnastics of real lubricity enjoyed to the full from the final fall of the curtain to daybreak, the delicate machinery of her sexual organisation might have been thrown out of gear. But when the second month had gone by, the poor creature realised that she was certainly *enceinte*; that soon she would be no good either as singer or courtesan; that she would have to drag her deformed body slowly along and worry herself to death in idle seclusion for months. She lost her wits. There was no room in her brain but for a savage and morbid resolve: abortion. A riddance of the burden. There must be some way to tear from her flanks, no matter how, the germ of life developing therein, growing larger day by day like a seed fallen in rich, fecund, healthy soil. Hiding her face behind thick veils, her forehead wrinkling with rage and anguish, conquering her instinctive fear of death in the torture to which she was self-condemned, the little woman went and bought drugs, sought succour from shady midwives who got money out of her and granted her no deliverance. She supplicated doctors who took advantage of her madness, subjecting her to prolonged examination, overwhelming her with salacious fingering of her thighs, so pink and white, and of her sex complacently offered to their investigation, until they finally thrust her from their consulting-rooms with feigned indignation and disgust. She tried everything to destroy the life within her. She buckled herself tightly in an iron corset that bruised her flesh like a nun's hair-shirt. In despair, preferring to perish sooner than live thus vilely swollen, as she repeated during nightly fits of sobbing in her dressing-room, she scalded and tumefied her sweet body in baths heated almost to boiling point. But neither the intoxication of absinthe, nor burning, revulsive injections, nor voluntary falls, nor wild rides on horseback succeeded.

When undressed at night before getting into bed, she looked at herself, stark in the mirror of her wardrobe, and saw her shining skin already stretched as tight as a drum from hip to hip, with the magnifying curve of pregnancy, Marie-Rose spat at her reflection as at something filthy, while digging her fingernails into her belly.

"Why don't the beastly thing drop down?" she cried out with the hysterical intonation of a woman writhing in the throes of insanity.

From the day when the child moved for the first time in her being, when this tremor of life shook her from head to heel, she became resigned. Unknown sacred repose, mysterious and profound stupor overcame her. She accepted the ordeal with passive submission which, little by little, changed slowly and strangely into sweet joy, like a stormy sky cleared and cleansed by showers.

So Lucien was born in an outburst of laughter and happiness, not like a young imp in a family of poverty-stricken outcasts, cursed because of thoughts of another mouth to be filled, another obstacle in the fight for daily bread, but like a babe born to wealthy folks—a mite to be petted at once and swaddled with loving solicitude.

Marie-Rose adored her son with the instinct of an animal. He developed haphazard among the ups and downs of the chorus-girl gradually working her way to the top of the bill. He educated himself all alone, without studies, tuition, or ever obeying anybody. College life, even as day-scholar or at an expensive boarding-school, terrified this mother of a doll. Either because she imagined it would bring her luck, or by some mania of maternity, or else out of fear of approaching old age, she prolonged her son's artificial infancy in silly fashion, far beyond the first fruits of puberty.

He turned out a fine example of a lad growing up in the manure of love. He was the bold boy full of insolent repartee, searching in the pockets of his mother's lovers, tossing off the contents of half-emptied champagne glasses, listening at doors, getting to understand too soon what he ought never to have known and being too young to witness the visions of vice that none sought to hide from him. When only twelve years of age, he would turn out the gas in the pantry and put his hands under the skirts of the ladies-maids. His actress-mamma roared with merriment when hearing of his audacity, encouraging and questioning him. The outspoken thoughts of little Lulu went the round of the clubs and were whispered between men of the world after dinner. He was scarcely able to scribble a letter in the awkward, stiff hand-writing of a dunce, abridging words and smearing hieroglyphics to hide mistakes in spelling. An addition of a few figures was beyond his powers and all he could talk about was the scandal of the world behind the scenes.

Marie-Rose saw herself reflected in her son as though in a mirror. His features had no particular character, being those of any clubman, or man-about-town you like, but his disposition was marked with the maternal stamp. Like the star of opera-bouffe, he was nervy and always ready to fly into a passion for nothing at all. He had inherited his mother's coarse humour, the fun of the streets, and resembled a girl with masculine tastes to such an extent that sometimes the actress laughingly addressed him as *mademoiselle*. To while away an idle hour, she would dress him up in one of her frocks or a lace-trimmed *peignoir*.

"You're much too good-looking!" she would then foolishly exclaim, as she smothered him with caresses.

His mother alone was blind to the fact that he was on the threshold of manhood; that his nostrils were dilated when a perfumed beauty passed; that he became absorbed in long reveries; that he was drawn towards unknown delights as if following a will-o-the-wisp. Mme. Hardanges was only a little jealous, and kept anxious watch over him when women—friends from the theatre and companions of orgies—kissed him full on the mouth instead of lightly touching his cheeks with their lips. He carried himself like a young fighting-cock, flapping his wings, just beginning to crow, stalking round the hens in the poultry-yard and at first his conquering manner diverted her hugely. She laughed to see his glances stray towards the petticoats, and suddenly lapse into silence; then toss his head proudly and blush deeply because some kept-woman signalled to him with her feather fan, while a sly smile hovered on her carmine lips. When the son accompanied his mother home from the theatre at night, she would warble like a thrush that had been too long among the vineyards.

"Did you notice how they were all making eyes at you—every one of them? Especially Nini Seigneur in the O. P. box. If you cared, you could make a fine cuckold of her friend, fat old Baron Silberstein. As for Jeanne Roulin, she'd give her right hand to be able to get rid of her Italian count and take you on instead." Shaking a warning finger at him, Marie-Rose continued, murmuring in accents of pleasure: "Only fancy! My little boy keeps the girls awake all night thinking about him and he hasn't a hair on his upper lip yet!"

Then, under the influence of her habits and her natural promptings, flying suddenly from one idea to another, and becoming reasonable once more, she took fright at her boy's first start in the race of love and realised the seriousness of the situation. She regretted all her foolish impudent companionship, upbraiding herself for not having seen farther through her natty veil than the end of her nose. All women seemed to be her enemies. Their utterances and movements required careful watching. She burned all the libertine letters addressed to Lucien. She protected him from dangerous contact. With all her strength and cunning, she tried to delay the inevitable result of this struggle. She sought to divert her youngster, lead him back into infancy, and extinguish the flames she had kindled and fed like a demented female preparing tragical incendiary fires and ruin, laughing and singing the while. Her wee, birdlike brain seemed suddenly to have struck against a great black wall. She was maddened by the mist hiding the morrow where she saw the embraces of love. Sounds of kissing and the moans of voluptuous enjoyment struck on her ears. In life were unique moments upon which depended all future illusions, beliefs, and downfalls. What mistress would capture her offspring? Which mouth would efface the bloom of her boy's fresh and sensitive lips? What bed would receive the novice, and veil with its coverlet his feverish curiosity and simple, tender caresses?

Marie-Rose could not sleep at nights for thinking of all this and suffered from fits of rebellion as if she had just seen her son off on a long journey from which there were fifty chances in a hundred that he would never return. She was bound to expect the most terrible shocks and deplorable adventures in the case of a young fellow like Lucien, by reason of his upbringing, weakness, precocity, natural charm, and a dormant heart that might suddenly begin to beat strongly when a spark of desire would light the torch of lubricity.

Perhaps some siren might fall madly in love with him, steal him away from his mother, strip him of all boyish affection, debase him by humiliating submission, chain him in unbreakable fetters, imprison him, drown him in such a sea of salacity that he would sink and be lost like a rudderless ship in a raging storm. Suppose some heartless jade were to cause him to suffer until he contemplated suicide, tearing his flesh and his heart on the sharp stones of an endless path of torture, disgusting him with everything, blinding him with tears, spoiling his dawn of love like a witch bestowing bad luck, cheating, betraying him, and replying to his ecstasy and his devout, confiding appeals by treachery, mockery, and falsehood? No one better than Marie-Rose knew what they were capable of, these wretches who trafficked with their bodies, putting a price on their love as if it was a rare commodity. There might be one having an eye to his mother's fortune, prompting him to get hold of the packets of banknotes in her jewel-case. Such a creature would empty his pockets daily, make him run into debt, and drag him towards the abyss that swallows up money, honour and everything else. Or another danger: that of contracting low tastes. There are crapulous prostitutes in the streets who hang on to a boy's arm, bewildering him with promises, holding him fast, leading him to an unmade bed, still warm from a recent battle in the lists of Venus. And what of beer-shop waitresses, with plastered fringes of hair over bold eyes and mouths reeking of cigarettes and spirits? And the perils of brothels; the consequences of vile debauchery: illnesses corrupting the blood and changing the strongest, healthiest man into a yellow-faced invalid with stooping frame and palsied hands?

To sum up: illicit union separating and removing the most affectionate and docile son from his mother; the martyrdom of unrequited love; the fall into the lowest depths of depravity; a state of rottenness.

Ashamed at such a show of misery, Marie-Rose Hardanges began searching in person to find a mistress for her son as carefully as if she had been in quest of a maiden to whom he might become engaged.

When Lucien was a baby, she had had him suckled by a young and pretty wet-nurse. Marie-Rose desired that his little impatient hands should mould rosy breasts of a delicate odour, swelling like ripening fruit. Between them, his hunger appeased, the child slumbered as if his head rested on a soft, resilient pillow. Each time he woke, his glance fell on a face surmounted by a forest of golden hair; pulpy lips of healthy redness parted in a smile illuminated by the pearly whiteness of the teeth and the gleam of eyes making one think of starlight. Following the same line of thought, she would have liked her son's initiation in love to have been an ascent to heaven, leaving a lasting impression on his heart, without spoiling his freshness and leaving no bitter dregs behind. In her conversation, she skilfully put leading questions concerning women, getting to know his thoughts without appearing to do so; interrogating him about his feminine acquaintances and their lovers. She offered cordial welcome to all damsels unknown to fame in the demi-monde, newcomers in the world of gallantry, and began again to create a whirl of diversion, seeking in every possible way never to stop music, dancing, and merriment from resounding in her pretty little house on the right bank of the Seine, not a stone's throw from the Champs Elysées.

It was at one of these gay gatherings that Andrée Clarette noticed the son of her friend and fellow-actress. Up to the present, Andrée had paid no more attention to him than to any other child. Now she saw he had become a man and she felt that she desired to be possessed by him. In her own parlance: "She was beginning to be gone on him." She was bored—in a fit of the blues. It was only because she wished to please Marie-Rose that she had made up her mind to put on a low-necked ball-dress and drag her melancholy self from her sofa where, stifling all dull thoughts, she slumbered by the side of the fire, lazily noting remembrances and dreams arising in the glowing embers. Her protector, Prince Tchernadieff, escorted her, and he was still puffing and blowing from the scolding and nagging with which she had unceasingly annoyed him on the way, during the discussions that cropped up between them without a cause. As soon as they reached the threshold of the first reception-room, the actress, with her usual impertinence, made haste to get rid of him and looked towards the couples waltzing in the light to see if she could find any men she knew.

She was simply attired, her golden locks drawn up over her temples in a careless tuft shading her forehead where a diamond crescent sparkled. Her gown was of stiff silk, straight and rigid, embroidered with scattered daisies as in an April landscape. The skirt was without a crease; short, almost hieratic, showing tiny satin shoes. Her V-shaped bodice was boldly open and in the point at the end of the dividing line of her naked back were Parma violets, nestling as in a vase. In front, under the adorable twin globes that seemed as if about to free themselves and bound proudly forward, was a glittering arrow of brilliants, a symbol and a challenge. Her waist was girt with a schoolgirl's narrow sash. She was radiantly beautiful, evoking visions of flowers, bright skies, and stained-glass windows. As she passed, there arose in her wake a murmur of joy and supplication.

Lucien, who had just prepared all the trifles needed for the *cotillon*, caught sight of her from afar and rushed to offer his arm. Fatigued, she leant upon it heavily.

"How nice of you to have come!" said the lad, drawing her away from the crowd and striking an attitude of devoted attention with all the cunning of a man who knows the value of a few minutes' halt between dances at a ball.

As he ceased speaking, Andrée's sharp ears made out amidst the buzz of chattering voices a sudden exclamation of Jacques Borys, the painter, as with an almost imperceptible nod, he drew the attention of Thouvenin, the fat comedian of the Gymnase theatre and the Marquis de Ramelles, an old man-about-town.

"A splendid couple, by the Lord! Who wouldn't play Peeping Tom when they go full speed ahead?"

"Rest easy!" retorted Thouvenin. "Clarette has no use for fancy men."

Andrée did not hear the actor's reply. With rapid steps, Lucien and Andrée had reached the conservatory, now deserted. Amidst water-lilies, a jet of water as thin as a silver thread fell with a monotonous sob in a marble basin. The leaves of the palms striped the silken blinds with the tragical shadows of threatening, crossed sword-blades. Azaleas looked like big red-and-white bouquets, while strange orchids bent forward as if proffering lips to kiss, or hovered like great moths. Suddenly, beyond these verdant screens, there arose above the murmur of small talk, the rhythm of a languid waltz. Its alluring melody, swinging on the violins' shrillest strings, enticed couples with the effect of church bells on a holiday; inciting to sweet clasping as intoxicating as kisses.

Clarette's features lit up with a mysterious smile akin to that of a nymph listening in the twilight to the hoarse cries of satyrs' desire. Without a word, throwing her fan on a chair, she abandoned herself to the young man's grasp and carried him away with her in a giddy whirl.

Both were equally skilful in the manœuvres of the American waltz. They knew how to advance continually in languid, voluptuous, furtive contact. Their steps kept time in slow measure resembling the murmur of the waves; the tide eddying in currents, coming up and retreating, at first interrupted, then dashing away again. Andrée, with feline suppleness, pressed her entire frame against Lucien, revealing beneath the silken fabric which now appeared to be glued to her body, the whole mystery of her beauty and everything that was desirable and shameless in her from bosom to knees; offering all her soft and perfumed flesh to his nostrils as if she had presented him with a bottle of scent. While they were waltzing thus, the actress at one moment half-closed her eyes with an expression of languid enjoyment. She was absorbed in selfish delight, revelling in the acuity of the sensation; and then she opened her entrancing orbs quite wide, dilated, burning with desire, fixing their glance on the lad's face with feverish sternness, as if she wished their fire to brand him to the marrow with an indelible mark.

The waltz concluded, he was well-nigh witless, not knowing what he was saying and no longer supporting Clarette with his arm, but rather leaning on her.

"We must have another dance—mustn't we? It was lovely!" he stammered prayerfully.

Andrée did not reply. She seemed absent. Her thoughts were far away—heaven knows in what lost regions! She stood quite still, betraying her emotion and her lack of willpower by the deep wrinkle that made a dent between her eyebrows; by the languor that swam in her big eyes, enhanced by dark crescents beneath. She seated herself among the cushions of a broad sofa, her legs outstretched, her body half-reclining. One might have sworn she was ready to let herself go with defence against hands about to seize her; to flatten her down on her back with brutal force in order that she be violated, supremely caressed, and thus her fever abated. She thrust her fingernails into the silken pillows, like a cat having her loins tickled and her fur smoothed by tender touches. Despite her innate frigidity, she felt herself moved by the lust it had diverted her to excite in Lucien. She submitted to the despotism of animal longing. She shuddered as if she still felt the young man's fingers, stiffening now and again as they moulded her waist and pressed her hand; as if the sign of virility that touched her body was rubbing against her still, adhering to her, at each step and turn of the dance, like a magnet full of mysterious strength and indescribable vibrations.

She thought how exquisite it would be to enjoy without cheating, lying, exciting her imagination, or feeding on fancies which could only be intoxicating for a second, spurring a *blasé* brain and awakening sleeping senses. Was it possible to really enjoy—only for once—in such a way as to shriek with glee, to die in delight; to enjoy as she had never been able since she had become a toy passing from hand to hand, condemned to sing unceasingly the same noisy and commonplace songs? She wanted to know the effect of the clumsy voluptuous strength of this boy, now she saw that he had lost all patience and courage, growing pale and suffering with the desire to be taken in her arms, to penetrate her being and engulph himself in an abyss of delight. Thus might she profit by a halt of happiness, without a morrow, but bequeathing magnificent memories that would serve to comfort and sometimes intoxicate her.

Lucien leant over Clarette as if she were guiding him and hypnotizing him with the phosphorescent gleams of her melting orbs; the pink flesh of her bust; the smooth whiteness of her dress. He trembled and could scarcely contain himself. As each second went by, Andrée was more and more wildly delighted, drunk with the caress of his hot breath, on the point of swooning madly with divine anguish, as happy as if really possessed by him, as if their bodies were already joined, melted, and welded in one.

"I love you! I want you!" groaned the youth, his lips on hers, in a kiss that was like a savage bite.

Encouraged by Clarette's silence, her seeming submissiveness, and her slowly closing eyelids, with a fierce clutch he pulled up her ball-dress and his hand began to explore the under-world of silk and lace.

At that moment, an English nobleman, Lord Shelley, appeared at the entrance of the conservatory, throwing apart the bamboo strips incrusted with pearls, forming a luminous curtain that barred his way. Followed by a crowd of laughing women, he was amusing them by acting the part of a guide explaining to tourists in a museum. Room-by-room, he showed them over the house of Marie-Rose Hardanges, pointing out with dry humour pictures and objects of art.

Lucien just had time to sit up straight, masking the young actress with his shadow while she smoothed her petticoats, with a start of fury and annoyance. But the embarrassment of the couple had not escaped the club-man's observation. He was all the more pleased, because he owed Clarette a grudge on account of having been formerly slighted, so he stared at them through his eyeglass and smiled.

"Don't trouble about us, I beg you!" he said, bowing with exaggerated mocking respect. "I'll change the itinerary for the ladies."

Forcing the curious young women to retreat, he led them away, giving rise to shouts of laughter as he declared loudly: "This section of the apartments is only open to the public on week-days. It is reserved for the lady friends of the mistress of the house."

The girls put saucy questions to him, begging for more ample details, as one of the naughty damsels, Suzette Listrac, had stuck her pretty head under the nobleman's arm and recognised Lucien Hardanges. Shelley continued to play the clown.

"She's a dry nurse and takes them on as soon as they're weaned!" he exclaimed with feigned solemnity.

"Who do you mean?"

"Clarette, of course!"

"Oh! Then it was Andrée Clarette who was there with the stripling?"

"Nobody else—in a quiet corner."

"Take my world, old sport," broke in Marthe Gournay, who was always cast for the parts of innocent young ladies at the Comédie Française. "I'd rather be in my shoes than in yours. Your bit o' fun will cost you dear."

Lord Shelley shrugged his shoulders with the don't-care gesture of a man who attaches no more value to a woman's threat than to the bark of a chained poodle. He continued his imitation of a cicerone.

Clarette had not spoken a word, having dropped back as if dazed. She was appalling by reason of her livid pallor; her fixed stare; her bust leaning forward, moving from right to left with the monotonous swaying of insanity; her knees parted as if she suffered from some smarting burn; her mouth bleeding through having bitten her lips

Once more, the orchestra struck up a waltz as if to make fun of her and twist the dagger in the wound that hurt them both. Lucien, stupefied, leaning against a great Dutch vase under the spreading leaves of a tropical plant, looked like a roysterer having lost his way at night, resting against a post until the effect of too much champagne should wear off. At last, the actress seemed to wake up and, like a banker at the baccarat table tearing up the cards after an unlucky run and who wants to glut his rage on somebody or something, no matter what, she picked up her fan, broke it, scattered the fragments, trampled on them, covering the Pompeian mosaic pavement of the conservatory with scraps of white feathers and odds and ends of blond tortoise-shell studded with the brilliants of a jewelled monogram.

"If ever I get myself in such a mess again, I'll make a hole in the water!" she muttered hoarsely.

The boy was staring at her in dull consternation. Without looking at him; without the consolation of a promise, or even saying "good-bye," she flew past him as fast as a frightened fawn, fleeing from the conservatory as if the spot was accursed. She hurried hither and thither among the gay crowd of revellers until she stumbled against her Prince. In the midst of this gathering where high and low society had sent representatives, he had found friends from Petrograd, and was having a good time discussing scandals relating to the Théâtre Michel and the Grand Dukes.

Clarette hailed him in harsh accents. "Wherever did you get to? I've been searching after you for the last hour."

"I've never stirred from here, my dear," he replied. He rose, his acquaintances following his example. "Allow me to introduce you to Count Mohiloff, lieutenant of the Imperial Guards, and Baron Serge Tcherkowski."

She hardly seemed to see the Russians.

"I'm bored stiff in this bazaar!" she said, interrupting her lover. "Let's be off!"

The Prince took care to make no objection and deeply bowed with the indifference that he always showed when with Clarette.

"As you please, little woman."

A week later, in the reserved enclosure at the Auteuil race-meeting, when the bar was crowded during an insipid walk-over, the Prince, worked up by his mistress and delighted, by obeying her, to get a few crumbs of love and to be able to show off in the Parisian world of highflyers, went up insolently to Lord Shelley after having imbibed a small bottle of Pommery.

"His lordship has a way of staring at women that makes me sick!"

"To what kind of women do you allude?" replied the

Englishman without turning a hair and as impertinently as the Prince.

"That's got nothing to do with you!"

"Then go to hell!"

The Prince flipped the lord's cheek with his fingers' ends as a matter of form and they fought a duel with pistols next day in an alley of the Saint-Cloud park. At the second exchange of bullets, Lord Shelley's arm was broken.

"It's cheap, considering my stupid indiscretion!" he grumbled, laughing despite acute pain.

Clarette thus had the best of the deal, although in her spiteful hopes of revenge, she had hoped that the Prince would have aimed at his adversary's heart, nailing him for months on a bed of pain and not have been satisfied to wing him gallantly. Nevertheless, she was obliged to confess inwardly that she was more bored than ever; "that she was always thinking about that boy." He pleased her and this caprice of an hour still dominated her with growing violence, impressing her brain and her entire being.

III

S he tried to shake off her thoughts and battled against the temptation. But through being thus repelled and suppressed, the desire was reborn with still keener, livelier intensity, gripping her flesh which for so many years past had proved refractory to carnal promptings, and took root as deeply as that of a wild flower in the chink of a wall. It seemed as if some fatality led on the twain, throwing them into each other's arms and forcing them to fall in love despite the difference in their ages.

Lucien's remembrance of the actress was deeper than her dreams of him. He was haunted by the memory and the savour of that kiss so quickly interrupted; by the dazzling gleam of her fair hair; her crimson lips; her supple, scented, marvellous body which he had been on the point of possessing. The sap of his youth seethed, boiled over, laid him low, maddened him with voluptuous hallucinations during long nights when, burdened by solitude, the adorable image of Clarette appeared at his beside; and also in the daytime, when idle, without work or occupation to stifle his aching need; having no pecuniary cares, heartfelt anxiety or longing imagination, he lapsed into idiocy, unable to break the spell or attain any other end.

He could not keep his secret and only one evening sufficed for his mother to know all. She did nothing more than mention Clarette's name and narrate a few funny stories about her as if they were mere matters of no importance, but making out that there was more behind; only she was too discreet to tell tales out of school. Marie-Rose paused for Lucien's questions to follow and the stripling, blushing rosy red, broke down and gave himself away, so happy was he to tear off the stifling mask of concealment and open his mind to mamma, whose blind, tender indulgence and passionate affection he knew so well.

To see them after dinner, their chairs pushed close together; their elbows on the tablecloth, mother and son might have been taken for two companions who, at the end of a peaceful meal, in shaded lamplight, empty their hearts, voice their hopes, and lumping together regrets and the sweets and bitters of life before starting on some dangerous errand to stake the share of happiness and ill-luck that falls to the lot of every living creature; and who, in order to be more resolute and prudent, exchange avowals, advice, and hopes. Lucien was uneasy. The prettiest of Parisian actresses was so far away from him. What money she spent on her dresses, pleasure-trips and household expenses! Never would she treat him seriously. Besides, merely for a passing caprice, no woman would risk losing a lover like Prince Tchernadieff who, according to what Lucien had got to know behind the scenes at the Opera, was able to spend seven millions of francs yearly without knocking a corner off his capital. He was the owner of emerald mines in the Oural mountains; considered that it was impossible to fool him and that his mistress was paid to be his slave.

"It seemed good fun to flirt with me, on the night of the ball," Lucien exclaimed despairingly, a sob choking his utterance. "Since then she has forgotten all about me. Don't you believe anything else."

Marie-Rose, greatly moved, wiped away a tear, and suddenly catching hold of her son's hands, she sat him forcibly on her knees, as in those days when he was so babyish that by coaxing him and smothering him with kisses, she always pacified him, changing her child's sulky little face into one bathed in smiles that seemed to her more beautiful than anything in the world.

"You great stupid!" she whispered. "No woman can help loving you!"

Thus reassured, Lucien continued with persistence that admitted of no objections: "Clarette is your friend—isn't she, mamma?"

"My very best friend, I may say."

"Well, then, talk to her about me. Tell her everything—how she has driven me crazy, so that I don't know whether I'm on my head or my heels. Let her understand that she ought to love me as much as I love her. You can work on her feelings like you do with lots of people when it suits you. Beg her to listen to you, if necessary. Don't say no! If you do, I shall fancy you don't love me any more."

"I give you my word, darling, that I'll do all you want, but you must swear never to love her more than me."

"You're jealous, mamma!"

"Swear?"

"To please you, I take my oath never to love any

woman more than my mother," he replied with a laugh.

He assured Marie-Rose that she would always monopolise his sweetest, most tender and constant affection and hugged her with such strength and joy, kissing her so frenziedly that the actress murmured:

"That's a kiss which is wrongly addressed!"

She rejoiced at this unexpected drama revealed by the curtain rising on the prologue. Her hopes were fulfilled; her son's first steps in love led him to satisfy a passing fancy of Andrée Clarette. He would begin his apprenticeship of love with a queen of delicate debauchery skillful in meretricious art, incapable of sentimental attachment, or of romantic, foolish fidelity which might endanger the future of two lives. She would simply inculcate her perversity in Lucien together with her experience and knowledge of the world without letting him commit any act of folly. At the same time, such a conquest would be a feather in his cap. Could a loving mother wish for anything better?

With great compliance, she put her shoulder to the wheel, joined in the game, allowed both to confide in her in turn and, far from putting obstacles in their way, she cunningly arranged meetings for them, watched over them stealthily, and gave them the run of her house where they were in safety, sure of not being seen or caught by surprise. Mamma pretended to be blind and not troubling about childish romps that were of no importance; or the frivolous flirtation of a woman of leisure trying to pass the idle hours away pleasantly. She invited Clarette to luncheon continually whenever the actress had no rehearsals or matinées. Marie-Rose knew how to have herself called away on some urgent business or the other, and so disappear, leaving the couple alone together on a sofa in the half-light of a cosy boudoir with curtains drawn, amidst the faint scent of cut flowers. Mamma's delight was to hide behind some tapestry, listen to their talk, and peep at them through a little hole that she had herself cut in the heavy hangings.

It made her heart beat fast to witness this exciting scene; to hear the uninterrupted music of the kisses that filled the snug room as with the fluttering of tiny songbirds, and see her "big baby," as she often called Lucien, by the side of a woman whose waist he enlaced with delicious clumsiness, only venturing to kiss the tips of her fingers and her hair. She revelled in her boy's delight and felt something akin to gratitude towards the woman he loved who filled him with celestial joy.

Full of confidence, quite easy in her mind by this time, fancying that the amour would not last more than five or six months at the most, Marie-Rose left Paris for Buenos Aires where an impresario offered her a thousand dollars for every performance. Marie-Rose calculated that she would be back just in time to sweep away the still-warm ashes of this little romance and appease the smart of Lucien's first disillusion.

IV

All of a sudden, strident trumpets and the bugle calls of battle sound a hymn of blood and fury, mingled with the despairing appeals of virgins pursued by a horde of rutting males, died away, changing into a vague murmur, but so soft and sweet that it resembled the pastoral hum of meadows awakening at the dawn of a June day. Far away, the blue immensity of the ocean was clouded by mists gradually fading, wreathing until metamorphosed into perfect bodies of languishing nereids swooning with love as they rose from the sea. Venus appeared, triumphant in glorious nakedness, veiled slightly by dishevelled golden locks, scattered drops of water forming pearls; and seaweed fashioned with rubies, emeralds and amethysts; her arms uplifted to bless and embrace. She smiled and in the bloom of her lips, the gleam of her eyes, the palpitating rigidity of her jutting breasts beamed the joy of life and love's longings. While the goddess drew herself upright, glorying in

33

her beauty, throwing dominating glances over skies, cliffs, mountains, and forests, rays of light shone forth, marking out a mysterious path for her, a milky way in which floated the dust of stars.

Violins and harps softly played a voluptuous nuptial march.

By the magic of the hands of womankind, outstretched over the universe, the epoch of love followed the epoch of iron. Males sought for partners. Couples were formed, overwhelming each other with dreams and caresses; whirling away, eager to glee in sylvan solitary retreats and cool dark grottoes where the men, now tamed under the yoke, seemed to feel their hearts' blood flowing drop by drop as from mortal wounds while they knelt supplicating at the feet of their seductive queens.

Such was the vision of a pagan festival and of unbridled rut, finally rhythmically accompanied by the entire orchestra in melodious, solemn unison—well-nigh religious; a kind of slow litany praising the glory and infinite delight of carnal possession. This harmonious fray, the sexes mingling and embracing; lovely heads thrown back waiting for the kisses of coaxing lovers' lips, and the pink and golden uprising of Venus, the undefiled sorceress, irradiating infinity while hovering over the first harvest of love, produced such a great effect on the spectators that the curtain had to be raised four times amid thunders of applause.

Behind the scenes, there was a rapid, noisy stampede of little Italian ballet-girls hastening to change their costumes for the second act and a rush of supernumeraries carried away by the ebbing of all these gauzy skirts. The wings filled with gentlemen in evening dress; a procession frequently brought to a standstill by the scene-shifters hard at work. On the darkened stage, that looked like a great courtyard, stood Campardon, the manager of the Nouvel Eden theatre; his big, heavy hands crossed on his walking-stick as on an old man's crutch, outwardly careless, keeping a sharp eye on the setting of the scenery, and holding forth in the middle of a circle of men-about-town and his moneyed backers. He stopped now and again to roar some coarse observation to an awkward stage-hand.

"Nom de Dieu!" he exclaimed with nervous irritation. "D'ye think the public will stop here all night to please you? If we can get through this first night's show without a hitch, we're booked for eleven thousand francs every time the doors open. Clarette—the little devil!—is a wonder. She's got all the fat in every one of the four acts."

The old Marquis de Pescaleilles who might have been said almost to belong to the staff, by reason of his liaisons with the stars La Caspacelli and Rosita Lecco, interrupted the manager suddenly, hastily trying to satisfy his curiosity which he had so far mastered. What had changed in the actress's life, inducing her to leap like a female acrobat from real comedy at the Vaudeville theatre to a variety palace famed for its spectacular ballets, and be content to play in dumb show, half-naked? It was a big slump for the star who could set a whole audience sobbing. Sardou, the great dramatist, had honoured her by calling her his working partner. Campardon had accustomed the public to extraordinary surprises and astonishing attractions, but this was really the limit. Why would he not divulge the secret and give the amount of the fabulous salary which he was most certainly paying Andrée Clarette?

Campardon shrugged again. He was not such a fool as to spoil the market. The engagement of Clarette was just a bit of luck such as happens once in a lifetime. He had only profited by a moment of folly of capricious Clarette. She dashed into his den one day, superbly insolent, and in accents that brooked no denial, said simply: "You're looking for a Venus? The part suits me. Pass me over a contract. Book me! I'll sign now!" And the thing was done there and then in a jiffy.

"The funniest part of it all," he went on with short, staccato, harsh laughs, "is that she did the trick because she's in love."

"In love? No, really? How's that?"

"Because, my dear boys, she is mashed on little Lucien Hardanges, Marie-Rose's kid. He has set her flesh on fire—"

Just as he was about to continue, Camapardon suddenly stopped. Brandishing his stick with one hand and pulling out a great gold watch with the other, he bawled at the stage-manager.

"Hi, Amaudru! Are you ready? It's time to ring up."

"As soon as you like, sir. We're waiting for Madame Clarette."

While he spoke, the actress came forward, followed by her dresser and her ladies-maid. She glided slowly down along the boards with an undulating swing of her hips. She seemed engrossed in dreamy thoughts, seeing and hearing nothing of what was going on around her, as if lost at some witches' sabbath to which she might have been enticed by occult spells. The stupid public doubtless fancied that she had drawn on fleshings and exhibited her flesh just for fun, or imagined that she had grown vicious and wished to show her nudity behind the footlights—nay, that she was "broke," and ready to prostitute her art for money. No one was far-seeing enough to guess that she had played this bold stroke for the sake of one being alone: a boy hiding at the back of a dark private box in the centre of the house, behind the balcony stalls. Clarette did not care a straw what

happened so long as she dazzled his eyes and drove the
memory of her radiance beneath the limelight into his brain
as if by the stroke of a hammer. That was her aim: to force
her well-nigh virgin lover, the lad she longed for to satisfy
the lusts of her flesh, to worship her. If she could succeed,
she would no longer fear anonymous letters, daily disillusion, or treacherous attacks stirring up the scum of her past.
He would belong to her in spite of everything and everybody. Never would he be able to escape the influence of the
fairy ballet. He would always be haunted by the vision of
her nude glory, arousing his pride and jealousy, preventing
him from measuring the deep ditch of separation between
them, and the fact that she was seventeen years older than
he, for she was of the same age as Marie-Rose Hardanges,
his mother.

"My word, little woman!—you're splendid!" shouted
Campardon, running up to her and shaking her violently.

"So much the better!" she replied in a low voice with a
ghost of a smile on her lips.

The curtain rose on the second act. The scene represented Olympus, an immense marble temple. Through the
columns could be seen glimpses of the sky with doves
flying. There were showers of flower-petals and swarms of
bees. To try and clear the heavy atmosphere of boredom
reigning in the abode of the Gods, the Hours, the Graces
and half-naked nymphs of forests and brooks performed
evolutions, alighting like butterflies and bounding away
almost immediately, pretending to hearken unto the
faraway wail of echoes. They formed countless changing
groups in their measured flights. Amid the delicate lace-
work of treble notes, short and light, a *pizzicato*, dropping
into a waltzing cadence now and again, the *leitmotiv* broke
forth, at first hardly recognisable, but becoming accentu-

ated, gathering volume by the sighs of hautboys and flutes, enlivened by the fierce clash of cymbals and prolonged appeals of horns.

The goddess appeared through the glistening gates, her brow wreathed in roses, shameless and coy at one and the same time, causing the Immortals to marvel because she taught them the ineffable mystery that draws lips to lips, appeasing the most cruel grief, causing the illusion of an endless mirage to comfort sad or poverty-stricken folks. Her pantomime related to the candour of loving avowals, to vague desire that none dare reveal, innocent idyllic mutual touches, instinctive audacity and all the kisses and varied delights that please, enchain, enslave, and kill. Rebelling against all restraint, tossing her fair hair whence emanated the scent of flowers, she predicted the events of future ages when the sole idol would be woman; the only religion: love.

With rapt attention, already charmed into submission, the Gods deserted the throne of Jupiter and rushed towards her, a disorderly crowd, their hands joined in prayer and their arms outstretched towards the Enchantress, imploring her, humbly kissing the marble steps on which her white feet had passed. They begged for a promise or a sign and seemed like hungry wild beasts clustering round a female lion-tamer.

Urged on by rage and terror, Jupiter, thunderbolts in hand, abandoned Venus to be the prey of Vulcan. While the lame, hairy blacksmith carried her away in despair, stiffening her limbs in his viselike grasp, the dances were resumed to lull once more the interrupted torpor of Olympus and the sensual chant of the orchestra was merged in solemn, funereal lamentations, changing next into a gallop suggestive of the lame lecher's flight, intermingled with moans that were strange and hoarse, like challenges to combat.

There was no entr'acte, but a sudden change to a flaming scene, representing the forge of Mount Ætna. This was a great hall of dazzling basalt pillars, incrusted with metals and nuggets; streaming fire darting forth forked flames; great heaps of cups and armour piled up like a fabulous treasure and guarded by the demons of the earth. The vaults plunged down below the crust of the globe in fathomless arcades, where great, wild, enormous eyeballs glistened in the darkness. In vain the Cyclops fashioned silver mirrors, golden girdles and necklaces in order to soften the heart of the exiled goddess and cause her to be kinder to their master; to awaken furtive joys in her suffering soul and drive away the bitter, home-sick longing that wrinkled her lips and darkened her brow. In vain, the Dreams had closed in upon her, in an attempt to calm her pain by the stroking caress of their fingers, closing her eyelids and evoking ecstasy.

Venus fled, turning away her shapely head, wringing her hands, sobbing with grief, cursing the Gods, as bitter memories arose of Cytherea, Cnidos, Byblus, and those luminous isles with their myrtle and laurel groves; their sands washed by blue waves; and starry, tepid nights when the breeze wafted the odour of the sexes and the murmurs of kisses.

And so the symbolical legend was pictured on the stage. The Implacable One, hated by mothers and wives, Ares, as the Greeks called Mars, who revels in the groans of the dying, racial hatred, battles of nations and burning cities, had fought his way to the side of the goddess with the golden locks, in order to pluck the flower of love withering in its prison.

She was happy, nestled against his massive breast, swelling with sap and strength. Venus yielded to his fierce attack, allowing herself to be carried in his arms, her nostrils drinking in with delirious delight the bestial affluence exhaled by the red hair and the armpits of the Olympian. She was so slender in contrast with such an exhibition of force, but nevertheless so powerful by her beauty, that the Devastator staggered like a drunken man, stumbling at every step as if hauling a chariot of war. Venus, her head swimming, her hair dishevelled, her eyes haggard and rolling giddily, dropped down upon the pile of bear-skins and tiger-skins forming her nuptial couch. On the divine couple, protecting clouds of night descended like a big black veil, enwrapping and hiding them in its inky folds.

The symphony of the violins had become monotonous, restfully lulling like the roar of sea and wind, but yet so deeply impregnated with tenderness that the music caused one's heart to beat fast in anguish. All of a sudden, as if reverberating from cavern to cavern, could be heard a tempest of shrill, terrible sonorous sounds and chromatic scales which seemed to be the monstrous guffaws of the Cyclops. The lame blacksmith stood erect at the head of the lovers' couch, in the midst of blazing torches, while he crushed them beneath the weight of the unbreakable meshes of his retiary's web, like a fisherman throwing his net.

The act concluded, Clarette hurried along a narrow passage leading to the green-room.

"Stop a minute!" called Campardon, getting in her way. "Don't you hear the row they're making?"

The noise of hired applause accompanying the slow fall of the act-drop was being answered by hisses and loud booing. Some of the public howled; others protested; insults were bandied between gallery and pit, as freely as in street-rioting. The occupants of the stalls wanted Clarette to come before the curtain. They clapped their hands and pounded the floor with their feet and sticks. A minority sneered, rebelling against the unblushing, sensual display, and the indecent, feverish gestures of the star, so real that it unnerved the spectators who bawled authoritatively: "Shame! Enough!"

Lucien Hardanges clutched the edge of his box with both hands, clawing the red velvet, a look of uneasiness in his eyes, as if he were a second to a dear friend fighting a duel. His fine figure and clear-cut features stood out in relief like a living picture against the discreet half-light of the private box. In the watered-silk lapel of his dress-coat was a white flower as big as a cockade. His shirt-front was adorned with three black pearls, the colour of old pewter; his collar, with its wings symmetrically bent, enhanced the olive, seemingly sunburnt tint of his youthful face, evoking recent cruises on summer seas; interminable games of lawn-tennis; lazy lolling on sandy shores and autumn shooting-parties. He bit his lips and knitted his brows. Rancour and hatred seethed in his boiling brain as he glared at the wretches who dared to hiss Clarette. He stared them out of countenance, one after the other, and would have given the world to rush at them, dash his hand in their faces and fling them his card. Andrée must have had a presentiment of these stormy entr'actes when she insisted on making him give his word of honour that he would remain seated, speak to no one and not try to go behind the scenes. Here was an opportunity that would never occur again for him to show that he was a man, by declaring his love before all and proving that he was not afraid of dealing or receiving a sword-thrust. In that way, he would be respected for being different to lads of his age, fancy men tacked on to a courtesan's list, chosen by her because she was lonely, capricious, or satiated. He had been tricked, bound down by an absurd promise, and obliged to hide in a corner, controlling his feelings and holding his tongue. If, at least, he had been able to escape and seek refuge in what seemed to him paradise—her dressing-room where she was then busy changing her costume in front of the mirrors reflecting glimpses of her blonde nudity, and where baskets of flowers scented the air. If he could only have brushed against her, looking at her without speaking a word or imploring a single caress. Sudden doubts tore at his heart and brought tearful moisture to his eyelids. He said to himself that Clarette was fooling him; that he worried and troubled her. Therefore she had got him out of the way purposely and at that very moment she was laughing with other men; drinking champagne, flirting, and promising the enjoyment of her body, indifferent to the grief and disillusion that was eating into his vitals. He fidgeted in the box, his nerves on edge, opening and shutting the door of his dark retreat, getting up, sitting down, twisting a glove, resolved to disobey orders and rejoin the actress. Then he hesitated, became timid and ill at ease again, trembling lest she should drive him from her presence and treat him as an enemy ever more. And he thought he was about to swoon when Madame Lévêque, Clarette's elderly housekeeper, opened the door of the box and, holding it ajar, slipped into his hand a little note.

It was nothing more than four lines scribbled on an odd scrap of paper, but they were so coaxing and loving that the stripling felt his blood run warm in his veins as if he had just gulped down some magic elixir. His heart thumped in his breast and it was all he could do to restrain himself from throwing his arms round the neck of the fat old woman who smilingly watched him, his face aglow as if he had been sitting in front of a cosy fire where bright flames leap to comfort the soul.

The note breathed the comradeship of a friendly woman desiring to become a man's mistress:

> Don't let yourself get too much bored, love—you're adored and all my thoughts are for you. Only one little act more, and Venus's lips will join your lips for a long while—nay, for ever.
>
> Get into my brougham, rue Caumartin, and wait like a good boy for your Andrée.
>
> That's understood—isn't it?
>
> Kisses and kisses and kisses from the whole of me to the whole of you.

She knew exactly how to make an impression on her sensitive young admirer. She had, as one might say, auscultated Lucien's unbalanced brain where sudden violence, capricious obstinacy, voluptuous instinctive desire, and fits of sadness, as fleeting as outbursts of joy, took the place of willpower, solid thought, or steadiness of ideas. She knew how absurdly Marie-Rose had spoilt her only son instead of bringing him up properly. Clarette had found out that Lucien had a girl's disposition, although his body was that of a robust male, brimming over with health and youth. Neither good nor bad, overwhelmingly selfish, lacking all moral sense, she looked upon him with too many great mirrors all round him and too much stroking of his white, graceful hands and long, curly hair. Such a lad would know nothing of life's sadness. Innocently adoring himself, with the triumphant hypnotism of Narcissus, he would admire his own comeliness reflected in women's orbs. Having had countless adventures leaving no regrets or remembrances behind; worn out through having been satiated with every joy of sensuality and having fathomed the depths of love's abyss; having run the gamut of all known vices and sensations, she found it supremely interesting to try and train Lucien, enticing, ensnaring, and dominating the raw youth. It would be a novelty for her because he was neither rich nor stupid enough to keep her and she dreamt of moulding him as it pleased her, kneading his brain and forming him according to her whim. Even at this moment, when she felt the warning of age and fading beauty; although the game she had started out of curiosity and to drown dull care excited and distressed her, she did not allow herself to be led away by her imagination, but grasped the true meaning of her own manœuvres. Between a perverted, fantastically depraved woman as she was and an adorer like Lucien, sentimental, romantic, languishing love, dallying with flowers, the soul's affinities and affectionate intimacy would have been out of date. She would be his and he would be hers by the attraction of the flesh; always the flesh and nothing but the flesh. She would inoculate him with voluptuousness and drown him in such a sea of salacious intoxication that he would never be able to escape, but become enslaved by her wiles of lubricity as by morphine, cocaine, and all those delicious poisons which double the joy of living and erase the dullness of existence. She would grow young again in the torrents of sap she meant to draw from him so as to revel in the fountain of youth. So far, in that evening's performance, she had granted him the pleasure of rejoicing his eyes, letting him view, in magnificent presumption, the splendour of her body about to become his toy of delight, the well wherein he could quench his thirst, the orchard where luscious fruit would serve to appease his hunger. The stage, brilliantly illuminated, blazing like a cathedral by reason of scenery and dresses, would be followed by the roomy bed in the dim light of a shaded lamp; the soft couch where, mouth to mouth and flesh to flesh, Clarette and Lucien would come to grips in the divine struggle.

When Venus gave herself up to Mars so wildly, Lucien was bound to guess that she was putting all her strength into the part for his sake, and playing for him alone. He would surely understand that she was already thinking of the coming pleasures of lust to which she was inviting him as shamelessly as a prostitute who, behind the transparency of a lighted window, might undress slowly, show off her nakedness, twisting and writhing, to let a looker-on know how cleverly lewd she was. She laughed inwardly at the virtuous indignation of the public, hissing, thinking to hamper her efforts and render her more decent by reading her a lesson. She also despised the bewildered manager imploring her to tone down her gestures, at the same time as he noted the profits that must accrue from the seeming scandal, begging her to come out in front of the curtain and feed the fever of the spectators.

She answered never a word and, feigning not to notice that there was a small crowd of men outside her dressing-room door, that Tchernadieff and one of the authors of the ballet, the poet Pierre Garrigue, were waiting for her return and stammering compliments as she entered, Clarette dropped into an armchair and sought for a sheet of paper to write to her boy.

"Perhaps we're in the way, dearest?" asked the Prince, seeing how she looked about her.

"Of course you are! I've scarcely got time to make my change."

Three loud knocks heralded the rising of the curtain. The leader of the orchestra beat time to the first bars of the opening music. There were dull, long drawn-out clashes of cymbals muffled in crape, marking a slow cadence as of a funeral march, followed by intervals of solemn silence. Then trumpets with tragic, superhuman notes of affright announced in formidable moaning lamentations the fall of the Gods and the destruction of their temples. But amidst these deathly clarion sounds, panting and mingling as if trumpeted from the four corners of heaven and earth, seemingly driven and magnified on the wings of a gale or a destroying simoon, arose a chant of pain evoking Cybele, nourishing the barren earth with the milk of her breasts; the malice of Cupid, piercing indiscriminately all hearts, mere targets for his sharp arrows; Phoebe, lighting up the skies of night with her silver crescent; Bacchus, causing the vine to grow to console mankind; Jupiter, burning with love, changing his shape continually to quench his lust; and Pan, whose joyous piping taught shepherds their songs.

It was a sacred psalm, celebrating for the last time, verse by verse, defunct symbolism and the abolition of beliefs; and while the trumpets' blasts died far away in distant vibration, harps mingling with the majestic melody of the organ accompanied the broadly rolling plain-chant of an anthem such as a grateful people sings with bended knee on the morrow of victories, the raising of a siege, or at the enthronement of an emperor, causing tattered flags stained with blood and powder, superb trophies captured from the enemy, to swell out and wave from end to end of a nave. Behind the curtain, not yet drawn up, the chorus grew louder, sung by an invisible choir of men, women, and children repeating the same Latin words, prophesying a new religion that would last through the centuries and be wafted with the migration of souls to the sun and the stars:

Ave Venus.
Ave mulier, regina mundi.

The curtain rose at last. From the golden hair, white hands, gleaming eyes, and rosy flesh of Venus emanated the waves of light that had survived ruin and disaster. Her victorious feet trampled upon broken idols and the Olympian chaos. She was looked upon as hope incarnate by the delirious masses. On her brow for a diadem were the constellations of the skies. Her pedestal was a heap of roses and lilies. Thus appeared the goddess who had once been Venus Aphrodite and who was now the Spirit of Womankind.

V

His ears still buzzing with the sonorous memory of music, his nostrils drinking in the subtle scent of an enormous cushion of violets barricading the front of the carriage, Lucien awaited Andrée. Despite himself, he grew torpid with repose as in a warm bath, losing all idea of time and of the street noises, scraps of talk and laughter arising in the bustle of the departure of the first-night public. His whole being expanded with a delicious feeling of freedom from care. Doubt, jealousy, anxiety had all left him. Clarette loved him and, preferring him to all other men, had chosen him to be her lover, although so many longed to enjoy her and were now going to their homes all over Paris tortured by useless, deceiving remembrance of the radiant beauty of the goddess's face and her body, feverishly glowing with love. Clarette was thinking of him. She was hurrying to fall into his arms without further delay, and bring him the feast of her kisses as soon as she could. Being now certain that she had not lied to him, and that in a few moments she would be by his side, seeking, touching, imprisoning him in a joyful embrace; that they would be able to speak to each other, intoxicated with the delight of being together, tempered with infinite sweetness the overpowering impatience of the man arriving first and waiting for his mistress to keep her appointment, when he starts at the sound of all high heels on the pavement and of the rustle of every skirt, his nerves unstrung and regretting every lost minute as if his anticipated enjoyment was to be without a morrow.

"Home, François!" cried Clarette, lightly springing into her brougham.

The door banged to, closed by Mme. Lévêque and the horses started off at a smart trot, their harness clattering. The actress took Lucien's head in her ungloved hands and, drawing it close to her face as if inhaling a nosegay, as if caressing his features with her eyes before making use of her lips for the same purpose, she whispered in her silvery, soft accents, her mouth on his:

"Do you think you love me as much as I love you?"

Her words were caresses that set his flesh quivering. She did not give him time to answer. In her staring, dilated eyes appeared a sudden flash as of summer lightning and she glued her mouth to the boy's half-open lips; her teeth grating against his. She took possession of his mouth, conquering it, branding it with her imprint in a sort of fit of masculine, brutal, animal fury. She leant over him, her throat emerging from a boa of blue fox; and pale, with the face of a dead bride, she forced him backwards, stifling and almost hurting him. As she stiffened her bust in the violence of her approach, the sealskin cloak that enwrapped her flew open and Lucien, his fingers straying and exploring, found that she had not changed her stage dress. Her sole attire consisted of her silk fleshings and a gauze scarf, exactly as she had appeared in the closing scene of the ballet. She was thus practically stark naked and the warmth of her frame became absorbed by the body of the sturdy youth, exciting and burning him.

All of a sudden, with her eyes closed, as if swooning, her bosom rising and falling, breathing fitfully, she collapsed on her lover's shoulder, yielding her lips slowly, regretfully. She might have been taken for a dying woman were it not that her features were transfigured by celestial beatitude. She stammered words of ecstatic gratitude that revealed her supreme intoxication.

"My darling—oh, my darling! How delicious it is! How I love you!" she kept on repeating in childish tones, nearly inaudible.

The windows of the carriage gradually became covered with an opaque mist, hiding the intertwined couple as if the blinds were drawn down. Clarette remained quite still, one arm round Lucien's neck. The other rested inert and carelessly on the youth's thigh. Her hair caressed his cheek and he felt her heart loudly beating as, pressed against him, she confessed how she had just melted under the influence of her excited feelings and how delicious her absolute enjoyment had been. It was perfectly true that her prostration was ineffable and Andrée remembered no other complete sensual gratification in all her life that was better or more intense among all the cerebral and physical delights that she had ever tasted. She revelled in it integrally, doing her utmost to drive all thoughts and dreams from her heart and soul, as if her brougham, full of violets, closed and sweet-smelling like a boudoir, was driving towards a precipice where, by some strange fatality, they would be dashed into an abyss.

"How lovely you were on the stage!" said Lucien suddenly, blushing deeply.

She smiled, lifting herself a little away from him, so as to look him full in the face, and again she covered him with kisses, very softly and slowly. He joined his mouth to hers with uncertain, innocent earnestness, blindly wetting her lips and chin.

"You don't know how, darling! You've not the slightest notion how to kiss!" exclaimed Andrée in a whisper, her eyes glittering in anticipation.

"Let me teach you."

Her legs twisted in his, supple, salacious, with perverse stroking, pausing now and again to tease and give a fresh fillip to desire, she began her lesson by putting in action scientifically every tickling touch she knew, and all the measured cadence of caresses of fingers, hair, and lips. She surrounded him with waves of magnetic fluid, overwhelming him with kisses, drowning him in a flood of the keenest and most mad voluptuousness. Lucien's kiss had fallen on the back of her rounded neck like a frenzied bite. Her kiss, on the contrary, ran round the curves of his ear with furtive delicacy and then stopped finally near the lobe. She nibbled it a little like a red berry. Her lips wandered in his hair until they reached the temples where the arteries pulsate. Her mouth served to close each eye, and finally nestled on his mouth, as if the desired goal was attained. At first, Clarette's kiss rambled timidly near the corners of his lips, opening them slightly at last with moist tantalizing touches and, finding them no longer aggressive, her mouth stayed on his, drinking his breath, appreciating its freshness, and clipping first the upper lip and then the lower between the pulp of the velvet cushions that enframed her teeth. Then came the climax. Like doves, their darted tongues met and mingled in mysterious hymeneal union, joining the souls of mistress and lover.

Lucien felt his reason leaving him. He quivered from head to foot, shaken by great insatiable billows of passionate lust; his fingers incrusted in the silk fleshings. He never ceased seeking Clarette's mouth.

"More—more!" he prayed, as soon as she feigned to release him, drew back, or interrupted the manœuvres of her licentious lips. "Yes—like that! Keep on—for ever!" he muttered.

Andrée obeyed, exhausting and enthralling him; maddening and killing herself in this delirious play.

At the moment when the brougham stopped in front of Clarette's little house in the Avenue Kléber and François hoarsely called to the concierge to throw open the double doors, the couple started as if awakening suddenly. They remained dazed and silent like revellers returning half tipsy from a riotous supper and who might have been sleeping side by side during their journey home. Andrée was the first to regain composure, rearranging her dress in a twinkling, drawing her furs closely round her calmly, with a pretty shiver.

"Good-bye till to-morrow, darling. François will drive you home," she said, her voice hoarse with stifled sobs.

She spoke as if regretfully distressed by some imperious necessity; afraid of glutting his appetite too quickly, or consuming his love in one burst of flame like unto the burning of a heap of straw.

He thought she was joking and stared at her with anguish and stupefaction.

"So you won't let me stop with you? Do you really want me to go?"

Great tears rolled down his cheeks. He trembled as if

suddenly freezing with cold; and Clarette, feeling that all her courage was oozing away, repulsed him with a last violent kiss.

"No, no! To-night I want to be yours in your dreams!" she cried.

Lucien flew into a passion like a spoilt child when a toy is taken from him.

"All right! I'm off, as I see I'm in your way!" he returned with insolent mockery, as he dabbed his eyes with his hand-kerchief. Wickedly, without weighing his words, not knowing what he was saying, as if eager to destroy and trample on their love; to ill-treat the woman he thought was fooling him and whose subtle uneasiness he was unable to understand any more than the supreme refinements of a worn-out actress. "I shan't be long finding a girl to finish me off!" he added.

Alighting from the carriage and lifting his hat politely, the youngster made a show of quietly lighting a cigarette and, his hands in the pockets of his black overcoat, his stick tucked under his arm, he stalked off, taking great strides. Without looking back or turning his head, he disappeared in the haze of night, striped by the changing rays of the streetlamps. Lucien heard the distant clatter of the brougham wheels on the road, the dull sound of the heavy doors, now closed and bolted, and these noises resounded so keenly in his heart that he felt too weak to walk, and dropped onto one of the benches of the avenue. The damp, icy darkness, the silent solitude and the cloudy masses of black wadding hiding the sky, drove him out of his mind. He seemed not to know his way and to be lost far out of the world. None would come to his aid, lead him into the right road, comfort him in his sad plight. His face hidden in his contracted fingers, he sobbed with grief and disappointment, first accusing and then excusing Clarette; torturing his brain and asking himself in vain why the actress had been so loving at first and suddenly so cold, drawing back at last after having almost yielded her whole body, and sending him packing like a bore or a parasite. His state of fever grew worse. In his mind's eye, he saw once more the licentious scenes of the ballet where her beauty had dazzled him as on an August day the sun scorches one's eyelids. He recollected everything and the most insignificant details of the beginning of their acquaintance when every minute had been exquisite and sweet. How quickly events had taken place—all in his favour—from the night of the ball until this new ballet at the Nouvel Eden! Did she not insist upon choosing his private box herself? Had she not sent him the pencilled note, promising so much in so few words? She had abducted him, so to say. And what of the drive to her dwelling, his kisses and—above all—*her* kisses which had made him drunk as with alcohol, opening his eyes, revealing unknown enjoyment, teaching him the art of love. He was still panting under the influence of her lips, mouth, and tongue, his blood not yet cooled; their smart still prickling his flesh. To be thus kissed again he would have given life, honour, all he possessed that day and all that would be his in the future. He now believed that this dalliance amounted to nothing more than the trickery of a depraved woman to pass away the time and excite her sensual emotion—in short: a great, odious, cowardly lie because she knew he was defenceless, having faith in her love and giving himself up to her with all the strength of his being and in the best of faith.

He had only been chosen to put a light to the furnace of this wicked creature's lubricity; innocently and stupidly getting her ready for some other man. While he shivered,

weeping, in the cold night air—silly fool that he was!—
Clarette was disrobing in her room where the walls were
hung with ancient brocade of a rosy hue. He had not been
received therein, but on the threshold had never thrown a
glance at the bed without his heart beating wildly and causing his brain to swim. While he endured the torture of
passing in review the remembrance of this woman, she was
opening her arms to a lover, writhing and swooning with
lustful joy as he roughly attacked her. From between her
clenched teeth issued moans equivalent to confessions of
felicity which arise with emotive gratitude from the bottom
of the heart to the lips when all restraint is abolished.

He swore inwardly that he would find out the secret that
Andrée had so stubbornly hidden from him. He only had to
remain on the watch all night far beyond the dawn, if need
be, so as to come face-to-face with this man, laugh at him,
and provoke him to a duel. Lucien resolved to upset the
plans of this creature, too clever by half, and stand sentinel
under her windows as if on outpost duty. He turned back
almost on the run, took up his position in front of the house;
and eyed the streaks of light escaping through Clarette's
shutters, searching on the blinds masking the stained glass
of the smallest drawing-room—her "resting-place," as the
actress called it—for intertwined silhouettes; the coming
and going of a couple playing a shadow pantomime of lust.
But nothing appeared except the black outline of Andrée's
figure. For a few minutes, she leant her elbows on a table, as
if writing a letter; then stopped suddenly, seemingly reflecting in an attitude of anxiety; tore a paper to pieces, and
taking a portrait from the mantelpiece, kissed it lengthily.

Changing from extreme rancour to blind confidence, the
young fellow became ashamed of having insulted and
suspected her. She would probably never forget his caddish

behaviour and the way he had left her. Nor could she forgive him for having treated her like a common street-walker, a prostitute to be got rid of brutally if she ventures to rebel or have an opinion of her own. He had committed the worst possible fault: belittling himself without a cause and losing his temper like a coster.

He had no claim on her after all, nor the right to pick a quarrel or prevent her from having her own way. They did not live together. He had never given her a sou; nor had they exchanged promises or taken any loving oaths.

It was all over. Clarette would never wish to see him again. He had destroyed the bonds of affection about to be tied. Their union would have been so deliciously beautiful, quite out of the ordinary. Beside himself with despair, turning round at every step, he took to blowing kisses to her house where all lights were extinguished—like the fleeting flames of their miserable love. His mouth and heart were full of these kisses and he prayed that they might reach the bed where she was sleeping, leading her to be kind and indulgent; to consider that a nineteen-year-old sweetheart is apt to kick over the traces, be troubled by the slightest thing; and lose all self-control because he loved her. He hoped she would guess that his eyes were full of tears and that by dint of caresses he would try to pacify her and soften her heart. So pondering, he wended his way to the Place de l'Etoile.

VI

Clarette was not asleep.

The cambric sheets scorched her skin as if she were reclining on hot embers, and being incapable in her unnerved state of remaining still, she stretched her limbs, then huddled herself up and pressed her head against the pillows, biting their lace edging from time to time. Her feelings in these quiet hours of self-communion as in a church when the service is concluded and the candles put out, were as strange as a dream.

It seemed to her that she had been slowly metamorphosed into another woman and would not have recognised herself had she looked in the glass. She fancied that she was making her start in the world with the bright tempting illusions of the teens; heart and flesh enthusiastically waiting for what a girl does not confess even to herself. Fifty heavy

59

years appeared to have been lifted off her existence. She had a purpose in life; something to interest her now, embarking on an adventure which resembled none of the commonplace gadding in which she had gradually worn out her heart and killed her soul. She left her usual muddy anchorage and set sail for a new land of delight, boldly heedless of reefs and shoals; resolute, ready to risk all, affront every danger, yet full of anxiety. Her being was moved by the uneasiness that heralds the departure of a ship, forcing sailors to be taciturn and pensive, while the coast is slowly lost to view and soon nothing is seen but sky and water. She was entranced by her disquietude. The cloudiness of her brain and her state of feverish suffering impressed her as being more desirable than all the monotonous pleasures that had fallen to her lot since she had grown into womanhood. She would have liked to increase the acuity of her sensations and could not call to mind ever having tasted the joy of living better than during this wintry night, notwithstanding that she was languishing with unquenched lust, while her thoughts were drifting, carried away by furious currents. Sleep came not to her eyes.

She had wasted her life sufficiently and gone from one man to another, wrecking quite enough fortunes—Heaven only knew by how much huckstering, degradation, disgust, and sacrifices!—to entitle her, at last, to yield her body for her own pleasure and to realise her own ideals. Why should she not be allowed to purify herself from the stains of her past and retire behind the wall of unique affection absorbing her being when her withered youth and faith, not entirely dead, might burst into blossom again? Her wealth was sufficient to prevent any fear of the future hampering her plans. Nothing need stop her from barricading her door, becoming almost an honest woman and living maritally like a little shopgirl with a young chap who suits her. She revelled in the idea that in her boy's arms, she would lose restored virginity.

Had she not always felt as indifferent towards men as to women ever since the day when one of her aunts, a flower-girl in the streets, had dragged her into a hotel room to be sold to an old member of the Senate who violated her? Although there was no experiment of lechery she had not tried, she was free of reproach in so far as any weakness or caprice was concerned. Among all the much-photographed lady-killing actors, Don Juanesque men-about-town, and pale-faced, short-haired, mannish women, offering them-selves as a sort of pick-me-up to satiated, bored lights-o'-love, was there a debauché who could boast that Andrée Clarette had sought a palliative to ennui in his arms; or a Lesbian who dared declare that her carmined lips had beguiled the actress's eternal lassitude? Only apparently did she offer Lucien the leavings of others. Her brain and heart had never been used. They were as clean as glasses out of which no one had drunk. The thought rejoiced her, giving rise to happy pride.

The part she had chosen to play was beyond compare. Future days and months would fly quickly by, in the enchanting absorption of mind caused by this education of love. What maddening diversion to tame the boy as if he were a wild bird, accustoming him to his cage and making him become tender and caressing! Then there would be the sweet voluptuousness of initiating him in every trick of enjoyment; corrupting, startling him; treating him like a wife whose husband brings forbidden diversions into the marriage-bed. During certain days and nights she would be gambling on the defensive, calculating the value of every card, trying her utmost to win, because to lose spelt ruin with no consolation afterwards. It would be glorious to conquer in never-ending battle where she would be always on guard against traps and treachery; puzzling to please; how to be never the same and to possess some charm lacking in other women; or do something—no matter what—that an ordinary mistress could not do; always striving to stop the fire smouldering in her lover's brain from dying out; holding his senses on the alert by promises, challenges, and inventions. Such a life was indeed worth living; one's whole heart and soul unceasingly stirred, as if knowing that the morrow would be one's last day on earth. An existence exempt from stagnation, with no brooding; no black thoughts to be stirred in the brain like poison pounded in a mortar. Carking care would be nailed over her door like an owl whose power to bring ill-luck causes terror.

Clarette got out of bed and, barefooted, glided quickly to her "resting-place" to fetch Lucien's likeness. It was an old portrait given to her two years before by Marie-Rose Hardanges with the pride of a doting mother. The actress placed the photograph on one of her pillows under the rosy gleam of her night-light. Leaning on her elbows, her chin in her hands, stretched on her stomach, she contemplated her love with the fixed stare of a wild animal on the watch. In this pensive attitude, she might have been taken for a sorceress performing some diabolical incantation; her bright eyes casting a spell over a man whose jealous mistress had provided the likeness for this fell purpose. Clarette studied and scrutinised every line in the pictured features. She revelled sensually while looking at the face of the boy; thinking how she would take, love, and keep him. As in a vision, she saw Lucien's head on the pillow framed among the lace, heavy with sleep, dropping back, his eyes closing under the fatigue of the conclusion of love's fit of ecstasy; starting slightly because her lips skimmed over his brow bestowing the last kiss of the night. And she smiled, replying to her lad's insolent smile.

Suddenly, she remembered his impertinent insult when enraged at being sent away, and she burst out laughing. She would have wagered any amount that the poor young fellow was not just then in a prostitute's arms; nor had he even paid the slightest attention to the discreet greeting of any nymph of the pavement. According to her wish, he was now dreaming of her; his fury cooled down; impatient to see her again and resume the lesson where their lips had left off. He was possessing her in his dreams with his loins afire, fevered lips, and burning with a thirst that all the glasses of water he gulped down would be powerless to quench. Perhaps too—he was only a boy still—with hands wildly straying, he might be trying to trick his imagination and, while thinking of her beauty and her caresses, enjoy a pale imitation of the infinite delight she had refused him. She, also, lost her wits through sketching this suggestive picture and her blood coursed hot in her veins. Clarette closed her eyes, feeling as if she had breathed some strong, intoxicating, heady perfume and stretched her shapely limbs. She threw off the satin coverlet and the lace-trimmed sheet, and engrossed by the idea that their bodies were joined in the closest coupling of love, she slowly satisfied her lust and imagined that Lucien's ecstasy mingled with her own.

VII

Clarette did not leave her bed until eleven o'clock, full of fatigue, with heavy limbs, and she had scarcely touched the bell when Mme. Lévêque appeared. Her features were convulsed and she was puffing and blowing at every step she took. Violent emotion was bad for the fits of asthma to which the worthy dame was subject.

"Mon Dieu!" exclaimed Clarette who felt in good humour. "What's the matter with you? Has your banker absconded with all your savings?"

"You shouldn't laugh," replied the old housekeeper. "Lucien's ill and you've been sent for three times this morning."

"Lucien ill?" exclaimed Andrée, her voice thick with emotion. "Why didn't you wake me, you nasty beast? I might have slept till tomorrow for all you care! What are you doing there, staring at me like a stuck pig? What are you waiting for? Pass me a hat—cloak—anything! Order the brougham. But no!—send for a cab. That'll be quicker."

She whirled about the room like a madwoman, knocking over chairs, hustling Lévêque and driving her little fists into her eyes to brush away rising tears.

"Don't get yourself in such an awful state," grumbled Lévêque. "Who says there's any danger?"

Clarette never hearkened to her, but arranged her hair with four pins stuck anyhow in her luxuriant locks twisted and bunched together. Covered with furs, her feet in slippers, already prepared to depart as if her house was on fire, and as if every second that went by increased the lad's sufferings. Exaggerating the serious nature of his illness, she behaved as if afraid not to see him alive again; and as if she might reach his bedside too late to struggle against the approaches of death. Rudely telling the old woman to hold her tongue, Clarette took her by the shoulders and bundled her out on to the stairs.

"Well? That cab?" grumbled Andrée, her voice shrill and hoarse by turns. "Must I go and fetch one myself on the rank?"

"How anybody can get so excited, I can't imagine!" groaned Mme. Lévêque; and shaking her head, mumbling scraps of ill-tempered talk in an undertone, she went downstairs to the servants' quarters.

Andrée panted, her heart aching, her face glued to the window; and having turned mechanically, caught sight of her face in a mirror. She was so livid, her features drawn by a night of insomnia and by such a cruel awaking, that despite all her anxiety, she rushed to her dressing-room, made herself up with red for her lips, powder and a hint of rouge on her cheeks, and crossed her bust with a broad, gauzy fichu like a great butterfly with outstretched wings.

She was deliberate in her arrangements that finally enhanced the perfect oval of her striking features. Even merely to sit by his bedside, showing herself to be a maternal and friendly nurse, she was bound to be attractive so as to please him and prevent disillusion from spoiling the boy's dream. Supposing he was given up by the doctors, it was her duty to appear young and handsome in his eyes until they were closed for ever, so that he should have a vision of paradise before setting out on the journey to black unknown nothingness or some haven of glory.

Her footman having returned with a cab, Clarette jumped in hurriedly and gave Lucien's address to the driver.

"Five francs' pourboire if you drive like the devil!" she shouted.

The cocher, huddled in his grey greatcoat, shrugged his shoulders, winked to himself with a mocking grin and flogged his horse as hard as he could. The poor animal ambled off in a vague attempt at galloping.

"More moods and fancies of these 'ere women!" grumbled the cabman to himself, swaying to and fro as his ramshackle vehicle bumped over the stones. "This sort o'thing don't suit my old mare!"

Andrée shook and trembled almost convulsively. Her brain seemed to be escaping from a gaping, sudden fracture and she endured martyr-like sufferings at having to sit still without being able to fly quickly through the streets. She put her head and shoulders out of the window.

"Faster! Faster!—for God's sake! Kill your horse, if need be! I'll pay. I'm going to see a poor boy—ill in bed," she kept repeating, at first in tones of prayer and then imperiously.

As soon as she caught sight of the windows of the

ground-floor apartment that Marie-Rose Hardanges had leased and furnished for Lucien, Clarette did not even wait for the cab to come to a standstill, but leapt out at the risk of losing her equilibrium and breaking a limb on the asphalt.

"Keep the change!" she cried, thrusting a twenty-franc piece in the driver's outstretched hand.

"She's cracked—that's sure!" he mumbled, overjoyed at the godsend as the actress rushed away to the house.

When she found herself in front of the young man's door, Andrée grew weak. She thought that it was impossible for her to make another step. She felt as if about to fall flat on the door-mat, lacking strength even to press the electric bell, step over the threshold, and interrogate those who would welcome her and brutally reveal the truth all at once. Her heart beat feebly, her temples aching as if held in a vice; her eyes were blinded by an incessant whirling vision of black-and-white specks that formed a combination of physical torture showing her what vast space Lucien occupied in her being; how she wanted him and loved him, so that she was conquered and captured instead of being a despotic mistress. Before she had regained her composure and was once more calm and reasonable, someone she could hardly see in the darkness of a narrow passage papered with coloured theatrical posters—a doctor or a manservant—opened the door.

The patient having heard the noise of the cab stopping and starting off again; the clatter of a woman's high heels in their mad rush on the pavement, sat up suddenly in bed. Erect against his pillow, he called out Clarette's name with all his might and main as if afraid that she might be off again at once, merely ringing at his door to enquire after his health, because it was no trouble for her, nor much out of her way on the road to dressmaker or milliner. His hoarse, whining voice took on a childish tone, reminding one of the complaints of a frightened child trembling in the dark, calling for help and praying not to be left alone.

"Andrée! Andrée!" he clamoured. "Is it really you at last, Andrée?"

Clarette dropped on to her knees at the side of the bed, her arms thrown round him, drawing him to her, pressing him to her breast, smothering him with mad caresses as if kissing him for the last time because she would never set eyes on him again. Weak, distressed, he rocked backwards and forwards under the showers of kisses and fell drooping on his pillow, his feverish fingers clutching the actress's shoulders.

"Yes, yes—'tis I, my darling!—the woman who loves you!" she murmured.

"You love me?" he sighed.

"With all the strength of my being—madly!"

"You love me?"

"I adore you!"

"You love me?"

"More than anything or anybody in the world!"

"You love me—no one else!"

"You only! I swear it on your life and mine. If I lie, may the false oath bring the blackest ill-luck to us both!"

"You're not angry with me?"

"How could I be angry with you who are dearer to me than life?"

"But I made you suffer, you know. Say that you've forgiven me—say it again. Tell me you love me—say so at once."

"Of course I love you—you great, big child! Can't you see I do? Oh, I love you! I love you!"

Lucien's bodily strength momentarily revived and stimulated by this fit of happiness, began to fade and melt, metamorphosed in unconquerable torpor, forming profound weakness. His voice became well-nigh inaudible. He stammered confusedly; the words dying away on his burning, colourless lips. He drew Clarette's hand on to his pillow, pressing his cheek in her palm which was soon impregnated by his fever. He kept on kissing it and closed his eyes, falling asleep without loosing his hold. His slumbers were disturbed by fantastic dreams of anguish and sudden fits of coughing that seemed to tear his breast open. Clarette made no movement. She would have liked to relieve his pain and give her health in exchange for his malady. She watched him sleeping; and at intervals, with the most light and careful touch, wiped away with her handkerchief the drops of sweat that stood out on his forehead. As she remained kneeling, she seemed to be praying like the most chaste and pious nun invoking the protection of the merciful Virgin. Clarette might have been imploring a miracle in fervid prayers, her great eyes fixed on the patient, watching over and caressing him with their glances, when the doctor who had discreetly kept out of the way, entered the room on tiptoe.

At the sight of the unexpected picture, he smiled like a sceptical philosopher who had seen many scenes of this kind and was astonished at nothing. Clarette's glance questioned him. She was full of fear, greedily begging for some word of hope.

"Pleurisy, most likely," he said in a low whisper. "Now, however, my fears are lessened. A patient who is beloved and fights against his illness, gets over it nine times out of ten."

"Yes, yes—we'll save him," she murmured, tears welling up in her eyes.

From that moment, Andrée became his nurse. Seated in an armchair, she lived and slept lightly in the warmth of the room that was kept closed and curtained. She was attentive to his slightest complaint or murmur, covering him up each time he tried to throw off the sheets and blankets. Andrée gave him his medicine hourly, only slipping away now and again to eat a mouthful standing up, as if in a railway refreshment room for a few minutes before the train started off again. She made up her mind she would cure him. So that no one should hinder her, and to be sure of being able to nurse him until the doctor declared him out of danger and convalescence began in slow resurrection, with one stroke of the pen, she cancelled her contract with Campardon and broke her engagement at the Nouvel Eden theatre; indifferent to his threats of law proceedings; not caring about the heavy forfeit she would have to pay. Despite the great advance booking of seats and the box-office sheets filled up for a month ahead after the sensational first night of the sensuous mythological ballet, the second performance was postponed, as the public were informed on bands of paper hastily stuck across the playbills.

Campardon felt inclined to kill Clarette like some dangerous animal. He was all the more furious because the actress was his last card. He thought that in his exhausted mine he had struck a vein of gold which would have set him up again at the very moment when he saw bankruptcy looming, with irretrievable ruin in sight.

Poor Mme. Lévêque came in for all the threats and insults destined for Clarette. The old woman remained phlegmatically and mockingly calm, being used to theatrical quarrels out of which she always came with flying colours—and with profits in ready cash.

She made no defence or objections; and proffered no

excuses when the manager attacked her furiously. She was satisfied to reply quite quietly, adjusting her spectacles on the bridge of her nose.

"I'm entirely of your opinion, M. Campardon. I put myself in your place. This is no fun for you, but you know Mme. Clarette as well as I do, eh? You must have guessed there was a screw loose when she suddenly got into her heard that she'd like to play a dancing-girl's part in a ballet. Upon my word, I'm surprised to see that an old stager like yourself with all your experience hasn't a better idea of what women think and do."

The housekeeper, at bottom, was delighted that Clarette's fantasy should have turned out to her advantage as she argued—*her* Clarette having broken an engagement that was beneath her. Mme. Lévêque looked upon Clarette as her daughter, and also as something to be governed and exploited like an estate on which her housekeeper lived so comfortably that she felt as if it belonged to her. She was so completely identified with Andrée's existence that, by a peculiar miracle, she was convinced she shared all her adventures.

"It'll cost us a tidy bit o'money, but we've got the brass," mumbled the old lady. "Seems to me rather uncommon to have a little flare-up like this. Such a fine ad. must be paid for. Nothing like keeping oneself before the public!"

Despite her advanced age, Lévêque was sentimental and the new romance of the actress interested her greatly. All her sympathy went out towards the boy-lover who seemed to have stepped out of a comedy. Nevertheless, she was alarmed to see the fun lasting so long. Clarette's fickle disposition appeared to her to be altered. The housekeeper measured the frightful progress of her mistress's new frenzy of love, like a great oily surface starting from the secret grotto of her sex and spreading to the brain with a likelihood of the heart being flooded. Mme. Lévêque felt her influence lessening. Andrée no longer listened to her, being obsessed by one fixed idea: to love her little man and be loved by him in return. So her housekeeper battled without gaining an inch, losing, on the contrary, more ground daily, and exasperated to such an extent that, without daring to confess it inwardly, she almost hoped that Lucien's illness might terminate fatally, and thus brutally obliterate Clarette's voluptuous longings.

The actress had not been to bed for four nights, dozing reluctantly at intervals; exhausting herself in mind and body; tiring herself out in her struggle against feverish fatigue and breathing the vitiated air of the sick room. She was in open revolt because everybody was up in arms against her, worrying and begging her to snatch some slight repose by giving up her post at the head of Lucien's bed. Lévêque, as persistent as a faithful dog, only succeeded in getting herself sent about her business.

"Can't you let me alone?" cried Andrée, always retorting in the same strain. "If Marie-Rose was in France, d'ye think she'd slip off to bed and let her son be nursed by anybody else than her? I've taken her place. Now, do you understand?"

The actress did not add that she experienced selfish joy at the thought that her young sweetheart's mother was hundreds of miles away and unable to get back to Paris to exercise the right of putting everybody—including even the beloved mistress—in their places as simple and superfluous subordinates. The idea that Lucien's mother was out of the way and the boy was entirely in the possession of the woman he adored brought supreme gratification to Andrée.

"Don't be cross, my dear old Lévêque," she went on, her

ill-temper disappearing and passing her arm round the housekeeper's shoulders. "You drive me mad, pretending not to see what's going on inside of me." Andrée profited by Lucien dropping off to sleep to bundle Mme. Lévêque into the drawing-room. "Sit down and I'll tell you all about it. You can't imagine how miserable I am. The poor dear fellow told me something yesterday in the night. It's all through me that he's so ill and suffers from this horrid fever. The other night—you remember?—after the first night of that ballet, we came home together in the brougham. He was awfully hot, poor darling!—burning. The fact is we'd been kissing awfully and the windows were up."

"Go on. I'm waiting for the finish."

"The finish! Well, if you must know—the finish is that I'm Clarette and can't change myself to please anybody. It's not my fault if I always hanker after what's impossible even when I'm dead in luck." She gulped down sighs of sadness and wrung her hands. "I was frightened at my own feelings and his. I dared not go too fast, thinking that I might quench my thirst too quickly. I didn't realise that he couldn't see things as I did, being only a boy just starting in life, so I sent him away and drove him out into cold night air—"

"Ah! that's you all over."

Clarette got up in great anxiety and went back to the open door leading into the bedroom. "I thought he had just woke. No wonder he conjured up a lot of nonsense," she continued. "He thought I was sleeping that night with the Prince and that I had put him off with lies. So, instead of rushing off to find a girl, as he threatened me he would, or going home to bed, he watched my windows, standing sentinel in the fog which gradually froze him to death, soaking through his thin dress clothes and overcoat."

Lévêque knitted her bushy grey eyebrows and, not

knowing exactly what to reply, kept on repeating automatically: "Quite extraordinary, dearie—quite extraordinary."

Lucien's frightful, hoarse, hiccuping cough interrupted their conversation.

While the actress hastened to the boy's bedside, the old housekeeper murmured to herself that the best she could do was to keep quiet and wait for the good or bad results of the love story.

"Oh, damn their love!—their bally rotten love!" she hissed through her teeth in a fit of scorn and spite.

VIII

Then came a series of days all alike; a long, monotonous, mournful week, full of unceasing uneasiness; alternatives of hope, quiet, happiness, torment and desolation. One day the patient improved, only to be overtaken the next by crisis after crisis, each one more dangerous than the first. He lost flesh. All gleams of vital energy had taken refuge in his big, dilated eyes, deeply shaded with black circles. He made himself understood by gestures only, unable to articulate plainly, and was so weak that he could only drink by being propped up by a pile of pillows. He seemed to recognise no one but Clarette. She read in his glances that he was happy to enjoy her contact at his side all day and all night; to see her there every time he opened his eyes and only drink what she poured out for him. She held her hand in his for hours.

"I love you! I love you!" she would say again and again, replying to the sad, mute interrogation of his staring eyes.

Hearing this declaration, he would squeeze her fingers with greater strength, as if the tender confession was healing and stimulating. Finally, Clarette got the upper hand in the desperate battle and checked the advance of the malady. The joy of having performed such a miracle brought back her strength, bathing her in waves of magnetic energy just as she was on the eve of breaking down and succumbing to fatigue when her animal force was exhausted. At that moment, she only kept on her aching legs by dint of stimulants, alcohol, and forced feeding; her brain being enfeebled under the stress of shock and emotion. The doctor's prophecy came true. The loving, devoted, maternal mistress had driven Death away from the patient's bedside. Lucien got up, gained fresh life and became slowly convalescent. There were fewer fits of coughing. He could sleep. Andrée followed the progress of his cure, madly interested in it as at some enthralling spectacle that sets the nerves vibrating and makes the heart beat faster. She was overjoyed at the slightest sign or smallest detail betokening her lover's resuscitation; detecting cheering signs that none remarked but her. Her soul was singing as she no longer felt the lad's fingers palsied with fever, but saw his cheeks, erstwhile so white, take on rosy tints and heard his voice getting firmer, regaining its normal tone. No longer did he breathe with a whistling sound akin to that of the biting breeze foreshadowing the fall of the last few russet leaves of autumn.

Lucien soon became strong enough to sit up for an hour, his back supported by many cushions. With the help of Mme. Lévêque who, with her plain common sense, resignedly grasped the fact that she had nothing to gain by opposing her mistress's whims, Andrée dressed her convalescent patient with her own hands. She warmed his silk shirt in front of the fire, put it on for him, combed the curls of his hair, too long and matted together by the sweat of sleepless nights; making him comfortable, petting him with the joy of helping to bring back his good looks and effacing the traces of pain that were fixed like a mask over his refined features.

He began to take a little nourishment. To vary the menus of his little meals which served more for diversion than for need, Lévêque went round the markets, passing hours at shops noted for edibles, bringing home everything she could find of the very best, fitted to give a fillip to his tasteless palate, sickened against everything through having been washed by countless bottles of nauseous mixtures. She took possession of the tiny kitchen, about as big as a bathing-machine, and laid out the table close to the bed. The Russian tablecloth embroidered with red and blue flowerets, the ancient crockery and sparkling crystal glasses and decanters formed a sight of gaiety. It was enough to tickle the most jaded appetite to sit at such a table, especially as delicate dishes were quickly placed thereon.

Clarette prepared Lucien's new-laid egg with her own hands, cutting and buttering little strips of toast; forgetting to eat herself to gaze on his childish way of swallowing and his enjoyment as if he had been starved for weeks.

The two women held whispered consultations, hesitating about pouring Bordeaux into Lucien's glass, frightened to be too generous and both exclaiming in an alarmed chorus:

"Gently! Don't drink too fast! It won't do you good to drink so fast!"

They squeezed the gravy of red and savoury grilled rumpsteak into porcelain cups; cut white breasts of fowls, as if he were a mere baby, and to clean out his little mouth, as Lévêque would say, offered bunches of golden grapes.

They smiled when he looked happy and satisfied, yawning after a dainty repast, and gradually subsiding all in a heap among his pillows, sleepily murmuring:

"It's good to be alive!"

"And to be loved!" added Clarette, her lips lightly skimming over his forehead in a butterfly kiss.

"Yes!—and to be loved!" he echoed, lifting his eyelids a little so that she should see how affection and gratitude swam in his eyes darkened by languor.

Sometimes, if he so willed it, Andrée, in her deep-toned sweet voice, with its infinite crystal vibrations that lulled like the softest music, read him a chapter of a novel or some newspaper articles. She would stop and grow dumb as soon as she noted any trace of fatigue on her patient's face. She scarcely spoke unless he questioned her about some lapse in his memory, or concerning the length of time that he had passed without news of the life of Paris from which he had perforce been cut off. When the couple chatted freely, it seemed as if the room was full of delicious melody; the sound of violins or the light warbling of tropical birds.

"I'd like you to talk to me for ever such a long time," Lucien would say to her. "Your voice calms my nerves and soothes me. It's so lovely that I'm afraid I'm dreaming; or that it mayn't be true and won't continue."

"Oh, big crazy boy I love!—d'ye take me for a fairy?" she exclaimed, laughing.

He was able to get up and walk a few paces round the room, leaning on Clarette, although he was still very weak; his legs as if boneless; his head giddy, aching with shooting pains at every movement he tried to make. But he was happy to be out of bed and upstanding; to be able to put his hand on the furniture, halt before the fire blazing merrily, or remain a few minutes in front of the window where he lifted the curtains in great curiosity to view the bustle of people and the traffic in the street; but also in anguish, noting in a mirror how his thin and suffering frame bent over.

"Tell me now—sincerely—don't you find me shockingly altered?"

Andrée reassured him with cajoling, coaxing words, forcing him to sit down and rest, threatening and scolding him affectionately because he obeyed her only too regretfully. She covered his knees in the folds of her *surah* dressing-gown, and curled herself up on a pile of cushions like a poodle nestling close to its master. She made him remain quiet by her babbling, forcing him to forget all worry in listening to stories slowly told and marvellous plans for future pleasures.

Gradually, as his strength came back to him and he began to need less care, Clarette's feminine nature reasserted itself. She arranged his diggings according to her fantasy, until the two little rooms were redolent of violets and lilac. She destroyed everything recalling his illness and the danger he had run, the torments she had endured and the sadness that had reddened their eyelids.

IX

As soon as Lucien was in a fit state to support the fatigue of the journey, Clarette took him away with her to the South. In the Garavant quarter of Mentone, she possessed a villa built in the Italian style with flat roof, terrace gardens, and walls frescoed in light and pleasing tones, surrounded by lemon-trees and rose-bushes.

It overlooked the sea and there they shut themselves up of their own accord as if in a religious retreat isolated from the outer world, where one can indulge in endless ecstasies and perpetual adoration of a symbolical monstrance. They lived solely for the sake of love, discovering daily new delights, better caresses, or some more perverted and more maddening way of joining in carnal union. They told and retold the beads of the chaplet of lust and all their thoughts and dreams had no other horizon, object, or ideal than love, desire, and stupration. The more they fathomed the depths of the divine mystery, the more they were intoxicated in the joy of coupling their bodies. They were consumed with raging, devouring flames; thirsting and hungering for caresses and sensations, longing for each other. Their efforts increased their mutual desire and their beatitude grew keen, superhuman, and magnificent.

Clarette tried her utmost to keep her lover always on the alert, amusing him with sudden surprises and inventions. She was never the same woman two days running. She forced him to travel in charming, imaginary countries where all the female inhabitants were marvels of beauty. The ship on which she made him sail was her white and rosy frame, as if it was one of those wonderful vessels we hear of in fairy legends and folk-lore ballads. Sometimes he landed in Japan; in a harbour of yellow water where at eventide, under trees laden with cherry-blossom, the geishas were on the watch for courtly knights and brought them to a halt with lascivious beckonings full of artful promise. Clarette drew her hair off her forehead and kept it coiled up with great golden pins as long as daggers and her brown eyelashes were enhanced by a touch of kohl. The slender contours of her hips and bust were lost in the soft folds of a long, silken kimono and she squatted down on a pile of rugs, her head resting against Lucien's knees. In this attitude, she served tiny porcelain cups of green tea which acted on their nerves and made them feverish.

Just as if they had been snugly hidden in some house of ill-fame in Tokyo, Clarette complacently unrolled picture after picture, revealing unblushingly erotic scenes painted in water-colours on rice-paper. With steady, alluring glances, she interrogated the boy, waiting with sweet docility for him to choose in one of the sensual drawings, according to his fancy, the position or caress that appeared the most desirable and wanton. They immediately copied the tricks and positions of the selected picture without omitting the slightest detail.

Another time, Clarette would seat herself at the piano and charm Lucien as she played swinging, lascivious Spanish dances. Their swaying measure evoked clacking tongues, joyful cries, and strident laughter. It was devilish music; mad melody fit to drive angels crazy. The actress at that moment would be wearing a peignoir of lace with ribbons and frills. Her golden hair was arranged in smooth bands, marked with waves. A saucy kissing-curl was plastered on each cheek and a red rose, like a flag of rebellion, surmounted her tiny, sea-shell-like ear. Now and again, she stopped playing to smile at her lover and show him her beautiful white teeth, resembling blanched almonds.

"*Io te quiero, querido; io te quiero, nino del mi corazon!*" she murmured with coaxing accents.

She rose and tripped in a sensual dance for him, having thrown her dressing-gown far from her. Her bust was supported in her stays, her arms naked. Her petticoat of cambric and Mechlin lace was flying and whirling at every twist of her loins and wriggle of her hips. Her breasts, hinder globes, and belly were offered provokingly in turn as she retreated, turned, and bent her body backwards, making play coquettishly with a fan. She feigned the swoon of salacious enjoyment, exactly as if she had been posturing to the lilt of an invisible orchestra of guitars and castanets. She mimicked all the gestures of the divine comedy of sexual union and, panting, hot, a musky, wild-beast odour emanating from her perspiring skin, she fell upon her lover, almost violating him, like a girl thrusting her thirsty mouth into the pink pulp of a slice of watermelon, or drinking amontillado from a goat-skin. She curved her frame, arched her loins, and writhed like a professional dancing-girl under Lucien's fierce, delirious attacks.

"Long live they mother for bringing thee into the world, little one of my heart—desire of my eyes, I adore thee!"

She murmured these soft love-sentences of the lasses of Spain, until her silvery whisper died away in the exquisite joy of satisfied sensuality.

At other moments, when the sun was sulky and the sky overcast, she cleverly imitated a bold flapper; the very image of a fast minx, trying, although so young, to enjoy life at top speed, showing the perilous allurements, hesitations, and coquetry of flirtation. Clarette was the very spit of those dashing, naughty, English maidens whose seemingly innocent demeanour and pink-and-white complexions have conquered Paris and maddened the rakes of the City of Light. Her big, velvety eyes sparkled merrily, reflecting the bliss of charming and careless youth. She wore a tight-fitting blue silk jersey—the colour of the sea at twilight—which clung to the buds of her breasts. A leather belt encircled her small waist like a bracelet. Her skirt was of striped flannel and a small straw hat was cocked over one ear.

She played with her lover a game of half-promises, semi-refusals, pretended fury, false yielding, figuring a bread-and-butter miss brimming over with strange curiosity; tasting vice with the tip of her tongue, but without emptying her glass, chary of getting tipsy, even as a wine-bibber samples some rare vintage before stocking it in his cellar.

She perplexed Lucien by questions apparently innocent and unknowing, but which nevertheless could only be answered by extracts from the archives of sadism. She let herself be kissed and touched, only to slip away immediately he tried to enjoy the full possession of her body according to the duty of a male trying to take shelter in the nook of Nature to which he was accustomed.

In order to deceive him with illusions, taming and moulding him as she fancied—and also to satisfy her own desire—she went through the manœuvre of tricky, voluptuous accommodation inherent in a young woman physically a virgin, but whose brain and heart were miry abysses, into which a common prostitute dare not peep without being overcome by sickening vertigo. Clarette drowned Lucien in a flood of artificial delight; almost killing herself besides as she died away under his caresses.

Every kind of languor, anguish and carnal enjoyment, belonging as much to the brain as to the flesh, was put in action. Neither of the twain would confess fatigue nor ask for quarter and, unable to become torpid or exhausted, they finished by falling away from each other as if they were dead. For a few minutes, they would be bereft of the feeling of being alive; their thoughts and, in a minor degree, sight and hearing left them. They succumbed in heavy sleep like a brace of drunkards in the mud.

"To which country shall we travel to-day, my darling boy?" Clarette would often ask of Lucien; these games of meretricious make-believe delighting her more than she would ever dare to confess.

"Choose yourself, little woman."

"No! It's your turn to-day."

"Well, we'll go round the world!"

X

The garden sloped halfway down a hill and it was as spacious as on a lordly estate. Facing marble terraces and flights of steps were vast lawns garnished with bedded red geraniums and rare tropical plants with strange foliage. Under golden bunches of mimosa, the date-trees' fanlike leaves unceasingly rustling and the metallic, verdant gleam of eucalyptus, were broad, winding alleys, full of radiant statues, chosen expressly with the intention of evoking legendary amours. Leda leant back submissively, flogged by the palpitating wings of her swan. Psyche's drawn lips appeared to be wafting despairing appeals to Cupid. Narcissus, stooping slightly, languished in the soft fatigue of self-love. The white figures stood out in bold relief against the blue sea which seemed like a great silk curtain draped from end to end of the horizon.

Farther away, the scene changed into a kind of paradise, a Promised Land from which the traveller departs regretfully, his soul full of an everlasting desire to return. In the hollow of the high mountains sheltering the town from gales, and whence seemed to flow waves of warmth, followed in alternate succession vine-arbours, rose-bushes and orchards of lemon and orange trees loaded with fruit. In the shade of the branches, through which the sun formed filigree patterns, the soil resembled a great carpet of anemones, narcissus, and violets stretching in velvety brocade, as if embroidered, spotted here and there with oranges and lemons gleaming like bars of gold. Perfumes, equally heady and sweet, reigned in the air. Linen, hair, and skin became impregnated with the fragrance to such an extent that one's brain swam in languid intoxication.

This Eden was reached by little paths, paved with sharp pebbles and invaded by marjoram and fennel. One narrow track came suddenly to an end in front of a square cistern, its still, dark water reflecting clouds and shrubs as in an ancient silver mirror.

Clarette enticed her boy one day into this wilderness where none would trouble them while they kissed and embraced, as only butterflies and thrushes passed through it. When they had arrived in the depths of the sylvan retreat, the actress threw herself down at full length among the flowers, crushing them beneath the weight of her perfect body as if, while filling them, to extract from their death agony the most subtle and bewitching scent. When Lucien knelt by her side, attacking with the ardour of a young faun to possess her, she repulsed him with outspread, stiffened hands.

"No, no, I beg you—not like that—not just yet," she whispered, a fresh pagan vision springing up in her brain. "Inhale my odour as if I were a blossom amidst all these flowers—as if you had plucked me. I want to know if my smell can intoxicate you as strongly as their perfume acts on me. See, my love—here is your nosegay. I give it to you!"

So saying, Andrée untied the ribbons of her dressing-gown and appeared stark naked to her lover's dazzled eyes. Shimmering spots of light, filtering through the leaves, danced and illuminated her radiant, lily-white flesh; covering with sparks the creases of her silk robe spreading among the blades of grass and the petals of the violets; enhancing by golden gleams scattered on her milky skin, the twin rosy glories of her bust; the tawny, gilded bushes of her armpits; the vermilion nails of feet and fingers; the mysterious, maddening, inverted triangle of sex, and her black stockings held up by garters of Chantilly lace.

According to her wish, Lucien gradually inhaled her natural scent, voluptuously covering her whole body with his caresses, pressing and forcing his mouth into all the nooks whence emanated the aroma of her adorable body, while the mad dream drove him into delirium.

She was the flower of love, its petals sweet-smelling, in pink and golden bloom, granting visions of happiness, joy, and complete oblivion. He was powerless to tear his lips from its full-blown, throbbing calyx, moistened by celestial dew. He was swooning, ready to give up the ghost by reason of the divine sensation created in his being. It seemed to him that a great weight dragged him down in the eddies of a bottomless sea, where what remained to him of his strength and intelligence was submerged amidst all these perfumes.

While he nearly fainted away, falling all of a heap, pale and livid, Clarette was convulsed in infinite lascivious enjoyment; her contracted hands plucking bunches of violets and crushing them beneath her dilated, palpitating nostrils.

XI

Many months sped by without Lucien and Clarette heeding the flight of time or putting a stop to their hunt after varied carnal diversions. Now and again, some fortuitous event interested them, turning them away for five minutes from their sensual obsession and casting them anew into normal life, by reason of slight astonishment or passing regret and remembrance. They never read a newspaper. They had no knowledge of what went on in the world since they had left Paris one misty, grimy day in winter, when the windows of the brougham were flecked with mudstains at nearly every turn of the wheels; the streetlamps blinking feebly amidst flurries of half-melted snow like the haggard eyes of beggar-women.

Lévêque's instructions were to send visitors about their business, stifle all curiosity, put everybody off the scent and arrange Clarette's affairs as best she could according to her judgment. She was not to write except at the last extremity and only for the most grave and serious reasons.

The servants at the villa were all Italians, hired for the season, like plate and linen from an agency. Clarette had only taken her ladies-maid. She was an artful, dependable girl and her mistress felt almost as safe with her as with her devoted housekeeper.

Sometimes, out of foolhardy bravado, egged on by the innate imprudence of womankind, always liking to play with fire and tempt the devil, the actress would sit on Lucien's knee and, her arm round his neck—her favourite customary posture when she wanted to be petted or gain his confidence—she put the following question to him:

"There's something in your mind that you daren't confess, boy. I'm sure you miss Paris and often think about the Bois and the Boulevards, wishing you were back there again."

"You've never been more mistaken, dearest. It strikes me that I've lost all power of thinking," he added innocently. "The compartment in my brain where my ideas were stocked seems to have been emptied. If I thought about anything at all, it could only be about you, and you alone—you I love."

"Really and truly?" she persisted. "Don't you regret anything at all, Lulu? Not the slightest thing—such as restaurant dinners and suppers, dress-rehearsals, the girls and your pals? You may as well say so. I shan't mind—indeed I shan't!"

"All I regret is that I haven't always known and adored you!"

XII

After the passing of processions of gaudy cars, maskers, and the silvery dust of confetti, spring had come. Love was wafted on the wings of tepid breezes. The roads, with their white hedges, pink trees, clouds of midges dancing through golden rain, the fields strewn with flowers like a carpet for a bride to walk on, the forests of olive-trees, the sea daily spangled by divine dawn, darkened by the purple enchantment of the setting sun, and the sky, constantly blue, seemed to impose gladness on all. Worthy of the days were the nights, passing away calmly, scented, suggestive of illicit delights, inviting loving couples to voluptuous, merry love-making. Moonlight nights were emblazoned with the gleams of millions of precious stones, recalling the vision of innumerable swarms of fireflies winging their way to the great corolla of a lotus.

There were mysterious mysterious affinities between Clarette's radiant, immaculate flesh and the magic planet whose light is as soft as a woman's glances. The orb of night is enchanting and alluring, filling the brain with uncanny dreams and insanity. When darkness was banished, sent shuddering away by the soft, mysterious, artificial light of the moonbeams, the actress escaped from her room, hastily deserting her prosaic bed in the alcove under the feeble gleam of the nightlight, to take refuge in a kind of studio on the second story of the villa, overlooking the bay. Cap Martin could be seen, bent under its verdant thick fleece, and the sinuous coast line as far as Bordighera.

The large room was only furnished with piles of cushions, a broad divan covered with bearskins and ancient silks, satins and brocades; a Florentine sideboard with its panelled doors always ajar and containing a bottle of champagne, glasses, and a plate of ginger-nuts and highly spiced cakes that tickled the palate and created pleasing thirst. The furnace in the basement warming the whole of the house caused summer heat always to reign there.

Having bolted the door, Andrée extinguished all lights and lamps, lifting the silken blinds and drawing back the curtains. Amidst the milky flow of light splashing the window-panes, streaming from the moon as from a lighthouse, falsifying colours and imprinting strange, irregular stains on the matting covering the floor, she let glide down along her body her dressing-gown, drawers, and cambric chemise, emerging from a white, round, hollow pedestal, pleased to think she resembled a statue; throwing her firm breasts proudly forward; arching her loins and stiffening her hips in the bluish haze that clothed her with a celestial circle of rays of light quivering in the warm atmosphere.

She insisted on her lover following her example, and when he was entirely nude, she stretched him out amid the black furs, admiring and contemplating him. Then she

drew herself up to her full height in front of him, her nakedness gleaming with peculiar tones, shimmering lines,
fantastical shadows, and limpid irradiations that startled
him with novel aberration and made him tremble giddily.

As if she was immaterial, intangible—some apparition of
feverish sleep or delirium—she sat down, close to him,
encircling him with her arms, half reclining across his rogu-
ish frame in the prime of youth, setting it on fire by sudden
cunning, lascivious contact; and then escaping, getting
away, fleeing to the other end of the studio in furrows of
white phosphorescence, goading him thus with lust and
deception, until furious, losing his wits, complaining
hoarsely—foaming at the mouth like a rutting animal—he
twisted her wrists with abrupt brutality, wrestling until he
drew her down upon him like an adversary to be crushed
in a fall.

In this superb, victorious posture, she seemed to be
possessing him much more than he possessed her, holding
him down, nailing him under her body in a conquering
ride; her arms outstretched like a ship's yards when the
wind fills the sails; and her fingers incrusted in the
stripling's shoulders. With their supple limbs naked: she,
knees wide apart, breasts projecting, dishevelled head
thrown back, eyes dilated by flaming joy; he, flattened out
on his back supine and still, conquered, they formed a
picture showing the end of a heroic struggle between a
wood-nymph and a shepherd whose heart was tempered
by audacity.

She laughed loudly, drunk with sensual enjoyment,
shrieking like a she-devil bounding in the frenzied merry-
go-round of the witches' sabbath. She was transfigured,
with a wild, enthralling, morbid expression spreading over
her features. Her brain seemed to be agitated by a terrible

swarm of phantasmagorical ideas, excited by impossible longings and intoxicated by lies.

"Lulu—my own Lulu—my adored little *wife*—do you love me? Answer me quickly—do you love your little Andrée as *he* loves you?" she cried out to her sweetheart with sobs, moans, and laughs.

Lucien joined quickly in the game, revelling in the perverted suggestion of this latest mad freak of her imagination with quite as much enjoyment as the actress.

"I love you, my little *husband*," he murmured, "and I'm yours entirely!"

XIII

There were evenings when Clarette pretended to be suffering from headache, vague heavy lassitude, or sudden torpor, so as to diminish the vigour of the lad's assaults, release herself from his greedy grasp and keep him at arm's length. Remaining awake, it diverted her to watch and see him grumble, twist, turn, and complain until, gradually giving way to fatigue, he closed his eyes and dozed. She would then lift herself up and, resting on her elbow, listen to his breathing and let him begin to dream and glide into slumbering oblivion. She scrutinised the gradual relaxation of his features, the slackness of his boyish, slender body, while waiting patiently for hours until he was inert, steeped in deep repose. Then, with feline movements, she gradually drew close to him, caressing him with imperceptible and furtive kisses, encircling and stroking him, communicating artificial life, as it were; sacrificing her mouth while her agile, coaxing hands manœuvred softly, conferring the pleasures of paradise without causing his eyes to open or interrupting his slumbers. Andrée, smiling, became madly intoxicated at the sight of his long shudders of ecstasy, gnashing teeth, and flushing cheeks. She was as happy as if she had really pressed him to her bosom.

When they got up in the morning, she questioned Lucien, forcing him to tell untruths in self-defence. She grew sulky, feigned to be vexed, and scolded him.

"I can see perfectly well that you don't love me," she exclaimed. "Last night you mentioned a woman's name in your sleep. You were dreaming of love. I dare you to say it isn't true, or that I'm mistaken!"

"Well, if you must know, I did have a dream of that kind," he replied, half-awake, rather ashamed, getting out of temper and rebelling. "It's all your fault!" Calming down under his mistress's magnetic glances, he quickly added: "But I give you my word I was dreaming of you—of you alone. I'll tell you my dreams, if you like."

She stopped him out of superstition, as merry as a boarding-school miss in consequence of the success of her naughty lewd trickery.

"I forbid you to describe it. It's unlucky to tell one's dreams before breakfast. Besides, I'll let you into the secret and reveal my awful doings."

With much reticence, stoppage to receive and return kisses, and sudden ripples of laughter, she confessed her new sin and told him all.

"Really and truly," she summed up, "it would have been too much of a good thing for you to dream of some other girl while I was kissing you!"

XIV

Marie-Rose posted them many letters.

It's far from kind of you, to stop writing and not share with me a few minutes of your happiness. I know it's not funny to tell stories to one's mamma when suffering from indigestion brought on by too much kissing and no doubt you're worried because nights and days made up of twelve hours each are far too short for honeymoon couples.

Anyhow, I should be very grateful for the slightest news of you both. It would warm the cockles of my heart in this God-forgotten Argentine Republic where I feel like a lost soul.

Drop me a line, one or the other.

My thoughts are always with you and I envy you.

The star of operetta, in fact, felt herself getting old, besides being lonely, all abroad in faraway Buenos Aires, her tiny bird-brain full of gloomy ideas and sad home-sickness. She counted the days, sometimes fancying that things would turn out badly. Her mania consisted in the idea that she might fall ill, suffer, and slowly pass away without Lucien being at her bedside to give her the last kiss on earth, close her eyes, and bury her. These mournful thoughts tortured and maddened her, bringing wrinkles to her smooth forehead. The love of fair France, the regretful memories of all she had left behind—on the other side of the water, as she expressed herself with profound melancholy—gnawed at her vitals, poisoning every hour of her voluntary, lucrative exile.

She had to strain every nerve not to leave everything in the lurch, engagement and impresario, and brazen out the scandal of such a break, in the face of advertisements published and posters stuck up in profusion. She would have liked to have made her escape as from a prison and embark on the first steamer leaving for Havre. But she was so unbalanced and frivolous, fearful of the least bustle or hindrance; incapable of taking part in any violent quarrel or struggle, she recoiled at the probability of uncertainty, worries, the results of an inevitable lawsuit, the instinctive fear of lawyers who hang on to the last, becoming part and parcel of a lone woman's existence if once they force their way over her threshold; without counting all the cross-examination so damaging to an actress's reputation. So she managed to gain mastery over herself, earning her money with reluctant efforts, straining against the collar like a poor horse working its way up an interminable rising stony road in the blazing sun, dropping on to its ensanguined knees and starting off again under the whip; thinking maybe of the journey's end when he will be unharnessed and find hay in a full manger and a litter of clean straw.

She gave the public their money's worth, unveiling her bosom reluctantly, and going on the stage sulkily as if following a funeral. But directly she heard her cue and the orchestra accompanied her, she resuscitated and was once more the truly wonderful artiste, working herself into a fever, letting herself go and singing as she only knew how. Her triumph was always indescribable, with frenzied calls, showers of wreaths and bouquets, presents amounting in value to a small fortune, and countless tokens of enthusiasm that would have driven crazy any other footlight favourite than Marie-Rose.

She was the idol of the public as a woman as well as an actress, and waves of fascination seemed to surround her with her dead-gold hair; a funny little nose, delicate and aristocratic by reason of its curves, but saucy because tiptilted; her merry, full lips like ripe strawberries; the graceful slope of her shoulders and the satin skin of her opulent bust, reminding one of the pearly lining of a sea shell, pink marble shining in the sun, or tea-rose petals.

It was no wonder therefore that Sarosa was pleased with his bargain and rubbed his hands at having booked her, although her salary was unprecedented. So he tried to get her to renew her engagement and go on a long tour from end to end of South American. Marie-Rose laughed in his face, treating him with as little ceremony as a stuffed doll.

"Strikes me, old sport," she exclaimed insolently, in accents recalling the highest summits of Montmartre, "that you must wake up every morning with your eyelids glued together and never wash your expressive face, which no doubt prevents you from seeing what I feel from morning till night. I'm fed up with this sort of life—got the dead sick

—understand? I'd go out charing, push a fruit-barrow, or live in abject poverty sooner than begin a tour with you over again. Roll that up, laddie, in a bit of cigarette paper and smoke it! No more bids, eh? Going, going—gone!"

Sarosa did not know when he was beaten; counter-attacking, wanting to have the last word and, losing his head at being sent flying so unceremoniously, offered first a million of francs and then a blank contract for the actress to fill up on any sharing terms she liked. His importunity jarred on Marie-Rose's nerves to such an extent that one evening they almost insulted each other.

After knocking discreetly, he opened the door of her dressing-room a little way, and bowed, his face very red, his bald head shining in a bushy crown of grey hair, with the rough and cunning appearance of a speculator accustomed to the leverage power of money. A man he was who listened to no one but himself, never deviating an inch from the line he marked out leading to a golden goal.

"I hope I'm not intruding?" he said as softly as he could with false obsequiosity, for in his state of rancour and disappointment, he would have preferred to crush her wrists in his great common hands until he compelled her to sign.

The actress was in one of her worst moods, full of anxiety, stamping her little feet in despair, feeling quite ill, because among the heap of letters just arrived from Europe, piled up on a table unopened, only to be read when she chose to find time, there was not the one she expected and longed for from the son she adored. This apparent forgetfulness, ingratitude, and lack of affection crushed her, filled her eyes with tears, and struck home to her heart like a dagger-thrust. Anyone could have had for the asking all the loot of her journey: jewellery and the trunks crammed with valuables, like booty from a pillaged city; and she would have discounted all monies coming to her for the rest of her life, sold her soul to the devil, submitted to the vilest and most debasing humiliations to have had news of Lucien immediately; to have pressed him to her breast with her trembling arms; to hear him say and say again that he loved her just as much as when she was in Paris; that he kept a corner in his heart for her—that old quiet corner where she had reigned for so long in sole possession—to listen to him stammering out childish lies and vain excuses, finally exclaiming, while his lips never ceased kissing:

"I knew you would forgive me, mammy. My time has been so taken up! You can't tell how little time a fellow can get to himself when he's in love!"

She stood the lad's photograph up against her mirror, full in the light of the electric lamps on both sides, stopping in her undressing hurry to look at the likeness, blowing kisses to it, taking it up with a caressing touch, moaning sweetly, and still full of pride to think of his handsome bearing, so seductive to women. How sad she was that he had forsaken her; that there were so many miles between his lips and hers.

"My little boy!—my little boy!" she gasped in a sob.

As Marie-Rose did not seem to be aware of his presence, the manager repeated in tones that grew a shade more harsh: "I hope I'm not intruding, madame?"

Annoyed at being caught with tears in her eyes, the actress looked him up and down impertinently.

"That all depends," she replied with a mocking toss of her head.

"Please explain, I beg you."

"Because I guess you're here again to bother me with your offers."

"Exactly. You read my thoughts," he retorted in his usual cool way.

"In that case, my dear sir, I'm sorry to have to show you the door. When I'm covered all over with vaseline, I like to be alone."

"You confounded little devil!" he broke out, grumbling. "Beware if I ever get you in a corner!"

"Oh, I say! You're rather too familiar. That sort of thing don't go down with me!" She took him by the shoulders, and bundled him out. "I never thought you were such an idiot!" she called after him.

Marie-Rose went on filling sheet after sheet of paper with her long, sloping, jerky handwriting, well-nigh illegible; the downstrokes crossing each other, muddled and mixed, as if thoughts and memories had shaken her brain in impetuous stampeding gallops that she panted to follow and note down, scribbling to Lucien enough manuscript to form a small newspaper. What she wrote was incoherent, affectionate, melancholic, mocking, mournful, tearful, and merry, reflecting her different moods. She poured out her wild and fitful love without omitting the least detail, anecdote, or adventure of her daily life.

If you could only imagine, my darling, what it is to be far away from all one loves, and how sad one gets, losing one's wits for the merest trifle when nobody— companion or friend—is nigh in those wretched hours when we would like to be with someone who would laugh us out of superstition, anxieties, fits of blue devils, and comfort us with a kiss or a hearty handshake, I am absolutely certain that you would find a minute's leisure to write two lines on any odd bit of paper.

Something like this, you see: 'I kiss you, dear little mamma, with all my heart to show you how I love you and how I don't forget you.' Or even not as much, only: 'I love you, mother.' Four words like that would make me as strong as a lion and bring me enough happiness to last me a month.

You've never travelled all alone. You don't know the terrors of this chessboard town where I feel quite small, all out of gear, with my French face and Parisian ways. Here a woman is a mere atom and counts for nothing. Two and two make four more steadfastly in this city than anywhere else in the world, I fancy, and time is put in the scales like merchandise, with dollars for weights. I feel I'm carried away, urged on and crushed by some invisible force.

I'm afraid and I don't know why, as when a child is left alone in its cot in the dark. Sometimes I feel inclined to throw my arms round the necks of passers-by in the street when they speak our dear, pretty language. I tread on their heels, following them like a mad creature only to listen to them talking.

It's your fault that I can't sleep; that I'm getting ugly. I look like a dirty, wrinkled nightcap. You deserve to be thrown over and treated as you treat me. 'All over between us two!' is what I ought to say, as in that play we saw together—if you remember—last year at the Palais-Royal theatre.

Time did not hang heavy on my hands then. I laughed more often than I cried. I had a handsome young scamp of a son who adored his mother; who would have defended her; who hid nothing from her; who was good, loving, confiding; who would have been sorry to hurt her feelings or cause her to feel the slightest sadness.

You've fair grounds for refuting my argument: you're in love; your love is returned, and it's your first love. I'm not quite sure but what if I were in your place, I shouldn't care a straw, send everybody to the devil and live for my love alone just as you're doing.

But you must consider that I'm not an ordinary mamma. Your love is as necessary for me as food and drink; without you I feel myself going mad. I'd cover one word from you with kisses and kisses. One line would bring me a part of your being. I can't stand your silence any longer. I shall be seriously ill.

Before Marie-Rose gummed down the envelope, she added the following across the margin of the fourth page:

I swear, my dear Clarette, that I'm not jealous. I'm really overjoyed at the idea of your reciprocal love. I don't want to put any obstacle in your way. I should like to change places with you and you are too great a friend of mine not to help me and take my part a little bit. Be merciful and scold Lucien gently and caressingly. He deserves it and he ought to obey you. Force him to write to me.

A kiss for him and for you.

Luckily for Marie-Rose and Sarosa, she knew nothing about the sad prologue of her son's adventure and the prolonged anxieties of her friend and fellow-actress. The excessively sensitive disposition of Marie-Rose, leading her to see the blackest side of things and fly off at a tangent where her boy was concerned, added to the maddening, torturing mirage of distance, was such that the poor woman would probably have succumbed under the weight of the bad news. Anyhow, come what may, she would have broken the contract binding her to her impresario.

But Clarette greatly preferred to have no one in her way to interfere with her task, take her place at Lucien's bedside, or challenge her right to be there, so that no other woman could hope for the privilege of being included in the effusions of loving gratitude pouring out from the heart of a convalescent youth in favour of the nurse whose soft, pitying hands had dressed his wounds, given him to drink, and guided him gradually back to life; whose soothing voice had lulled him to sleep; whose affection had never failed. All this remained and was magnified in his brain, memories never to be forgotten and always to be evoked like healing balm at the slightest tormenting illness. Andrée, therefore, distrustful of the perfect intimacy and great confidence already existing between mother and son, took good care not to let Marie-Rose have any news. Nor did Lucien's mistress send for her or alarm her, but kept her aloof with tricky telegrams wired from Paris; and later on, from Mentone.

Andrée easily prevailed upon her lover to show her all his letters and not to allude to the danger he had overcome, thanks to his youth and her ceaseless efforts as energetic as those of a sister of charity defending a patient against the skeleton with the scythe and, finally victorious, routing the grim destroyer. At her dictation, Lucien, satisfied to do her bidding, told of his departure for the Riviera with no unnecessary details, picturing it as a sudden fantasy; a desire to play truant.

All said and done, this enabled him to excuse himself easily for forsaking his mother and breaking his promises. He had no correspondence to keep up—a task he hated—and when instinctive filial feelings stirred his soul feebly, now and again, he was delighted at the unhoped-for idea—a godsend that absolved him.

From week to week, from month to month, he spaced

out and shortened his letters. At last, he stopped entirely and wrote no more to his mother, notwithstanding that he was certain she madly adored him. He knew she only painted her face, exposing her half-nude breasts and her rounded thighs in fleshings for his sake; still working hard at her singing with the idea of sharing her earnings with him on her return and giving him money, and still more money, as much as he desired for his pleasure and to lead a fast life. When Andrée, astonished despite herself at his selfishness, upbraided him halfheartedly for his laziness, the young rascal invariably replied:

"I can't help it, I don't feel in the humour! You can write a line or two for me!"

XV

Because her brain was crammed with illusions and maternal pride, Marie-Rose pitied Andrée.

Lucien's mother was a strange being and had wrought sad havoc during her career. Incapable of doing harm to a fly, emotional, charitable, shedding tears over a little flower-girl selling bunches of violets in the streets or a pauper's hearse trundling along unaccompanied without a friend to follow it, going to the place of rest: an anonymous grave. Nevertheless, in order to conquer boredom and be able to laugh for five minutes, she was indifferent to the fact that she had often made men miserable for the rest of their existence, or had kindled strong passions consuming the soul. She considered that life was too short for anything except uninterrupted enjoyment and that it was quite time enough to be serious and reasonable on the dark night when the bottom of the hill is reached and the mirror reflects a wrinkled, deformed face in a frame of white hair.

It seemed that Lucien would take after her. A son is often the effigy of his mother, inheriting her weaknesses, preferences, dislikes, and as much vice as virtue. In the adventure of her boy with Clarette, there were reminiscences of Mme. Hardange's career. She, too, when first she fell in love, had bolted off like a mad horse with the bit between its teeth. Nothing could have stopped her or brought her back. Like her son, as soon as she knew what it was to love and be loved, and had lost her virginity, tasting the pleasures of caressing and coupling, she fancied that the gates of heaven were open to her and that she yielded never to give herself to any other man. This resolution did not prevent her from rearing and kicking over the traces whenever one of her partners tried to hold her to him, or tame her. Rack her memory as she might, she could not recollect having behaved otherwise with seventy-five per cent of the men she had loved; or having been compassionate when she found they were weak-minded and easily dominated.

Her darling, good-looking lad would be cynically inconsiderate with women. She hoped so, for was it not the height of folly to abandon oneself entirely to heartless women whose brains get muddled with the slightest temptation; to deny that happiness is a mere fantasy that cannot last; to believe that one can escape the common lot and not fall mortally wounded in the unequal struggle of the sexes? As if by some inexorable decree of fate, one or the other— lover or mistress—was bound to go under, but not Lucien. That could not be.

Her diagnostic was all wrong. In the bustle of departure and farewell embraces, she had not seen things clearly and could not guess that Clarette would throw herself body and soul into this amour as in an abyss; playing her last card—

imprudent and insane creature!—with this nineteen-year-old stripling. Her silence, the pleasure-trip and the elopement proved to Marie-Rose how wrong she was, even if proofs were needed. Clarette loved Lucien. That was certain and doubtless she intended to live with him maritally. Marie-Rose pitied and envied her no longer. Lucien's mother reproached herself for having fanned the flame of her son's infatuation and having been too accommodating at the beginning of the liaison, which she looked upon as a funny case of "mashing," out of the ordinary run. It amused her like a witty curtain-raiser played on a Sunday night at a club by amateurs and of no importance, never to be revived despite its success. Clarette was a friend of fresh date, charming, frank, and generous, who had given her absolute and unforgettable proofs of affection, rendering her many good services without even venturing to allude to them; or bothering her by fawning on her hypocritically; or worrying her, as had other frivolous chits, with loving appeals and ridiculous fits of jealousy. Clarette had always taken her part. By reason of her disposition, tastes, and faults, she seemed like a cousin or a relation with whom one had been brought up, or gone to school with, passing holidays together and swapping girlish dreams and curious longings. She had not the slightest reason to hope that harm would come to her, or to wish that her fellow-actress should be driven quicker or more painfully from the paradise she desired to enter. Unconsciously, Marie-Rose had forced her to embark on a sea of troubles, condemning her to martyrdom so that her boy should be happy and play with a finer, more elegant, and gaudier toy than is generally granted to a 'prentice Don Juan of his age.

How could she, who had never been able to reflect quietly three minutes in a year, manage to grasp the fact that Clarette was sincere; "trying," in the parlance of racing men, and not only satisfying a passing caprice, taking him for what he was worth, but building seriously on his future affection and abjuring her former theories often summed up in one concise phrase: "My love has no morrow." Marie-Rose shuddered in sudden fright, as when one sees a ship sinking in the distance or a house on fire. She said to herself that Andrée and herself were of the same terrible, dangerous age when Cupid lies in wait for women and pierces the tender hearts of the poor creatures who are like roses completely in bloom. A gust of air as light as a boy's breath scatters the petals. It suddenly struck Marie-Rose that in her turn she might also fall a victim to this contagion and suffer the same fate. It was dreadful to fall in love too late in life, yielding to a lover soon to be off and away, seeking pleasure elsewhere and getting rid of a woman brutally or with polite lies, but torturing her all the same, and leaving her to her loneliness, her heart aching with unsatisfied longing, hungering after affection, and yet vibrating from the effect of recent sensuous excitement. Alone!—at the very moment when one had begun to appreciate all the heavenly enchantment and joy of living with one man, as if married. Alone!—with one's dream and the distaste of what one had formerly considered was real felicity. Alone!—with the certainty that all is finished, that such unspeakable intoxication will never be enjoyed again. Alone!—dazzled by the glorious dawn at which one has only been able to peep without being allowed to be purified by the sunshine of the coming day.

It was terrible for Marie-Rose to be forced to realise that she was approaching the age of forty—thirty-seven had just tolled like a funeral knell. Months and days were running on, added to the old account. To-morrow she would be mellow, as worthless as over-ripe fruit or a faded nosegay and would be compelled to descend the roughest declivity of the hill of life. There was nothing else to be done but to sink into the mire again, in stupid monotonous debauchery. Her sweet lips, as yet healthy and pouting, would dry up and wither; and very soon rouge and face-powder would be powerless to mask her wrinkles. Such torture would be intensified still more by meeting incessantly wherever she went in quest of amusement the only object she had ever really loved in the whole course of her life. She would have to witness the display of his great joy as he paraded openly with his mistress usurping the position she regretted and coveted. It would be agonising to feel oneself peered at slyly with mocking pity that stabs and lacerates the heart. The result would be a lingering death, in affright of self as in front of a mad dog; and become cognisant of one's fearful state—for invalids have lucid moments—finding that reason was departing from the brain and that a frightful mania was incrusted therein, nailed fast. To escape the obsession, she would have to rush out of her dwelling, live riotously; drinking, singing, laughing, so as not to feel lonely, and to get drunk with noise and the obscene touches of strangers; break herself down with fatigue, ill herself—stupefying her wits and her heart.

The vision was as gloomy and as sinister as a glimpse of hell, bringing fits of mortal dejection that lasted for whole days, depriving her of sleep and making her tremble in fear.

Luckily, Marie-Rose was prompt to regain her energies and dismiss all dark thoughts. She shrugged her shoulders, jumped from black presentiments to rosy ideas, and soon laughed at all her terrors.

Undoubtedly, Clarette would suffer because she was unlucky enough in her first experiment to fall across an ideal, innocent sweetheart. A lover like Lucien might be the one man capable of performing such strange transformations and prodigious miracles. It seemed improbable and impossible that the double, or exact copy, of her son could ever be found, or that anybody equal to him or better than he could be met with anywhere.

XVI

Lucien and Clarette had no idea of deserting the land of roses and the everlastingly blue sea to return to their Parisian home. The season, however, had come to an end. The hotels were shutting up one after the other and their noisy table d'hôte bells no longer disturbed the soft twilight and the sunny haze of the South. The great white buildings seemed dead, with their closed shutters, vast dumb frontages, and deserted gardens. One by one, along the dusty beach, spotted by fishing-boats, the villas were emptied. There was no longer any chance of meeting those pitiful bath-chairs where could be seen the emaciated face of a consumptive patient surrounded by his pillows and shaded from the sun by the white umbrella of a manservant yawning at every step, or followed by a Sister of Charity mumbling vague prayers with bloodless lips.

The lover and his mistress lacked both the desire and the will to follow those happy patients who left the Riviera cured, freed from illness or merely buoyed up with the hope of dragging out their existence till the autumn, and live, if only one season more.

Our pair of lovers were not haunted by the alluring vision of Paris, the dangerous enticement of the Allée des Acacias with its three lines of carriages stopping and proceeding like a carnival procession. They had forgotten the gay and bright Boulevards and their sparkling shopfronts; the spring race-meetings and the amusing throng in the paddock; the new fashions; the chesnut-trees in bloom; the pretty landscape of the Bois de Boulogne in vernal splendour, trim and neat, lacquered pink and green; the thrills of "trying-on" at dressmakers' or milliners' establishments, stopping till late to gossip and get acquainted with all the scandal one had not heard for so many months. They felt happy at not being threatened with indiscreet visits, since they could go in and out just as it suited them, stroll through the streets, show themselves without being stared at, drive through fields behind a pair of ponies, the bells on their collars making merry music, or choose a boat in the little harbour and, the sail set, glide out to sea, or come to anchor in a peaceful cove, sheltered from the breeze by granite rocks and the pine-trees' drooping branches.

Clarette always patronised the same old boatman. He wore little gold earrings and his wide, shaven face, tanned by sun and spray, reminded one of a Roman emperor as seen on medals that even now are sometimes ploughed up in the furrows of Southern France. Having formerly cruised on yachts, he knew how to behave diplomatically and keep in the background. No one knew better how to amuse his customers and plan excursions to kill time.

He took the lovers one night to fish by fire. The fireflies lit up the darkness like a shower of fleeting, gilded sparks, and the surface of the sea in the bay was smooth, only gleaming with sudden splashing of phosphorescent drops following the leap of some fish in distress and forming mysterious figures in the water. There was something fantastical and uncanny that thrilled them both in their gliding progress by means of slow strokes of the oars through what seemed like heavy oil. The brazier of fir-cones and resinous branches crackled and spluttered, casting blood-red reflections, forming a long, broad line that followed in their wake. The skipper stood erect at the prow, surrounded by smoky clouds, attentive, watching for his prey, and firmly grasping the trident that he cast and drew in at intervals. On its sharp points could be noted the death agony and convulsive struggles of mullets and weird fish peculiar to the Mediterranean.

Arm-in-arm, pressing close to each other without speaking, "they let themselves live," as Clarette would say, and felt so tranquil and happy; so far out of the world that they were on the point of shedding tears of joy.

Lucien was the most amused, as he was full of unceasing childish curiosity, always on the alert and diverted by any change of scene or action. Clarette was less receptive, but nevertheless she revelled with all the strength of her soul in the delight of having her lover almost in her skirts in the middle of the divine night where on shore, in invisible gardens, innumerable nightingales were singing as if joining in a voluptuous symphony. The evaporation of the scent of flowers was so mingled and blended in the saline breath of the sea that it was impossible to recognise or define their odour.

Following the winding shore, exploring holes in the rocky depths where the sand gleamed like a golden carpet under the sudden flare; and seaweed waved, undulating like strange violet and green tresses, the boat made its way into a narrow, dark bay, surrounded by a wall of foliage— rock-rose, myrtle and pines. The thicket, marked out by cloudy white blossoms, exhaling as from a vase of dried petals, the perfume of myrrh and incense, evoked the vision of a distant, mysterious island of love, lost in the billows; a pagan Cytherea, doves flying over it, accompanying lustful couples eager to consummate the divine sacrifice.

It was late. The night wore on and the flame died down in the brazier. The boatman and his boy were heavy and dull with fatigue. Clarette bent over Lucien, encircling his neck with her arms.

"Suppose we stopped out, Lulu?" she whispered, a new fancy lighting up her sea-green eyes. "You will—won't you? The men can sleep in their boat. We'll lie down under the trees. Do! Say you will, darling. It's a mad longing that's come over me. It must be awfully nice and comfortable in the thick undergrowth."

"Just as you like," replied Lucien, who always submitted with docility to his mistress's whims.

He signed to the skipper to pull in shore and let them land.

They walked on without caring where they were going, helping each other, hesitating, stumbling against gnarled roots or pointed pebbles that clattered down carrying along other stones with a shrill sound as of cymbals. The pair sought a secret, sheltered nook where, in the tepid warmth of this spring night, their bodies intertwined could wallow again in carnal enjoyment. Their clamours of ecstasy would rise to the stars, tearing aside the veil of the silence of solitude like the moans of animals.

At last they halted at the end of the promontory that formed a barrier to the cove. The sand was strewed with seaweed and resinous fir-cones. The horizon was bounded by the sea glistening with the countless reflections of the stars.

"Won't this suit, love?" said Andrée. She added in delight, lisping girlishly: "Help me to make the bed, please, sir!"

A rough kind of couch was soon sketched out by means of the handfuls of dry leaves and seaweed they piled up together.

"Come quickly, dearest. You can't tell how cosy it is!" murmured the actress, the first to throw herself down.

When Lucien followed her example and they were both reclining side by side, Andrée pretended to close her eyes. She yawned, stretching her limbs as if overcome by sudden fatigue.

"I'm asleep already, Lulu. You won't be able to wake me."

"Don't tell stories!"

"Oh, my sweet!—do please try and wake me!"

"Any way I like?"

"Just as you choose, little man. Good night, dear."

The boy made no reply. His nerves astretch by her apparent resistance, the strong, aromatic odours, and the long sleeplessness of the night, he lifted up Andrée's unresisting head and showed her that he had profited by the tantalising, delicious lesson she had given him in the brougham filled with violets, going home after the first performance of the Venus ballet. His lips wandered coaxingly over the back of her neck, her temples, eyelids, under her chin, and at the corners of her mouth. His hot breath fanned her flesh, while his tickling fingers passed lightly round the contours of her hips and thighs. She quivered from head to foot, scarcely able to restrain herself, but stubbornly resisting her feelings, longing to drive her lover to extremities, and force him to brutalise her. She kept her eyes shut, without uttering a word or yielding to his sensual attacks; skilfully playing the part of a woman overtaken by sleep that stupefies the most robust of mortals, like the drunkenness of strong spirits.

Lucien's refined caresses continued with increasing voluptuousness. She did not give way, however, nor forget her passivity, or her assumed unconsciousness in which each kiss grew into a sudden surprise, almost akin to the kisses of dreamland. Not knowing what was coming next; struggling against her own desires; the growing fever that heated her blood and set her whole being ablaze, pricking her loins as with the points of spurs, shook her from top to toe with extraordinary lascivious delight.

In his disappointment of defeat, he felt as if he would like to strike her out of revenge for not getting the better of her and being made a toy of for such a long time. He panted as if he had been running a long race.

"I'm certain you're not asleep! Open your eyes!" he ordered in vain.

Suddenly throwing himself on her, crushing her, his hands rummaging under her petticoat, forcing her legs apart with his stiffened knees as savagely as a lustful satyr who might have sprung from a leafy hiding-place to violate a goddess in her sleep, he had his way with her and possessed her in the deepest conjunction.

"So much the worse for you! I wanted you!" he whispered hoarsely.

With unbridled salacity, his heart beating wildly, his brain on fire, his strength magnified tenfold as by a magic spell, he was now once more a male misusing his muscular superiority. In his triumph, he forgot all caressing delicacy and became like unto a beast of the fields, in the season when the sexes watch for each other with desire and couple in the act of procreation, when stables and forest clearings reek with bitter, rutting odours. He bruised and shook her. He flagellated her with a shower of blows as of a flail scattering the corn and sending up golden dust over the barn-floor covered by the sheaves. Each stroke flashed fresh vibrations through Clarette's body, forcing her to quiver from head to foot as if she was a bell that a drunken ringer might have caused to crack in furious wedding chimes.

This simple, common, brutal sensation of coition surpassed in acuity, languor, length of time, and enjoyment every conjunction in which she had revelled ever since Lucien had been her lover and her slave. It was so violent and intensely devouring that the lust-maddened woman threw her arms round the young fellow's waist, driving her nails into his flesh and almost piercing the cloth of his light summer jacket.

"My love—Lulu, I adore you," she gasped in accents that were unreal and no longer human, evoking the prayer of one of the elect on the dazzling threshold of Paradise. "Keep on! More—more! Yes—Lulu—like that—for ever! Don't go from me! Stop where you are! Oh!—Oh!—I'm so happy!"

The lull came and they fell back exhausted among the scattered seaweed and leaves.

"Hadn't we better go to sleep now—don't you think?" was Lucien's query as his lips curled in a victorious smile.

"No, no! It will be daylight so soon," she returned, quickly raising herself up on her hands. "You're not sleeping, surely, my darling?"

"Not more than you are—you bad creature!"

And they fell to loving each other again. They were closely joined once more, insatiable, goaded on by fresh rising lust; drawing new strength from the pure air diffusing the smell of the sea, the subtle fragrance of mastic-trees and rock-roses. The intervals between each act of love were surprisingly brief, for they welded their bodies with as much fury as if they were copulating for the last time and were forced to bid each other an eternal farewell at the peep of day and, tired of everything, dash themselves hand in hand into the depths of green chasms, seeking together oblivion in nothingness; or, perchance, new amours and dreams in another planet; a new existence.

One by one, the stars paled, effaced by the first blush of gold and pink daybreak resembling the opening of some strange, celestial flower. Thorny bushes, and the sombre green tones of the pine-trees appeared, standing out against the emerald limpidity of the sea. The expanse of water seemed to be fanned and it wrinkled under the fresh breeze, tiny waves becoming illuminated with gleaming spangles, while it also stirred the foliage, and the leaves appeared to be slowly awakening and gaining animation.

As he rose to his feet, Clarette shrieked in fright and anguish.

"Lulu! Lulu! I can't see you! I'm dying!" she called to him, with the despairing accents of a person drowning, sinking in whirling eddies.

At first the boy thought his mistress was joking and burst out laughing as he strolled away towards the beach. But Clarette continued groaning as if her brain was bursting under the stress of fearful hallucinations.

"Where are you, my own?" she called. "Where are you? Take me—speak to me!"

Strangely groping, with the jerky and timid gestures of the blind, she struggled on to her knees, dragging herself forward on the sand. Then, bounding erect with a sudden effort, she staggered about, her legs giving way, too weak to support her. Her face was livid, convulsed with vertigo, bloodless, as when life becomes extinct after arteries are severed. It appeared as if the wretched woman was struggling in thick darkness.

"Where are you?" she moaned, her voice hoarse and dying away in strangled sobs. "Don't leave me all alone. Oh, where have you gone to?"

Lucien laughed no longer. He trembled in fright, chocking, nearly bereft of sense, stupefied by this tragic awakening, a vision of agony succeeding so quickly to the supreme joy of carnal caresses. He could not manage to utter a syllable—his throat gripped as in a vise—nor regain in a slight degree his reason and a little coolness. The radiant serenity of daybreak and the lulling murmur of the waves ornamenting the shore with their foam dyed pink by the rising sun, made their mutual anguish still more cruel and lamentable.

Just when turning round, he hastened with outstretched arms to embrace and hold up Clarette, she beat the air with her contracted hands, swung round and dropped down flat on her back like a great distressed bird wounded unto death.

"Lulu! Lulu!" she sighed in what seemed a last appeal, and remained still and stiff, with the absolute appearance of death.

Like a madman, the boy threw himself on his mistress, putting his lips on hers as if to help her feeble breathing. He pressed his ear against her heart that beat with feverish irregularity and, certain that she lived, that all was not over and there remained some hopes of saving her, he half-undressed her so that she might breathe easier. He hailed the boatman. The two men ran to join him. Thanks to their energetic rubbing and the cold water they dashed in her face, wetting her forehead and neck, Clarette came to gradually, opened her eyes, stretched out her limbs slowly and regained her senses. She escaped from the limbo in which she had momentarily disappeared as if in a dark whirlpool.

Healthy colour returned to her cheeks. Her nostrils palpitated and her eyes glistened with unspeakable surprise and heavenly joy. Her glance was not the same as usual. The pupils were dilated, lit up with the inward fire of ecstasy. She did not speak, hypnotised, so to say, in the intoxicated, rapt contemplation of her lover. Seeing the anguish that still distorted the lad's features; infinitely delighted to find that his eyes were full of tears, as he trembled, panting still with grief not yet departed, she seized both his hands and clasped them in hers.

"So then, Lulu, you would have suffered if I'd died?" she whispered softly in friendly, rather than loving, accents.

He was only slightly reassured and feared to allude in any way to the great loss of which he had just had a glimpse.

"Don't talk about that, I entreat you!" he interrupted.

"Why won't you answer my question, darling?" she persisted.

Her false gaiety suddenly disappeared and such regret, bitterness, and keen melancholy were expressed by her features that it appeared as if she was at rest for a few moments only, feeling herself condemned beyond remission, and knowing that very soon another upheaval, more violent and painful still, would deal the last blow and carry her off. Nevertheless, the stroke that had convulsed her, prostrating her with such a perfidious, brutal shock; the exhaustion caused by the unlimited fatigue of her madly lascivious, uninterrupted acts, by which her body, lacking the suppleness and resistance of early youth, was over-wrought, began to wear off. Her frame had resisted continual sensual wear and tear, but now all the machinery of her delicate organisation was out of gear and had stopped as if some essential part was broken.

She recovered her strength, her thoughts grew clearer, as if under the influence of some elixir swallowed drop by drop through the teeth prized apart. Animal instinct no longer made her suffer and complain, but her anguish was derived from her brain and heart corroded by inconsolable grief combined in uneasy awakening.

Why had capricious destiny forced her to have a fore-taste of the terrible feelings of death, when her last black hour had not struck? Why had she been saved and succoured? It would have been a sweet and wonderful adventure to leave the world in that way, at the close of a night of enjoyment in such an ideal spot, surrounded by the sea, trees redolent of perfume, the song of birds, the rising sun, the fleeing stars, and give up the ghost without a strug-gle, in the shortest dying agony, her lips still moist from her lover's coaxing mouth, her flesh still aglow and aching from the violence of nuptial joys; her whole being impreg-nated to the marrow with the quintessence of love and end life in glorious triumph, breaking like a violin string made to vibrate too passionately and parting in two at the end of the concert when the last note has resounded.

She wept at the thought. Seeing Lucien's eyes fixed on her face with mute interrogation in his eyes; full of renewed anxiety at her new, perplexing fit of sadness, she sup-pressed her grief in order to give him a smiling glance.

"Don't worry any more, dear. It's all over—the last storm before the sun comes out. Come, let's be off. I'm feel-ing jolly now!"

As she was still weak, broken down by the violent shock, the skipper and his boy seated her on a pair of oars and carried her to the boat.

PART THE SECOND

I f a reporter had interviewed Marie-Rose concerning her feelings, insisting like a father-confessor to get to know the numerous impressions of the mother as well as of the actress, from the exact moment of embarking for the Argentine Republic until she arrived in Mentone, she would not have had a merry story to tell.

She could not understand, or perchance guessed only too clearly with great grief and instinctive fear of the future, what was going on in the indefinable soul of her fellow-actress and in Lucien's virgin heart. During her tour, Clarette had altered and so had the boy. They were so different to what they were when she had left them and seemed so run-down that the star of opera bouffe saw in alarm that she scarcely recognised them.

It was only natural that after an absence of so many months, neglecting matters of business and all her friends, she should consider that to stop in Paris meant a useless halt with risk of delay, losing much precious time. She was dying to embrace her son, press him to her bosom and smother him with kisses. That is why, full of affectionate ideas, she went to see him; because the ungrateful youth, steeped in love, neglecting his filial duty, had not gone to Havre to meet the incoming steamer and did not care to form one of the crowd waving handkerchiefs on the jetty. His only excuse was that being so deeply in love he had forgotten his obligations.

It was therefore only natural, Marie-Rose kept on saying to herself, that she should go and see her best and oldest friend, Clarette. In the past, Lucien's mother had welcomed Andrée in many of her different unions. After all, in Bohemian circles, the fact of lovers and mistresses living together constitutes matrimony, but a mother-in-law is not looked upon with the same disfavour as in legal households. Marie-Rose was very indulgent and put herself in the place of the loving couple, trying to plead in attenuation of their lack of consideration. But she did not succeed and being open-hearted, confiding, and superficial, she suffered greatly. All her illusions, the pretty, tender lies that break a heart hungering for love, were scattered to the winds one by one. Her feminine subtlety, leading her to scrutinise exchanges of glances, and the slightest whisper or gesture, laid bare all her errors of judgment and enabled her to see through Andrée.

Marie-Rose, returning home, consulted the time-table unceasingly, unnerved by continual stoppages of the train, counting the minutes and recapitulating all the happy dreams of the sea-voyage and the entrancing anticipation of her son rushing to enfold her in his arms. Instead of all these demonstrations of affection, kisses, and eager questions, she had only experienced a brutal shock, such as puts years on a woman's life and crushes the most easy-going and case-hardened folks.

Although she had telegraphed to Lucien stating the hour of her arrival, there was no one waiting to receive her on the platform of the dusty station gleaming white in the sun. No one to help her to step out of the carriage and, in order to kiss her without hindrance, rid her of the innumerable handbags and parcels a Parisian pet always takes with her on a journey. There was not even a servant, obsequious and attentive because reckoning on tips when the visitor should depart. Marie-Rose would have betted large sums on Lucien and Clarette both meeting the train, with kisses and laughter all round. Her mother's heart would have been divinely stirred to see her son grown taller, more handsome, and arm-in-arm with his lady-love like a real husband.

"Listen to me, my children—another time try and live a little nearer the Boulevards," was the funny remark she had invented on the way as an answer in case Lucien or Clarette remarked that the journey in the train had fatigued her.

She called herself cowardly and foolish for not having taken the next train to Paris, leaving them in disgust because they did not care for her and had humiliated her so grievously, but she had not been able to summon up sufficient courage to flee and escape. The thought that Lucien was now near her; breathing the same air; that in a few moments she would be able to see him again and caress him fondly, got the better of her energy and fury.

After all, she met him driving along the road. Her fly crossed his vehicle. There was only a slight delay due to the difference in clocks which in country villas are always wrong, too slow or too fast. There was no need for him to try and excuse himself, as she showed no vexation, opening her arms to him widely, and moistening his cheeks with tears of emotion and happiness. Without troubling about her luggage following behind her cab, she quickly jumped into Lucien's governess-car covered with an awning.

"How happy I am, darling!" she murmured, pressing her son to her breast, stopping him from speaking and looking at him with ecstasy. "Kiss me again!" she went on with short, hysterical laughs. "It seems as if I hadn't seen you for hundreds of years. You can't tell how I love you. You're more good-looking than ever—she must dote on you." Marie-Rose had already forgotten the gloomy disappointment of her arrival and the absurd delay that had tortured her. "So, it's still going on—your honeymoon, eh? She's madly in love with you—isn't she?"

"Yes! And I adore her!" he replied with such conviction that Marie-Rose felt as if she had been stabbed in the throat. She turned deadly pale.

"She would have come to the station to meet you," he added, "but she's not very well. You're not vexed?"

"On the contrary!" returned his mother, thrown off her guard in her excitement and imprudently shrugging her shoulders. "She would only have been in our way."

"In our way!" echoed Lucien, rebelling like a pious man forced to listen to blasphemy. Then, suddenly, attacking his mother bluntly, speaking harshly in imperious accents, causing her to open her eyes and without dreaming how he tortured her, he exclaimed: "I don't suppose you've come down here to bother us, eh? I hope you'll keep quiet, or else—"

"Or else?" she questioned timidly, as he stopped.

She regretted her interrogation and hoped he had not heard her, while she trembled like an innocent prisoner waiting for the judge's supreme verdict, and having well-nigh abandoned all hope in human equity.

"I shouldn't be long putting things right. You know I'm awfully fond of you, but Clarette counts with me more than anybody! That's what I say and don't you forget it, please, in case by any chance you should be feeling jealous."

The delicious, childish demonstrations of affection which Marie-Rose had anticipated would have degenerated into a sordid quarrel if she had not bowed to fate by postponing her hopes of revenge and plans of battle until a more favourable opportunity. She felt herself at a disadvantage and doomed to defeat. Therefore, being a talented actress and knowing better than anyone how to wear a mask and get the better of her impulsive disposition, feeling stronger than usual because she was fighting to free Lucien, and defending her sacred maternal rights, she succeeded in keeping her temper, making up her mind not to play a wrong card.

"You've got rather touchy, my dear," she ran on, bursting out into shrill and noisy laughter that sounded quite real and completely tricked her boy. "Can't you see I'm joking? I've got a rise out of you. Poor darling, it's easy to read your thoughts. Now I know all I was trying to find out and I'm awfully pleased. A man doesn't take a woman's part so warmly unless he's sure of her love, so you'll let me love her a little bit, too, considering you love her so much and she returns your love."

"Will I let you?" he replied quickly and gladly, immediately won over and confiding. "Of course I will! I was frightened what would become of me between the two of you—both so jealous of each other. I was bothered, thinking that you wouldn't be reasonable and that things would be at sixes and sevens. She's my wife, you see, and I must stick up for her. If I didn't, she wouldn't have anything more to do with me. I'd sooner die than lose her. I've got a lot to tell you about her that you don't know."

"I can guess! I've only to look at you and listen!"

It was a sad return for her and entirely different—alas!—to what the star songstress had hoped for and imagined like a mirage in the desert during her interminable exile. It was a cruel blow for her heart that her adored son trampled on like grapes in a wine-press. All her tenderness and affectionate fancies were destroyed and scattered. She saw herself as an old actress. The performance was mournful and painful; all her influence was gone; she was submerged in a sea of indifference. She was out of date; her "gags" went for nothing, being only listened to for the sake of old times; neither applauded nor hissed; treated like an understudy. Nevertheless, she hung on desperately, refusing to abdicate, throw up her engagement, hand her part to another, or disappear.

Poor Marie-Rose was not befooled for a minute and did not believe in the sincerity of the honeyed declarations of friendship with which Clarette overwhelmed her; nor did the affection vouchsafed grudgingly impress her. Lies upon lies, yawns disguised as smiles, icy kisses scarcely touching the cheek, conversations stopping dead whenever she appeared, the days counted as when a poor relation or a sponging guest is making a stay—all this could be easily gathered by the couple's doubtful welcome, the transparent significance of their manner, questions, and laughs. Marie-Rose would have been idiotic or have worn a threefolded bandage over her eyes not to have seen the conspiracy against her; not to have guessed how her presence wearied and troubled the loving pair and how they wished she would cut short her visit and return to Paris. Marie-Rose could see. She was quickly-witted and gifted with the subtle instinct enabling her to detect all the wicked tricks that one woman can play on another.

If she had been obliged to confide her troubles and lay bare her heart, lacerated with anguish, she could have made all good people cry their eyes out. She remembered a creole song she had heard in a Buenos Aires music-hall. Melodious, melancholy music accompanied the sobs of a girl whose baby is torn from her breast to be sent far away to a wet-nurse.

There was nothing that Marie-Rose dared try or do to put a stop to the affliction. She was like a doctor seeing too late the inanity of his first diagnostic, and not knowing what remedy to prescribe in the face of invading, contagious gangrene of which the poison mounts, spreading to the brain. The medical man abandons all hope of cure and reckons only on some miraculous change for the better. Her maternal pride had blinded her when she pitied Clarette and compared her love to the momentary blaze of a heap of straw; full of pity at the thought that Lucien, his appetite quickened by his first sips of the cup of love, would soon have broken his bonds and rushed to kiss other lips, leaving a mistress too old for the mad desire of a nineteen-year-old youth. The actress had a firm hold, and had glued his flesh so tightly to her aphrodisiacal body that he could not escape. He was a prisoner inside this woman. She had weaned him from all remembrance, affection, and ideas, with the exception of what was stamped with the impress of her beauty and their love.

And it was she—the mother!—who had done this grand deed and fastened them together. The unvarying, furious whirl of these thoughts in her poor little bird-brain maddened her. When she combed her hair in the morning, she found many grey hairs and laughed so seldom that her dimples were less marked. Her friends would scarcely have known her again.

Sleepless, feverish, full of anxiety, unable to contain herself any longer, she got out of bed as soon as all was quiet in the villa, stealing barefooted along silent and deserted passages until she reached the door of the bedchamber of love. With her contracted fingers pressing against her ecstasy and sighs, she peered through the keyhole eagerly, wildly, like a detective tracking criminals, and saw the room brightly illuminated as for a ball and the bed disordered by the erotic pair's lascivious intertwinings. Terrified, feeling demented at this unbridling of lechery, gluttony of lust, and display of vice, shuddering with cold as if she was gazing at the frightful lubricity of a Walpurgis night, Marie-Rose saved herself from falling by leaning heavily against the wall.

"That whore will kill him!" she groaned between her clenched teeth, shaking her baby fist tragically in the direction of her enemy.

This was no longer light and smutty operetta causing amusement and laughter, with a frivolous plot turning upon a young man's first steps in love, to be witnessed from afar with startled eyes and sudden awakened curiosity like the dancing light of golden rain in a firework display. It was a drama, a disgusting adventure bound to finish badly, the concluding scenes all dark, with rows of red lamps glowing along the footlights and the atmosphere full of funereal forebodings as if a great night-bird was hovering.

Clarette had taken a strong liking to the lad's virginal flesh. In her hands, the poor boy weighted no heavier than one of the lemons that flecked the neighbouring orchards with golden spots. She would empty him, press out his juice to the last drop, and only throw him from her when he was done with and flabby, like useless fragments on her dessert-plate.

When the frightened eyes of Lucien's mother stared at the sight of the couple's meretricious enjoyment and their complicated lustful efforts; and, panting, nailed to the threshold of their bedroom by some irresistible force, she counted the savage strokes of their encounters where seeming pride prevented either of them from asking for quarter. Marie-Rose writhed in pangs of desolation, not knowing what to do or try. The most adored mother has never been able to defeat a mistress and, above all, a scientific seductress like Clarette who now, for the first time in her life, abandoned herself to her instincts and longings, playing a supreme martingale in the attempt to live in the present all the lost years of the past. In despair at the weakness of her position, the wretched woman wrung her hands, sobbed, made savage wishes in an undertone, dooming Clarette to the bitterest grief, and regretting days of old, when sorceresses drove gold pins into the heart of a wax doll modelled in the effigy of a rival; when spells overcame the decrees of destiny and, without outward signs of crime or bloodshed, one could be rid of a woman proved to be an enemy.

"If he would only crush and kill her one night! Why can't she die in the midst of her mad lust?"

Marie-Rose said to herself that in such a case, she could easily console her boy, drive dangerous memories from his brain, console him for his loss, gradually restore his wasted strength, bringing him back to health and forcing him to regain the tranquility of mind without which no man can ever prove steadfast. In a few weeks, she would set him up again, and make a new man of him until there was an opportunity of getting him married. She had the exquisite vision of a daughter-in-law, submissive, charming, bewitched by her husband. Marie-Rose's frivolous face and shock of rebellious golden hair would not prevent her playing the part of a good granny. To show off behind the scenes, she would have brought to her dressing-room her son's pink, plump babies, exquisitely dressed and beribboned, reminding her of Lucien's childhood when she dandled him on her broad Japanese divan under the shade of dwarf palms.

While seeking a wife for him, she would choose with great wariness and after minute enquiry, a series of pretty mistresses, to be enjoyed for what they were worth; for the pleasure of a night. They cost dear, but no man ties himself entirely to them; only bestowing scraps of his strength, the merest atoms of his being.

■

Clarette, at first not feeling safe, uncertain of the effect his mother's presence and the revival of former affection would have on Lucien, his boyish past appearing like a latent menace, she tried to deceive both her lover and her old friend by showing herself affable and sweet-tempered with Marie-Rose. But when Andrée found beyond a doubt that she had the upper hand and that the lad would back her up and not turn round on her if she threw off her mask, she changed her tone and manner, beginning to show her distaste and annoyance at the length of Marie-Rose's stay. It seemed endless, because it clouded the rosy light of her liaison.

She inflicted haughty humiliations on her guest, trying artfully by trickery, hints and wicked ruses of all kinds to make her understand her hostess's wishes—which were also those of Lucien—and guess that both were waiting for her departure as for deliverance. Clarette feigned sudden headaches so as to break up all walks and excursions and shut herself up in the villa as if it was a cloister. She turned over in her mind every little thing that would make the sojourn in the country odious to Marie-Rose Hardanges. The force of inertia that the perturbed mother opposed to her; the tenacious will-power against which her spite was powerless, and the inutility of her schemes, inventions, and perfidy, made her ill with exasperation.

She soon threw off all restraint and purposely made Lucien's life unbearable, goading him with unjust reproaches, sulking with him night after night, and repulsing him as if she no longer loved him and was tired of him. The poor young fellow's brain was in a whirl, perplexed by this incomprehensible enigma. With increased devotion, he knelt at the feet of his idol, begging; imploring with tears, loving oaths, and wild prayers for a statement or a reproach.

When she judged that she had kept him on the rack long enough and felt that he was saturated with the influence of her magnetic fluid; at her mercy, isolated from the affection she feared; ready, in order to possess her again and enjoy her mouth and body, for ignominy, ingratitude and cowardice, suffering from the deprivation she had brutally imposed, Andrée, one night, while undressing, spoke out.

"So you want me to be frank and tell you all that's passing in my mind, dearest?" she exclaimed regretfully, making as if she was fearful of wounding his feelings.

"That's just what I want! I've been so wretched since you seem to have lost all love for me."

"Then it's your mother who freezes me to the marrow and drives me from your side. She humiliates me, with her distrustful ways, absurd jealousy and her affectation of always throwing herself between us as if trying to defend you."

Lucien tried to reply, but she interrupted him, drowning

his voice with her shrill tones that resounded through the snug, draped room.

"I can see perfectly well that she had only come to carry you off with her to Paris. You prefer her to me. So now that she's taken root, sticking here as if the place belonged to her and laughs in my face, the best I can do is to withdraw in her favour and leave you in the bosom of your family. It's the end of the season. Oh, I say!—won't Prince Tchernadieff roar when I tell him my story!"

Lucien started to his feet, very pale, and his heart beating rapidly.

"Don't talk like that, Clarette—for pity's sake. You know that you are all I love in this world!"

"After your ma—you mean!"

"My mother," he bawled, banging his fist in a fit of frenzy on the marble top of the toilet-table, "my mother—kick her out if she annoys you. And if you say the word, I'll help you!"

III

Marie-Rose strode backwards and forwards in her room that looked as if it had been pillaged. The bed was not made and the basket-trunks were wide open in front of the windows. The furniture disappeared under quantities of frocks, corsets, under-skirts, and piles of silk stockings toppling over.

She seemed to be stirred by the feverish haste of flight with danger increasing every minute and her heart thumped fiercely; her brain swimming with giddy terror at the slightest footstep on the gravel or the faintest tinkle of a bell.

She muttered unintelligible scraps of sentences, with smothered sobbing moans interspersed by stoppages of dull silence and accompanied by the jerky, angry gestures of her fingers obstinately twisted in the cambric folds of a pocket-handkerchief with which she almost crushed her eyelids whence flowed, one by one, great tears of grief.

The pretty little singer threw her light-hued summer dresses in bundles into the trays of her trunks and crammed her costumes as she packed like a washerwoman beating and wringing linen. Little she recked that she was spoiling the shape of her straw hats radiant with roses; creasing her lace; ruining stunning gowns and peerless sets of under-muslins trimmed with priceless old Valenciennes in styles that she had "inspired," as her dressmaker was never tired of telling her.

She had now but one thought, one wish: to depart and be off at once to the railway station where she could seek refuge in a carriage of a train that would carry her far away from the accursed town where she had endured the martyr-dom of what was best in her being. She wanted to get away without wasting another hour, as if some epidemic of disease was emptying dwellings one after the other; or as if foundations were giving way and walls threatening ruin were about to bury her as they fell. There was something automatic in her movements, and she seemed over-whelmed with madness suddenly seething in her brain.

The shock had been too great for such a frail little crea-ture, accustomed to let herself glide along life's stream and knowing nothing about cruel emotion, the black side of existence, and battles where men and women rend each other's hearts. Her feet were out of the stirrups; she was unable to master herself and regain her equilibrium. Power-less to understand what was going on, she sank in depths of immense disillusion; in the stupor of annihilation.

Her ears would long be ringing and deafened till her dying day by the echoes of the venomous, bitter quarrel she had just had with Andrée Clarette. The dispute began, Marie knew not how, started by some word so insignificant that she had forgotten it. The wrangle dragged on in a flood of sarcasm and cutting answers under the trees in the garden. Above the women's faces, red with the rush of angry blood to the head, their white parasols quivered and the discussion was kept up, growing fierce in the drawing-room and bedrooms, finishing with hoarse fishwomen's insults and the shaking of fists in the air, but sometimes dangerously near grimacing features.

Their hatred, hidden for so many weeks, repressed and disguised in hypocritical outbursts of false affection, blazed forth at last, and all that weighed upon their souls gushed out in abject, disgusting vomit. Retort against retort, thrusting and parrying, mother and mistress splashed each other with all the mire of a sink. Their mutual mockery was that of two streetwalkers fighting over a paying client in some haunt of vice in the lowest quarter of Paris. They dug up and loudly exchanged the dirtiest stories of their careers, filthy freaks buried in the past, such as their girlish weaknesses when in their teens; their lies; the muddy mysteries heralding their first appearance on the stage; their experiments with this young man and that old fellow in the rooms of shady hotels. They tore each other to pieces, pulling each other down to the lowest level of prostitution, with mutual calumny to satisfy their need of vilification and exaggeration, bursting into laughter, exchanging challenges; really not knowing what they were saying or doing. They arrived at the paroxysm of fury and yet both women kept their secret, taking care not to mention the name that was on the tip of their tongues and which had set them one against the other. Neither cared to confess the true cause of their tragic, insane exchange of invectives. Perhaps, in their exasperation, they might have fallen so low as to tear each other's hair out by the roots, claw cheeks and eyes with their nails; engaging in the real rough-and-tumble wrestling of public balls and third-rate wineshops when stay-busks snap as two nymphs of the pavement roll clasped together on the ground, scratching, biting, kicking, had not Lucien made his appearance, livid and frowning, on the threshold.

Like two adversaries on the entrance of the arbitrator whose duty is to make up their difference, Marie-Rose and Andrée stopped speaking. Their keen glances, darting rays of affection and evoking bygone days, served to interrogate and implore the boy. With equal confidence, they waited for the statement his heart would dictate. The mother believed in the son she had always adored, petted, and spoilt. The mistress trusted her lover, the being she had created; moulded in her image and glutted with enjoyment, desires, and dreams. He was her toy that she handled as she pleased, leading him by the nose and making him grow more stupid every night.

In the spacious room where only a few seconds before resounded the hoarse clamour and discordant bawling of voices breaking, as higher shriller notes were reached, strident and sickening, the solemn, threatening silence of an ephemeral truce weighed with strange heaviness. But the boy apparently refused to play this kind of part. He was full of painful, instinctive doubt, and hesitating as if distressed by the scruples of an honest man out of his element, crushed in whirling machinery from which there was no escape. He approached Clarette to defend her. It was easy to make a show of courage when the only adversary is a poor little mother brought out of Bohemia, whose nerves, momentarily jarred, were already calm again. She was like a pretty butterfly caught between four walls, bruising her fragile wings and not knowing which way to turn to regain the road to the sky. Lucien looked her up and down like a maid-servant who has dared to be insolent and lift her voice

in her employer's presence. Wretched Marie-Rose stood
with misty tears welling up in her eyes.

"You forget you're not in your own house," he said,
mockingly and harshly. "I'm sorry to have to remind you of
that fact!" Clasping his mistress's hands in his, he drew her
towards him with infinite tenderness, imprinting a lengthy,
loving kiss on her lips, and added with cowardice: "My
dearest Andrée, let me beg your pardon for her. No doubt
she's been in bad company during her tour."

Clarette, having no fear now for the final result, did not
prolong the mother's sad humiliation, and left the room
without looking back, leaving Marie-Rose and her son face-
to-face. Andrée left the door ajar so as to listen to the end of
the scene and continue to gloat over her triumphant victory
achieved with such slight effort.

Her departure was not noticed by Marie-Rose, who
stared aghast at Lucien's scowling face, his imperious
features convulsed, marked with deep wrinkles. She felt all
abroad, hardly recognising her son, and in her stunned
brain and parched throat not a word or sentence could she
find to express her disgust and stun him with her scorn. She
would have liked to upbraid him for his treachery, which
was well-nigh sacrilegious, and draw herself up erect in
front of the lad corroded with vice, forgetful of the most
obvious duty, to make him realise the pride of an insulted
woman and mother. It seemed, however, as if the sudden
shock of a violent storm had struck her down and almost
deprived her of understanding.

Instead of throwing himself into Marie-Rose's arms like
a good man, and explaining everything with moving, cajoling words, begging to be absolved—she would have
forgiven him at once with delirious joy—the boy continued
his attack.

"I hope that after such a vulgar row," he continued, speaking slowly and harshly, laying stress on every syllable like giving orders, "you don't mean to stop her much longer?"

"Don't be afraid! I obey! I shan't be her to-night," she stuttered, arousing herself from her torpor with difficulty, feeling herself driven in a corner.

She was obliged to drain the cup of bitterness to the dregs and thought that this vile dénouement ended the tragedy; that they were at last going to leave her in peace, satisfied to have turned her out like a parasite in everybody's way. But as soon as Lucien had left her, she could not help hearing their loud peals of laughter resounding in the entrance-hall, torturing her with a last triumphant blast of trumpets sounding the death-whoop of her broken heart, bleeding and wounded, and of her illusions, hopes, and dreams. Fragments of atrocious dialogue struck on her ears, dealing her the finishing stroke, and causing her to shudder as if exposed to an icy wintry wind.

"You went a bit too far, darling," said Clarette sarcastically, not meaning what she said. The joyous intonation of her voice gave the lie to her reproachful remark and prompted the reply she desired.

"Not at all! I knew the proper thing to tell her. We should never have been able to get rid of her if I hadn't shook her up like a mad woman—and she *is* mad, I'll swear!"

"Anyway, do you think she'll go?"

"Rather!—and as quietly as a lamb!"

Marie-Rose, utterly broken, threw herself down on her bed, her fists driven into her ears, her dilated eyes seeking in vacancy for some apparition to protect her. She spent her afternoon in absolute torpor, unknowingly letting the hours slip by. Suddenly awakened by the noise of distant railway trains, she started up and hurriedly packed her two trunks all alone, although she had never done a stroke of work in her life and the slightest fatigue made her ill. She folded her frocks, closed refractory locks with great trouble, and buckled heavy straps without even ringing for a maid to help her.

Marie-Rose did not cool down, or see things clearly until, after registering her luggage, she sank down in the shade on one of the benches on the station platform. The sun was setting behind the mountain's stony peaks. The roofs of the villas were resplendent, standing out on a golden background like the miniatures in a missal. Clouds of midges whirled in the air, forming changing, giddy figures. The serenity of nature stirred the depths of the unhappy woman's being, soothing her soul as with healing balm, bringing her to her senses. Fresh hope sprung up in her breast.

She became reassured, quickly turning from the blackest hatred to the most ardent delight. She sought consolation in lying belief, saying inwardly that Lucien was not guilty. He had only tortured her because he was under Clarette's sway. The dear fellow knew not what he was doing any more than a poodle sitting up and begging for a piece of sugar so as to avoid a cut from a whip. She absolved him of all blame and pitied him for having lost his will-power and, snared at his first flight, forced to support such a heavy yoke. It was Clarette who had betrayed her so traitorously and she should bear all the shame. Marie-Rose looked upon her like a witch, and cursing her, prayed to be able to live long enough to render evil for evil a hundredfold, overwhelm her with bitterness and pain, drive all her friends away from her, and force her to grow old before her time. In her burning brain, she turned over fifty incoherent projects of resistance and combat as if, before closing the gate of the villa behind her, she had declared war against her enemy and all weapons were to be lawful; all fair play abolished; without quarter, mercy, cessation, or peace.

The Paris express clattered out of the station. She reclined in a corner of the carriage, as limp as a broken doll thrown on one side by a tired child.

"Don't fancy that I'll let myself be robbed of my son!" murmured Marie-Rose through her clenched teeth. "You won't have him as long as you think—you scurvy jade!"

IV

From that day forward, Marie-Rose got ready to play her last card and was on the alert for the return of the mistress and her lover. The combat did not frighten her. She felt herself at home in Paris, for was she not a flower of its streets? Paris had been her procuress, so to say. She knew all the resources and secrets of the Gay City. Sooner or later, even without a lull in their madness of lust, if they continued to be drunk with mutual lasciviousness, they were bound to return home, if only to prepare for other travels. The weather would soon be almost tropical at Mentone. There were ninety-nine chances in a hundred that Clarette was thinking of departure, getting ready to imprison her fancy lad again and continue her exquisite dalliance in the cottage where every summer she kept open house for her friends and their girls during the big race-week at Deauville. But between the Riviera season and the fashionable period on the Normandy coast, she must perforce put in a few weeks at her dwelling on the Avenue Kléber. She had to choose her frocks for the plank promenade at Trouville, select dozens of hats, consult her lawyer concerning the action brought against her by Campardon, and which had been postponed again and again, quarrel with Mme. Lévêque, and settle outstanding accounts and claims. Paris was not to be treated like a station where the train only stops a minute or two. It is not for a woman to escape from the Modern Babylon when once she has breathed its limpid air, paced its asphalt with her saucy high heels, and affronted its temptations. Paris is the paradise of women where, once there, the days are too short for their pleasures and they lose all notion of time, forget their dreams, longings, what they reckoned on doing, and what they meant to do. Departures are put off from day to day, because circumstances, pleasures, dressmakers, flirtations—everything that a woman adores, in fact—seems amalgamated and bound up in a conspiracy to draw out and lengthen eternally an entr'acte that ought not to last more than ten minutes at the most. Besides, in this month of June, with the Grand Prix looming, being the height of the season when Society folks of the front rank were parading, striking attitudes, each at his post, determined to play a part in the comedy of fashion, Lucien, with his conceited disposition and his perpetual desire to show himself off, would not be able to refrain from the glory of appearing in public with Clarette, walking her about the paddock, lifting his hat when innumerable other hats were tilted to salute them both, and replying to the significant Bonjours that would greet them. The high-livers would criticise them as a newly-wedded pair, not quite at their ease in the moving throng, hurrying, bustling, and betting.

Marie-Rose was not mistaken in her surmises. Her maid

informed her one morning as she had just got out of bed that Clarette's house had lost the dull look of an uninhabited residence. The windows were wide open and Mme. Lévêque was expecting *Monsieur* and *Madame*—as she had declared in the kitchen—in a day or two.

A rapid flame as of a lightning-stroke shone in the eyes of the beauty of light opera. She drew herself up to her full height, her hair falling all over her face, and, forgetting imprudently that her servant was listening, shrieked out with savage vulgarity, in a burst of laughter that sounded like a challenge:

"'Madame' and 'Monsieur,' indeed! All right, my beauty! I'll look after the affairs of your sweet household!"

V

Lucien Hardanges seemed to be obeying his mistress's strict orders and, by a fresh show of indifference and absolute neglect, prove to his mother that there was no longer anything in common between them, that he persisted in disowning her and that the quarrel arising so lamentably without a cause, should never be made up. He did not go to see Marie-Rose and bestow a filial kiss on the loving woman who would have forgiven all and opened her arms to him with no unkind word, reproach, or afterthought. He did not even leave his card—that bit of cardboard on which a man scribbles a hurried line or two apprising a companion of one's return and how we shall be glad to welcome friends when trunks are unpacked and our home is all in good order once more.

He gave no sign of life. In other circumstances, such unjust ingratitude and lack of affection would have prostrated her as if the walls of her house had fallen in and crushed her under their ruins. She would have been ready to die, overwhelmed by her misfortune, sobbing for days and nights. Since her return from the Riviera, Marie-Rose had hidden her stricken heart under such thick armour; was the prey of such marked over-excitement, reckoning keenly on revenge and so completely engrossed by this hope, that this last blow was received like a spent bullet that pains without wounding.

It had a contrary effect, spurring her on, reviving her rancour, granting her renewed strength wherewith to inaugurate her campaign of treachery, traps, and ambushes against her companion who had become her worst enemy. She meant to hunt Clarette down without respite. Nevertheless, Marie-Rose longed to see Lucien—if only for a moment and in the distance—to follow him with her eyes and blow him countless kisses without him knowing it. So she went out in her brougham and had it stopped at the corner of a street near Clarette's house. Lucien's mother knew all the habits of the infatuated couple, at what time they passed along the avenue, when they went shopping, or strolled in the Bois. She watched for them to leave the house and sometimes waited so long that her coachman, overcome by the heat, fell asleep on his box.

She experienced great joy and was amply rewarded by a sweet thrill of emotion when perchance her son appeared alone, pulling on his gloves, lighting a cigar, clean-limbed and well groomed in his black morning coat that fitted without a wrinkle. She was able to stare at his retreating figure at her ease, caress him with her glances and admire him. When she saw him disappear afar, she experienced the furtive pleasure arising from deprivation of what one loves the most, and the anguish of knowing nothing of an existence where one is reflected as in a mirror, and where one's being has been absorbed, without counting doubts that madden and suppositions stubbornly formed in accordance with one's inward desires. Marie-Rose would not let a day pass without keeping this kind of platonic appointment, fixed by her maternal heart. To see her on the watch, hiding at the back of her brougham, her features hidden, and having studied in front of her mirror an arrangement of veil and hat so that it was impossible to recongnise her, nearly all the passers-by turned round to peer at her. They imagined some sad love-tragedy such as is daily played in the fashionable streets round the Place de l'Etoile, and took her for a society queen deep in intrigue, jealous, and tracking lover or husband in order to gather proofs before beginning divorce proceedings; or meaning to reply to lies and trickery by breaking off a liaison with seemingly careless swagger.

She was impatient, now that war was declared, to see for herself the progress of her scheme, measure the territory gained and, like a doctor noting the ravages of some mental illness, reckon up the worry, lassitude, and carking care that left the traces of deep wrinkles in the boy's face, as clearly as if seen in a mirror. She went home happy, smiling at her thoughts, sketching plans of felicity, singing in glee with trills and tremolos like a lark warbling when the sun rises, emerging from morning mists.

Although she feigned supreme indifference, and did not trouble to contradict stupid rumours of being head-over-heels in love, and notwithstanding that nothing by word or act betrayed the task she had undertaken, Marie-Rose had lost no time, inaugurating her campaign stealthily without attracting attention by useless tumult; without worrying Clarette by open threats which would have warned her to be on her guard in future. In fact, Lucien's mother steeled herself to remain calm; and affected great tranquility, exaggerating her quietude in order to reassure and dupe her former friend and her paramour.

Lucien and Andrée were now surrounded by the incessant weaving of a strong net which closed in and entangled them. Marie-Rose hatched marvellous plots as cleverly as if she was guided by some old procuress of high degree or a diplomatist having learnt his trade among the Levantines in Constantinople and who, little by little, might have been initiated in the mysteries of the harem, the purchase of consciences, victories won by the heavy artillery of banknotes, calumny, and bold, lying whispers. Neither lover nor mistress were allowed a moment's rest; nor were they able to revive the departed pleasures of their first loving embraces. Their concubinage was apparently condemned by the decrees of fate. They were startled by painfully debasing memories of the past and fears for the future, causing them to rebel against each other. This state of things gave rise to tragic scenes and fierce exchanges of coarse epithets in which the voices of the woman and the stripling were well-nigh equally strident as they bandied threats. It was true that they begged each other's pardon afterwards, but their mutual unjust reproaches were as venomous as infected wounds.

It happened sometimes that just as they went downstairs to get into their open carriage, or when they were seated at the dining-table, a messenger with a gold band on his cap delivered a basket of roses and on an envelope pinned close to the florist's name would be written: "From Prince Tchernadieff." By some inexplicable unlucky chance, Mme. Lévêque was never at home when these unfortunate occurrences took place. At another moment, a piece of jewellery without card or letter would be sent, evidently the mysterious present of some man who was sure to be known although his gift was anonymous and he chose to play a pleasant practical joke on an old flame. Marie-Rose would not have grudged paying a high price to play the looker-on through a slit in a curtain, as when she kept watch over their salacious intertwinings or their flirtations, so as to gloat over the sudden frown, pallor, and furious glances that made Lucien's features take on a demoniacal expression, or to hear the bitterness of his intonation as he exclaimed, gulping down a sob:

"Another fellow who can't forget you, eh?"

Some other day he would receive letters from women. These billets-doux were full of shameless longing requests, or brimming over with delicious, burning promises and sensuous appeals. The scented scribble was crammed with exquisite mistakes in spelling and grammar, proving that the sweet little writer had not read over what she had penned, fearing to miss the post; the sort of note that is dashed off at full speed with a beating heart, and inspired by a whirling brain full of mad dreams of lust, revealing the naked soul of a concupiscent pet promising endless voluptuous joys and begging for an appointment.

Some wrote like timid young flappers. Other scented missives seemed to have been sent by fashionable ladies suddenly moved by a mad fancy, holding back at first, restrained by the fear of being repulsed or of being forced to pass through trying ordeals before attaining their salacious object. Many notes were audacious and lively, tenderly familiar, stuffed with smart sayings, each sentence being peppered with suggestive hints of burning kisses. There were also descriptions of novel delights of lubricity and chaffing remarks. Lucien was informed that it was time to enjoy a little change and replace his "old lady" by a young lassie, still in her teens, as fresh as a flower moist with the morning dew; who had just begun to feel her feet and offered her love on an altar covered with a brand-new cloth.

Unwittingly, with the imprudence of his age, Lucien did not destroy these letters, but forgot them in his pockets or let them lay about.

"I'll make you repent," clamoured Clarette spitefully, in a rage, and dashing a perfumed epistle in his face, "if you go with other women—if you dare to try and make a fool of me!"

VI

To gain her ends, Marie-Rose did not care what she did. She could not sleep for pondering over her plan and lived in a perpetual state of flaming, feverish agitation. She went all over Paris in the most out-of-the-way quarters, not to visit the poor, fish out bric-a-brac, or make appointments with impecunious, albeit lusty artisans, but only to post letters so that they should bear postmarks of distant districts. An observer would have sworn that the rumours current concerning her clandestine amours were true and that she was "mashed" on some mysterious fancy man or visited a wealthy protector not moving in the van of Parisian society. A private detective or professional black-mailer would have got her a lucrative job at once, taking her into partnership and she could have earned double the salary paid to her behind the footlights.

She never missed her aim and all her bullets went home, deep in the heart. When she paused, it was to imagine fresh tricks, intensify her attacks and do more harm than ever. Never since she had reached the age of reason, had Marie-Rose been so tenacious, evil-minded, and cunning. Never had she endured such fatigue of mind and body, or worked so hard to surmount obstacles in order to demolish an enemy she hated and who had destroyed her peace of mind. She foresaw cause and effect. She was here, there, and everywhere, well aware that seed sown by a sure and skilful hand would sprout exceedingly well. She disguised herself and changed her handwriting with real talent, making no dangerous mistakes. There was not an error in the note-book where she jotted down the dates of her intriguing tricks and she was never bewildered by the posting of her anonymous letters or the addresses of envelopes. She marvelled at her own cunning and her profound intuition concerning the weaknesses of men and women in love.

She alternately scrutinised and questioned everybody she met, passing her evenings in the nooks and corners of the Gay City where the highfliers seek amusement. She led people on to gossip, without seeming to be gleaning information, and picked up valuable data and addresses. No one knew her son's tastes and ideals better than she did, so she confused and entangled him in gallant adventures without him knowing it. When pretty courtesans of the highest grade whose names creep into gossiping gazettes, excited and lured on by short, saucy letters bearing his signature, smiled at him in the Bois de Boulogne or in the crowd at the races, making eyes or showing the tip of a scarlet, moist tongue on the sly behind a fan, or by a turn of a blonde head framed by the silk canopy of a parasol, he forgot that his mistress kept watch, her suspicious glance never leaving him, and a smile of fatuity hovered over his features, while his lips seemed to respond unknowingly as if proffering a kiss to the unblushing mute advances of the unknown siren jostling him on the lawn at Auteuil or Longchamp. Imperceptible signs such as these can only be detected by a woman on the tenterhooks of jealousy, fearing to lose her lover. Clarette noticed how her living toy replied to these flattering offers which perplexed and delighted him. She felt inclined to beat him, and claw his face as a punishment for seeming infidelity, so as to remind him that he had lost the right to ogle other women, especially creatures whose bodies were on hire to the first man who cared to have them by the hour, day, or week. Lucien belonged to Clarette. He was her chattel, her property. She meant to dominate him and he was not to rebel or strain against the leash. Nor would she share his caresses with any woman. She did not intend to doubt his love for a second.

Turning all these raging thoughts over in her troubled brain, her face livid beneath her powder, panting with fury and in imperious accents, she gave her coachman orders to drive home quickly along quiet, unfrequented roads, after dragging Lucien with rapid strides towards one of the gates of the reserved enclosure and pushing through the mob of ragged urchins offering to fetch cabs or carriages.

"Let's be off. I'm sick and tired of these races," she murmured disdainfully.

They exchanged not a word all the way. Their bearing was comparatively decent. He was gloomy and sulky; annoyed at having to leave before the last two races. It was no fun to be treated so roughly and be deprived of his favourite amusements, the rare diversions relieving the monotony of their life.

She gripped and twisted the handle of her sunshade, her eyes fixed on vacancy, doing her best to hide her acute inward torture and not shriek in an outburst of sobs and insults.

They seemed to be the husband and wife, so common in high society, whose union resembles a splendidly-built frontage with waste ground and squalid huts behind. Their conjugal partnership had begun, most likely, by vile haggling and huckstering: the woman offering faded charms and the man only thinking about the banknotes of the dowry and of probable accidents and illnesses, ridding him one fine day in the near future of his fetters, and freeing him from all the false love, forced caresses, and hypocritical gratitude to which he was condemned.

Scarcely had Lucien and his mistress got back home than the actress slammed the doors behind her and, without even taking off her hat, insisted upon explanations. Rushing on as in a cavalry charge, she lost her head, accusing him of systematic falsehood and of breaking his word. He was the most cowardly, vile, abject lover on the face of the earth. Exasperated by his scornful silence, shrugging shoulders, and the low whistle of his lips that divulged not the secret she dreaded and yet burned to ferret out, she grew almost crazy.

Clarette poured out a flood of cruel insults, and startled him with sentences vomited forth in fearful nausea. She spoke words that afterwards one would recall with one's heart's blood, or all one's fortune, in despair at having uttered such phrases.

"I ought to have guessed what would happen before I took you on; before tying myself to you like a fool," she yelled, trembling convulsively as if in a fit of hysterics. "You're not a man. You're only a whore—soliciting and being beckoned to wherever she shows herself. You're a whore, I say, not worth the money she costs. You're a whore, exactly the same as your mother always was!"

The young man, sprawling in an armchair, his eyes half-closed, sluggish and still, cocked one leg over the other with the air of a spectator settling down to enjoy a comical scene. He had obtained extraordinary mastery over his feelings.

"Continue, ducky. You're awfully interesting to-day," he drawled coolly. "Excuse me—but may I trouble you to pass me the cigarettes there—just behind you." With a mocking leer, he added: "Seems to me this sort of quiet, married life is beginning to lose all its fun—what do you think?"

VII

As soon as Lucien and Clarette were together between the sheets, the desire of debauchery with its customary temptations and the mad longing for complete sexual gratification that blazed in their flesh when they sucked each other's breath and their bodies came in contact, patched up their quarrels nightly. The fissures of their matrimonial edifice were plastered over and the lovers were reconciled in bed. Their lust brought them together again, interlocked furiously in bestial, angry, savage struggles, as if they wanted to hurt, bite, and crush each other. They exchanged insults and threats even in the throes of absolute conjunction, gripping each other fast until the delight of the last throbbing spasms of voluptuousness dulled their brains, moistened their mouths as with drops of honey, driving away all bitterness and clamping them once more loving, affectionate, heated in happy ecstasy, grateful and submissive. Their felicity, like pleasant intoxication after a champagne supper, lasted until they awoke in the morning.

Clarette, always reluctant to get up and dress, kept Lucien in her arms as long as she could. She would have liked to keep him locked up in her bedroom, as she did at Mentone, that paradise of sunshine and sensuousness where they had adored each other, without a cloud to darken their love, or hamper it as with hobbles put on young colts at liberty in a field and who are fettered for fear they may start off in some mad freak, or bolt and maim themselves. Clarette was always on the watch; eaten up with jealousy. She was unnerved to the point of insanity by these ups-and-downs and incessant inexplicable storms which had succeeded the calm months of springtime replete with lengthy quietude that she had recently left, just as if stepping out of a hot, scented bath.

With the intuition of a woman who had seen the seamy side of life, she began to grow uneasy. She felt herself harried, surrounded, attacked ruthlessly by the inexorable hatred of a woman who was her rival and would never lay down her arms until she had gained the victory. Such an implacable enemy would stick at nothing, profit by every weakness, fault, or imprudent act to gain ground. Who was this rival? Clarette had forced Lucien to enjoy her when he had scarcely lost his maidenhead. Before she got hold of him, he had not had any experience of lubricity, only having paid for a few chance strokes with prostitutes whose names he forgot so soon as he had satisfied his sexual appetite. The unknown adversary had heard the story of Marie-Rose's son and his love-affair—it was common talk in Paris. She must have seen Lucien somewhere or the other, taken a fancy to him and wanted to lay down her body to him. She was doubtless about as old as

Clarette; or perchance a minx under age, cognisant of her own beauty and wanting for nothing; well-kept, eager to play a trick on her wealthy protector, love a handsome young fellow and be loved in return. In order to be certain and obtain undeniable proof, enabling her to defend herself against her unknown rival and not strike at empty space, Andrée would have endured the most cruel ordeals, spent her last thousand-franc note or pawned her last cambric chemise.

She could only guess at two female enemies: a rival or Marie-Rose Hardanges. Lucien's mother? That was impossible. Andrée felt she must be going out of her mind to ascribe such importance to the wretched little golden-haired doll so harshly treated and torn to pieces by her and Lucien. Clarette's lack of foresight and psychology led her to believe firmly that the forsaken mother was selfish and as fond of lazy ease and tranquility as an indolent favourite in a harem. Since her return to France, she had renounced all wearisome, useless resistance, and, abdicating maternal authority, tired out, had fallen back into her old habits, renewing friendships interrupted by her South American engagement. Being always inclined to take things lightly and cast all trouble from her, she must have forgotten by this time all about the ingratitude of her son and her old companion and fellow-actress.

Clarette wore herself out at having to turn and twist in this circle of doubt and surmises; unceasingly hesitating in her suspicions and searches; finding herself continually reduced to powerlessness as if in a pitch-dark blind alley where all efforts were doomed to failure. She found herself growing crazy; something like a bull, his hide smarting from the pricks of the *banderillas*, harassed by red cloaks waving, and with lowered horns rushing from one of his adversaries to another, without succeeding in driving his natural weapon into anybody.

As Mme. Lévêque mumbled, delighted in her heart of hearts to see the squabbles: "the run of the comedy was on the point of petering out; the bill would soon be changed and another piece put in rehearsal."

Finally, one evening, the lovers came to blows. Andrée had again lost her temper, breaking out in a storm of cutting complaints, either because the lad had tried clumsily to smuggle away a letter; or on account of some strange woman's significant smile during a languid stroll before dinner.

This monotonous, recurring nagging and unjust upbraiding irritated Lucien, despite his feigned indifference.

"And after all—suppose I had another woman besides you?" he replied, speaking like a man who determines to be the master and means to be left in peace at home. "Haven't you got your cursed Cossack—that bastard prince?"

"You lie!" she interrupted. "You know I turned him out for you."

"Stuff and nonsense! If it was all over between you, you would send him back his flowers and jewellery."

Livid, her fists clenched, the actress rushed at the boy and, with all the strength of her arm, slapped his face as if chastising a coward.

"You good-for-nothing cad!"

"Oh, you bitch!"

Before she could get away, press the electric bell, or run out of the room, Lucien felt like a murderer. His temples ached, his strength was increased tenfold by reason of his brutish rage, and he seized her wrists, beating, bruising and shaking her; driving her backwards until she staggered and fell on her knees, yelling with pain and fright. Her blonde tortoiseshell combs littered the carpet. Her dishevelled hair veiled her shoulders in golden curls. Lucien dominated her as if he had grown taller, his shoulders broader, looking more like a man than ever before.

He held her in this humiliating posture, defeated, crushed; one feverish hand pressed against his mouth to stifle her cries and sobs that sounded like the hoarse and gruesome groans of a woman being done to death, calling for help. He did not know what he was about. He trampled on her and would have been overjoyed to have a riding-whip with which to flog her until her bodice and skirt were cut to rags and her naked body displayed, striped and lacerated by bleeding wounds.

Suddenly, he felt he had enough and, nearly quieted down, let her go from his hold. She collapsed in a huddled heap, the back of her head striking the carpet with a dull thud.

"That's done! So good-night and give my kind regards to the Prince when you see him!"

He lifted up the *portière*, about to go, but with one bound, Clarette sprung to her feet, her eyes aflame, her heart beating wildly, the rosy points of her breasts showing erect through torn lace. She threw herself on Lucien, pressing her moist lips against his clenched teeth, winding her body about his like a vine round a young elm. She hung on him madly.

"I adore you! Forgive me, Lulu-love—oh! do forgive me! I beg your pardon!" she murmured, cooing in ecstasy.

Lucien tore himself out of her embrace, lifting her fingers one by one from his sleeves. He repulsed her brutally and rushed away.

"To hell with you! I've had enough!" he cried, while she fell prone on the floor as if dead.

VIII

I s it you, my darling boy—is it really you?

Marie-Rose kept on stammering out the same words; the same confused question, astounded, delirious; unable, in her overwhelming joy, to control herself or marshal her thoughts. She hugged in her arms the slender frame of her son, crushing him in her embrace, covering with passionate kisses the flesh of her flesh of which—unhappy mother!— she had been deprived for weeks and weeks. There was something fiercely animal in the way in which she fawned upon him, as if purifying him with her maternal mouth, effacing his uncleanness kiss by kiss, on his eyelids, cheeks, and lips, as in fervent exorcism occult spells are driven from the body of a bewitched victim.

Her great emotion caused her first to cry and then to

laugh. She gasped for breath, choking because her heart thumped furiously. There was insanity and ecstasy in her dilated eyes, as if scorched by too-dazzling light. In this great fit of motherly love, she resembled a woman of the people who, hustled in a crowd viewing illuminations, might have let go the hand of her little boy, losing him, so small and weak, in the formidable whirlpool of the mob, the human ebb and flow where a child is soon trampled and crushed, disappearing like a waif. After having sobbed all night and called upon God to take her, she finds the infant on the morrow in the hands of the police, safe, sound, and smiling, chattering childlike about its fright and trouble, while she catches him up, holds him tight to her bosom and runs, rather than walks, to her home.

Despite all her efforts, the illusions that buoyed her up, the hopes that kept the flame of her feverish hatred burning like a sacred fire, Marie-Rose could not imagine that she would win the difficult game so quickly. She had not expected Lucien back so soon. So she thought it was a dream when the cab stopped in front of the gate of her house and her boy, nervously excited, slamming the door of the vehicle behind him, flew upstairs, and caught sight of his mother, bent in two over the banisters, deadly pale and trembling all over.

"Now, mamma—no scenes, no bother, you know! I'm off again if you make a fuss!"

She did not even answer, quite pleased enough to stretch out her arms to him and draw him to her bosom with a simple, generous gesture of forgiveness and affection; welcoming him like a traveller tired of adventures and tramping, whose footsteps have turned in the direction of the old home. Lucien was a prodigal son whose parents' love never fails him; whose bed is always made, his plate and knife and fork ever on the table; his remembrance always evoking the same thrill of kindly feeling as of old. She put no questions to him. She evinced no curiosity with which to shock his suffering soul; bruised, perhaps bleeding. Besides, whatever had passed between him and Clarette mattered nothing to her. She did not want to know about their quarrels, rows, and final disagreement, since her dearly beloved son was near her, close to her. Little she recked now she held him in her possession and was able to fondle and kiss him unceasingly with might and main. She cared for nothing, for she had conquered in the perilous struggle and they were united again, mother and son, perhaps—delicious, supreme wish!—never to part for the rest of their life.

"Is it you, my darling boy—is it really you?" reiterated Marie-Rose, more softly and tenderly, as with kisses of dreamland mingling in the deadened modulations of her voice. With childish delight, she added: "How grand it is to feel absolutely happy!"

Despite his selfish disposition and hardheartedness, Lucien felt quite moved. His mother's flow of ardent affection thrilled him through and through. Tears welled up in his eyes.

"Do try and be calm, mamma, or you'll make yourself ill," he whispered coaxingly and prayerfully.

IX

For the first time, perhaps, since she had played the part of a mother seriously, Marie-Rose, the flighty little songstress, began to judge events clearly and wisely. Although safe in harbour, she did not lose one minute of precious time, realising that she would never have a finer opportunity of attaining her ends and finishing the free-love union of her son. The smallest error on her part; the most insignificant chance meeting or even one hour of boredom might bring the couple together again and rekindle the fires of their lewd madness.

Lucien was not to be allowed time to reflect, look about him, dream, ponder coolly over his divorce from Clarette, or think about past delights. Still suffering from the effects of the sensual love that had thrown his whole being out of gear; his brain still in a whirl, he entered on a period of convalescence, a critical moment requiring extra care and scrupulous attention. A relapse would be the end of all things and irremediable into the bargain. It was expedient to profit at once by the spite and rage smouldering in Lucien's wounded heart, and exaggerate the importance of the quarrel which was too brutal to be serious.

It was needful to arrange some separation not to be annulled by a repentant charmer's counter-attack; alluring, imploring letters, recalling in artful, incandescent terms those diversions of lubricity in days that were past. Lucien would be a lost man, falling once more under the yoke, never to recover his liberty again unless he was sent far away from Paris. His mistress must not see him again and, in the Gay City, she might fall across him at any moment.

Marie-Rose made up her mind to send her son to join the colours and anticipate the legal date of his compulsory service, although this new ordeal made his heart bleed. He would have to be a soldier for five years, in some distant garrison town where a woman like Clarette would never have the courage to live in exile. Daily barrack routine, friendliness of comrades, new habits, and fatigue of drill would stifle latent animal instincts. Dreams and remembrances would be replaced by the predominating sensations of hunger, thirst, and sleep. Easy-going sensual diversions, coarse and brutal, when men treat girls like female animals of no importance, would lead him to laugh at overpowering, passionate love. He would be torn and weaned away from the horror of being linked in imitation marriage to a bad woman.

Marie-Rose prepared her pleadings. She was fully armed with specious arguments and reckoned upon working on her son's pride by high-sounding patriotic sentiments, significant pauses in sentences left purposely unfinished and which abruptly open the listener's eyes, throwing a sudden gleam on the precipice close to one's feet; explaining certain doubtful attitudes of former friends who had turned their heads; shaken hands reluctantly; overheard by chance, words that stained like mud-splashes and which one left unchallenged with a laugh, convinced they were intended for some other chappie burning the candle at both ends.

His mother was astounded when Lucien framed no objections and did not seek to overrule her arguments. Like a stout-hearted steed, he rose at the jump without hesitation and remained submissive at once.

"You're right—absolutely!" he replied quietly, as soon as she had concluded her explanations. "It's the best thing I can do, but I'll join a cavalry regiment."

"The hussars, of course!" Marie-Rose went on, a proud light sparkling in her eyes, as if she saw him there and then on parade with his blue tunic and a shako ornamented by black feathers; haughty and swaggering; a dashing rake, like a soldier on the operatic stage.

"I'll be a hussar, as that seems to please you."

The boy laughed outright as if arranging some excursion or a trip to a new pleasure resort. All he knew about a soldier's life consisted of recollections of military novels, funny stories told by officers, and battle pictures carefully painted. He had never been in the company of troopers, hung round barracks, breathed the full-flavoured odour of the privates' sleeping quarters, or listened with a glass of cheap coarse red wine in front of him to the dull, stupid talk of young rankers and old petty officers always on the same subject: distaste stifled by fear or the vise-like grip of discipline. Like all young fellows who had never worn a uniform, he had not the least idea of what fate had in store for him in the ranks. He only saw the bright side of soldiering, the tinsel and ostentation of a mounted soldier's career.

In his mind, warped by being too much with women and actors, he saw officers in their best regimentals cantering round the Bois de Boulogne in the morning, following smart specimens of the weaker sex in tight-fitting bodices and flowing riding-habits; the Horse Show where the tiny hands of dashing beauties in and out of society applauded lieutenants and captains jumping the brook and the stone wall. He remembered hunt races and military meetings reported in the papers with long lists of the socially elect following the mention: "among those present." On such gala days, there were luncheons atop of four-in-hands with champagne galore and problematical "tips" given to pretty creatures listening attentively, marking their cards. An officer in a cavalry regiment is received in the highest society, forming real, useful friendships; crushing all prejudice beneath a spurred boot-heel; flirtations with real ladies ofttimes resulting in a duel or a rich marriage. All a chap had to do was to ride a charger, show off, live like a fighting-cock, get into debt, fight a little now and again; enjoy adorable mistresses, changing them weekly according to fancy; blossom into a ball-room pet; loll and loaf; but if war is declared, sacrifice life bravely and defy the enemy, dying on the field of honour or return home with the red ribbon of the Legion of Honour and scars that make a man look interesting all his life and cause him to stand out of the common crowd. Everybody would treat him as a comrade in the army. None would bother about his irregular birth or be chary of shaking his hand, so long as he proved himself a real good fellow, going straight, always to the fore in fun and frolic, showing oneself to be an open-handed, roystering blade, as careless of danger and trouble as his brothers-in-arms. Without an instant of boredom, adapting himself to this new life, flitting from a married woman to a queen of the half-world, his heart on his sleeve for the whores to peck at, he would soon efface the old fleshly attraction from his brain and rinse definitively from his being the lees of his first love, the last remaining thrills, and all vestiges of pain calling up the remembrances of "that wicked little bitch Clarette," as he described her inwardly.

He accused her so as not to have to accuse himself, and in reality, thought about her all the time, worried and disconcerted; already wearied by five nights alone in bed. Had she come after him, or written him a sad, imploring letter of abnegation, full of loving protestation, he would not have had the courage to repulse her. He was conscious of his weakness. It vexed him and he felt rather ashamed of it.

The very next day, accompanied by General Rosarieulles, one of his mother's friends, who took everything on his shoulders and smoothed away annoying formalities, leading Lucien through a maze of offices, the lad was found fit to serve and signed a five years' engagement in the 20th Hussars.

X

At the epoch, the regiment was in garrison at Saillans, in the south of France, a pretty little quiet provincial town. It reminded Lucien of stage scenery set to enframe a comedy of calm, honest country life. Many old gabled houses, bringing needed shade in narrow streets, stood out in relief against the immaculate blue sky. There were ruined walls, remains of fortifications covered with moss and flowers forming upright gardens reflected in the still waters of ancient ditches. Under the branches of the willows, a limpid stream coursed merrily and lazily, forced to sparkle and splash from morn to eve by factory mill-wheels and washerwomen's beetles.

On the slope of a hill, there was a district of churches, convents, and gloomy private houses separated by green spreading masses of foliage. In these pious thoroughfares, shrill, lively, or deep-toned chimes of church-bells resounded, calling the faithful to prayer and mingling with the whistling of martins scattering in giddy flight on the horizon.

At the extreme end of a long, populous avenue where grovelled paupers, outcasts, and prostitutes, in the midst of fields, behind a platform and shunted goods-trains and locomotives, stood immense lime-washed buildings, surrounded by high prison-like walls, pierced with innumerable windows, looking from afar like the glassy eyeballs of the blind. Here and there were sentry-boxes with somnolent soldiers on guard. Such were the cavalry barracks, with glass roofs shining like mirrors surmounting riding-schools; stables echoing with the ceaseless, deafening noise of rattling chains and horses neighing and stamping; the courtyard planted with stunted bushes near a dusty quarry; deep pits crammed with dung, the liquid settling in golden streams, alluring thousands of flies in black, fleeting clouds and the towing-path noisy from the exercises of buglers.

XI

Lights out! had been trumpeted. The last murmurs of the barracks died away in the great nocturnal silence. The only sounds to be heard were the measured treads of patrols going to relieve sentinels one by one; the laughter of returning troopers who had been on leave, back from the town with too much grog on board. Then all was quiet and in the sleepy stillness only remained the sounds of snores replying to snores, loud and long, rising from the rows of beds and at intervals the music of so many nostrils filled the dormitories with formidable stormy reverberation. In the midst of this moaning of billows, a piping, jerky treble could be heard in comic, timid cadence: the squeaky voice of a young soldier talking in his sleep and stammering out sentences from his drill-book.

Lucien could not settle down to sleep, still his thoughts, or drive from his brain the memories that harassed him as with painful pin-pricks. The rough sheets in which he turned and twisted his outstretched limbs, aching from prolonged horse-riding, brought back to his mind Clarette's roomy bed and the cobwebby cambric which her contracted fingers had often torn into strips during sleepless nights of love and lubricity. Despairingly, he compared those lost delights to the misery of his lot at present; to the heavy training-collar he loathed and which he had fastened round his neck with his own hands. The five years to be got through seemed, in the hallucination of insomnia, like a bare, rocky hill, its summit lost in the clouds. Five years! A big slice cut out of existence—the best part of life when a man's heart is like that of a virgin, and the body is robust, enabling fatigue to be derided; when the joys of love are experienced, every sensation being exquisite and desirable; and one is devoid of care, galloping on straight ahead as if to conquer the world. Five years to grow stupid, to vegetate, to mark time in the same regiment and wretched provincial hole; five years to languish after all one loved: happiness, a luxurious living; and condemned to crave for Paris.

The wretched young man grew weak, submerged in immense discouragement and great disgust of life as he reckoned up how powerless he was. It was useless to struggle against the iron netting that held him captive, or to evoke the radiant image of the mistress from whose embrace he had so stupidly torn himself. He felt so lonely, lost, and out of his element that big tears rolled silently from under his eyelids burning with fever and wetting his bolster. At last, exhausted, he closed his eyes, falling asleep while murmuring under his breath like a prayer of hope the pretty, sparkling name: Clarette.

XII

The actress had taken good care not to write to her lover. A letter would have shown that she had neither forgotten nor condemned; that she loved him still, wished to see him again and take him to her bed, and dreamt continually of the day of reconciliation when he would once more recline on her bosom. She preferred to suffer and torture her heart and her flesh, stifling wild and painful recollections sooner than make the first step towards Lucien and thus appear as if confessing she had wronged him; therefore encouraging by indulgent weakness the capricious inconstancy of a young man with the disposition of a light-o'-love.

It would, indeed, have been an irreparable mistake to humble oneself at the feet of this twenty-year-old lad, making him think too much of himself by imploring him, instead of treating him like a restive horse and tightening the bridle until the bit bruised and filled his mouth with blood.

Besides, Andrée wanted to win the last trick in her game
with Marie-Rose Hardanges. It had not taken Lucien's
mistress more than a week, after the first shock of the lad's
flight had calmed down a little, to find out—with the aid of
Lévêque—the secret of the absurd quarrel. Little by little,
she got on to the right scent, found the traces of the desperate mother's manoeuvres and laid bare all she had planned
and secretly set in movement so as to kill their love, make
them get tired of each other and break off the intimacy from
which she was excluded like a wet-blanket. Clarette was
still panting with rage at the humiliation of being tricked
like a silly young girl just starting in life; befooled by the
most stupid woman on the Parisian stage—a mere doll.
Andrée had but one dream: to become once more Lucien's
absolute, sovereign mistress, and that is why she calculated
every act and refrained from committing the slightest
imprudence.

Furious, revengeful hatred mingled with lustful fever.
Everything seemed black to her. She longed to overwhelm
her erstwhile companion with bitterness, disillusions, and
anguish approaching insanity. She wanted, so to say, to
bury the boy alive; steal him away body and soul without
giving his mother the slightest chance of regaining lost
happiness. The more Andrée worked herself up, the more
she accused and detested her enemy who had enjoyed the
triumph of revenge, destroyed voluptuous fancies and
sensuous delights; violated the paradise where Lucien and
Clarette thought of nothing but sexual gratification and
mutual adoration, the more she was filled with clemency,
tenderness, affection, and regret for the unknowing lad who
had escaped from her love—alas!—as if breaking out of
prison, leaving her grievously afflicted.

She had learnt all by bribing servants and gleaning information in the wings at theatres; knowing besides how Lucien had enlisted in a cavalry regiment and that he belonged to the garrison of a little town in the South. Full of temerity, despite her defeat, trusting in the power she considered she had over the young fellow, Clarette made light of the clever, wicked trick his mother thought she had played on her, and mocked at the seemingly insurmountable obstacle which it was hoped would dishearten her, stop her advance and bar her road if peradventure she made a fresh attack or furiously kept up the struggle. The boy's distant banishment rejoiced and reassured her soul. With great foresight, she calculated the consequences, and by some magnetic divination guessed at the throes of boredom and languor wherein withered the soul of the poor stripling changed into a soldier. She felt instinctively that he would be assailed by memories wounding like piercing darts planted in his brain, eyes, heart, and loins. She would have boldly staked her whole fortune against the most trifling sum that it was only a question of a few weeks before they came together again. That brief space of time would pass rather quicker than she supposed. It was the entr'acte of a fairy play when invisible music is heard, and the spectator knows that behind the lowered curtain enchanting scenes, marvellous apparitions, and brilliant lights are being got ready.

Thoroughly imbued with the spirit of the part she set herself to play, she was certain that she was followed, watched, and that the most petty details of her life were known to Marie-Rose who would be foolish enough to send full reports in her letters to her son. So Andrée feigned to be enjoying an existence of unbridled pleasure, parading in public first with one man and then with another; apparently not giving herself time to sleep, or take breath; inventing fantastical fashions; organising noisy balls and parties, to such an extent that Marie-Rose was tortured and delighted at one and the same time.

"How heartless Clarette is," she exclaimed, "to be so quickly consoled!"

XIII

Being warmly recommended to his colonel, Lucien had been appointed secretary to his commanding officer and all the boy had to do was to copy a few minutes, circulars, or letters; doze in his chair; and smoke cigarettes in front of the half-open windows. But he still suffered, the remembrance of his former mistress occupying all his thoughts. Worry and boredom gnawed at his vitals, submerging him in perpetual darkness where sunlight never penetrated, dictating mad, incoherent plans and frightful nightmares such as destroy the peace of mind of exhausted patients just before giving up the ghost. Nothing made him smile, not even for a few seconds; nothing could efface his insane obsession or soothe the smart of his feverish flesh.

After a lengthy inward struggle and the supreme rebellion of his pride, he made up his mind to confess his state of misery to Clarette. He resolved to write to her and beg for absolution like a repentant sinner confessing his sins on his knees, begging for salvation with joined hands and tears streaming from his eyes.

Clarette read the letter over and over again; but, prolonging the ordeal purposely, she did not answer it. She was overjoyed and revelled in her triumphant victory. It was all she could do to restrain herself from communicating the news to Marie-Rose and, with ironical condolence, sending the mother her son's humble petition of love, so tender and poignant. Andrée was dying to show her enemy the failure of all her efforts, lies, and snares, and force her to realise how the mistress, without saying a word, interrupting absolute inaction, taking any step whatever, or running after the lover who had forsaken her, had won the game and once more made his mother hide her diminished head.

It was not long before Clarette began to get ready to undertake the journey to Saillans. She did so with calculated slowness, her mouth watering already as she thought of the pleasures of lust in store, anticipating in imagination a thousand lovely, lascivious methods of gratification. She selected her dressing-gowns, frocks, and the hats her little man preferred. Some of them, indeed, his effeminate nature had prompted him to design and trim. She shut herself up in her pretty dwelling, passing whole afternoons among her gowns. Her bed was covered with all the mysteries of her under-muslins and brimmed over on to sofa and armchairs.

She dressed and undressed twenty times a day, trying on, twisting, turning, and meditating in front of her swing-glass. At intervals, she was thrilled so keenly that she nearly fainted, stirred from head to heel by lancinating memories of the olden days and the exquisite itching of desire. This wave of sensuous emotion dominated her being especially when her hand touched the transparent cambric and supple silk of under-garments, light and soft to the feel as a woman's skin, reminding her of amorous strolls in country leafy lanes; the laziness of long days at sunny Metone, and divine games during exquisite nights of refined salacity.

Mme. Lévêque helped her mistress, following her about like a faithful hound, but sulky and grumbling, shrugging her shoulders.

"She's got another touch of her old complaint—there's no mistake about it," the old housekeeper mumbled in an undertone; fragments of sentences escaping from between her teeth. "A big revival of the old play is now billed—with new scenery and dresses. More rotten foolishness! We were getting on so quietly and comfortably. She seemed calm and cured and now she's off again. Damn this love of theirs— this beastly love that makes 'em stick together tighter than glue!"

Mme. Lévêque emphasised her complaints with the rough gesture of a street-sweeper whisking garbage into the gutter. Discouraged, she bent over the open trunk at the foot of the broad bed. She folded and packed, almost automatically, pretty light-coloured costumes, lace-trimmed summer dressing-gowns, tiny Russian leather slippers, cloth cloaks and shot-silk wraps, pretending not to hear what Andrée exclaimed mockingly as she blew rings of cigarette smoke:

"Good old Lévêque! You've no idea how amusing you are!"

XIV

Lucien waited for Clarette's answer in a state of dull, gnawing anxiety. Every day his pain was more acute. His suffering and sadness were increased by disappointment at each matutinal distribution of letters in the barrack-yard. He tried to deceive himself nevertheless by thinking that perhaps his adored actress was on tour. Mme. Lévêque had not forwarded his appeal, either in obedience to orders, or so as not to disturb her mistress's peace of mind.

Marie-Rose mentioned Andrée in nearly all her letters, speaking of her former friend as of a person seen and met daily. Newspapers printed her name among those queens of fashion who had not yet deserted Paris for some up-to-date watering-place, and still showed up occasionally before lunch in the Bois de Boulogne and after dinner at the open-air music-halls of the Champs-Elysées.

If Clarette remained stubbornly silent and refused to

forgive him, it could only be because she did not love him any more; made light of his sufferings, longings and distress, and had given herself to another man. Doubtless, when she recognised Lucien's handwriting on the envelope, she burst out laughing and, without even opening it, had torn it up in a thousand pieces, throwing them out of the window of her boudoir giving on the broad avenue. Her love was dead. Why had he tried to resuscitate it? Why had he dreamed of living over again a period of existence that cannot be enjoyed twice in a man's life?

At the end of a week of painful expectation, fever, and nervous irritation, unable to hold out any longer, he posted to Clarette the following demented, irascible litany. Every line betrayed the lust that devoured his being, the wild beating of his heart, the fiery flames of his fierce longings, his unappeased rutting appetite, equally furious and innocent:

I wrote you a loving letter, putting my whole soul into it. If you had cared to look, you might have seen that the paper was stained with my tears. It's no lie, I'm not trying to fool you. You couldn't spare a minute to answer me, if only a few, commonplace words or a friendly sentence. You would let me die in an agony of grief in this rat-hole, without even turning your head or granting me thoughts of remembrance lasting two minutes. Despite all your dash and your money, you don't come up to the ankle of a common streetwalker, such as I've met here and whose hearts are cleaner than yours. I was foolish and credulous enough to adore you as in the past and dream of revived affection. I confess my hope. I was mistaken. Pardon my error.

How you must have laughed at me! The lesson is

profitable; worse luck for the women I get hold of in future! I'll make them pay what I owe you for my sufferings at your hands. Ever since my mouth joined yours, you lied to me. You've not had a thought for anyone except yourself—you alone. All you cared about was to profit by my strength and toy with my innocence. Such was your enjoyment, enabling you to warm your icy, listless body. Now you see why I hate you as much as I once idolized you, and I would give any price in order to buy back my preceding letter, written when I was mad and in which I debased myself so far as to supplicate you.

I esteem myself lucky to have been able to rid myself of you so easily. We shall never meet again. I feel it my duty to tell you plainly that the prospect of being done with you forever fills me with joy; that I don't miss you and that a prostitute of the lowest class has taken your place.

Adieu.

By the same post, as if Lucien was really crazy, Clarette received a third letter without a stamp and the envelope scarcely closed. No doubt the boy had scribbled it hastily and run to the railway station to catch the mail-train to Paris.

I have just written you some very vile things. I entreat you, my love, to burn my letters without opening them. I give you my word of honour—I swear on your beloved life that I don't mean one word of all I've written. I adore you more than I've ever adored you before. Do as you like. Whether you come to my rescue or not, I shall love you all the same and bear no malice. I'm so overwrought, lonely, and sad that my brain goes wrong at times and I can't see clearly what I'm doing daily. I think only of you. Only my love for you keeps me alive. If I could set eyes on you again—merely to brush against you as you went by, it seems to me that my heart would crack with joy. I love you so very, very much, my Andrée, that you can't refuse me a little mite of affection, friendship, no matter what, so long as it would prove to me that some insignificant atom of your being belongs to me still.

Lucien.

The same night, the actress took the train to Saillans.

XV

She awaited his coming in bed. It was the narrow, common bed of a provincial hotel with red reps curtains and carved wooden panels that had once been highly varnished. Clarette, reclining on this couch, might have been a dethroned empress in hiding who, dying for want of sleep and her strength and courage exhausted, had taken refuge anywhere. Vague sun rays filtered through the curtains and filled the room with mysterious dim light as in a church. The beauty of her fair head was enhanced by a kind of strange, languid charm. Her hair unbound, flowing over the pillow, enframed her face as with a quivering aureola. Her mouth looked like an open flower in a pink flagon. The heat had led her to throw off sheet and blanket and she who for one night had been the incarnation of the radiant, bewitching goddess Venus, outstretched in an adorable dreamy pose, leaning on her elbow, one hand supporting her cheeks, displayed with tranquil effrontery her splendid, dazzling body. It was sculptural. Its harmonious lines were faultless. It was supple, graceful, slender, feline; exciting by reason of its undulations and pearly sea-shell tints. A thin cambric chemise—transparent, low-cut, short, and flimsy—scarcely hid the nakedness of Andrée's frame or veiled secret folds and shaded spots.

The actress looked as if she had just woken up gently at the end of a happy dream. To see her smiling with half-closed eyelids; offering her pouting lips to invisible kisses; starting; quivering from head to foot as if being soothed by the prolonged stroking caress of agile fingers, one would have believed that her thoughts were still wandering.

Outside, church-bells were ringing joyfully, replying to neighbouring peals, mingling their chimes as if laughing in company with great shrill merriment, and causing the gaiety of holiday times to reign in the silence of the sleepy, deserted street. The unexpected noise warmed Clarette's superstitious heart, pleasing her like a happy omen and increasing the smile that lit up her features.

All of a sudden, yielding to a furious, impatient push, the door flew wide open and Lucien dashed towards the bed with the eager rush of a lost animal finding its stable once more. His brain in a whirl, a mad light in his eyes, his hands trembling, he threw his arms round his mistress's bust, making her bones crack in his frenzied clasp and crushing her to him as if he wanted to melt into her and be absorbed by her. He stifled and bruised Andrée, scratching her breasts and belly with the buttons of his tunic. Nevertheless, the actress felt no pain and made no complaint. Neither did she repulse him, but yielded herself up entirely and became possessed by him.

At once, without uttering useless words, their mouths

met and were cemented together. Their delirious, delicious kiss so long desired, dreamt of and waited for; this simple, endless, ecstatic kiss of the lips, in which they inhaled and drank each other, so to speak, in celestial intoxication; and by which they were fused into each other once again, thrilled them with such enjoyment, benumbed them with such torpor, shattered them with such voluptuousness that the lad sank down on his knees as if fainting, while Clarette fell back swooning lasciviously, limp and inert as at the conclusion of sexual gratification.

It was only at this juncture, after a lull of a few minutes, that the lovers spoke. It was no ordinary conversation, but rather an affectionate exchange of coaxing sounds, a series of reiterated, monotonous words of infinite sweetness; faint echoes of the brain incapable of regaining the slightest gleam of reasonable thought; sighs of happiness amidst which the voice articulates one syllable only, dying away in childish, chirping prattle.

"My darling, my darling—" murmured Lucien, his gaze riveted to her face.

"My boy—my own boy—my Lulu—my dear love—" replied Clarette, her glances plunging into his eyes; her voice taking on faraway, seraphic, crystal accents, as if coming from the clouds, bringing a message of peace, reconciliation, and the supreme favour of femininity.

They spoke no more, spurred on and burning again by their mutual desire. Suddenly, the young soldier undressed, throwing on the floor his trousers garnished with leather and his tunic. He was stark naked like a marble demigod as he stretched himself by his mistress's side.

With a sweeping, lewd gesture, Clarette tore to rags her chemise which was in her way, preventing her from feeling the contact of his flesh against hers and hindering her from offering herself to Lucien as he had done to her. They intertwined their bodies madly, rolling together furiously on the ancient wooden bedstead that creaked and groaned like an old fishing-smack in a gale.

In the midst of his fierce, brutal onslaught, Lucien stopped at intervals to look at her and revel in the sight of her. He appeared as if he feared being the victim of a mirage, of some morbid, feverish vision, or of some lying resemblance. He might also have been compared to a wrestler revelling in the delight of pinning under him a panting, defeated opponent. His nerves tingling, his strength increased tenfold, he never loosed his hold, but plunged her again and again in a sea of delight, making her loins ache, exhausting her by his incessant attacks, causing her to sob and groan.

"Again!—again!—more! more!" she moaned, half dead, enervated, her limbs hanging loosely. "Yes—yes!—keep on! How kind you are—how I love you! My own boy—do you want to kill me?" she continued.

The measured cadence of his savage shocks reverberated; hammering far down in her being, crushing her entirely. She had forgotten everything except that she was experiencing ceaseless sexual enjoyment. Clarette was convulsed by uninterrupted sensual spasms, and she fancied that she was penetrated by something burning that seared her being searchingly, emptying her of marrow, heart, and brain; changing her entirely and carrying her away into empty space. In front of her eyes were visions of sudden showers of stars, flights of comets, pitchy darkness, snowy plains, fluid mists, sparkling phosphorescence of strange flowers shedding their petals one by one, red and blue precious stones and frightful phallic apparitions. In the intensity of the sensation resided madness and pain.

She suddenly woke up, regaining fresh animation as if she had just swallowed some magic elixir, or been immersed in a tepid bath soothing the nerves and appeasing her whole suffering being. She covered him with kisses more ardent and lewd than ever; holding him to her, her arms joined round his waist as she drank his panting breath and shuddered in response to his thrills of lust.

Andrée was in ecstasies at the transports of her lover's delight and, while vanquished in his turn, he rolled away from her and fell back by her side, his heart beating like the rolling of a drum, she gently lifted his head and with well-nigh maternal care, arranged the second pillow, so that he could rest comfortably.

"You don't know how I love you!" she repeated several times, kissing his forehead. "You've made me happy, darling!"

PART THE THIRD

I

After showers of kisses, Lucien had to leave his mistress and forego the delight of breakfasting alone with her in the little room as she had wished and hoped. He returned to his odious printed forms and red-tape documents in the office that he now looked upon as a prison. He had fled from Clarette's arms with his eyes suffused with tears and without daring to look behind him.

By trying very hard, next day, he wheedled his colonel out of four days' leave.

"Take care not to get above yourself, young sir!" he exclaimed, as he signed the permission. "I promised to keep an eye on you!"

These four days, enabling them to live entirely together, with none to trouble them, pry on their movements, or get in their way, were a foretaste of paradise. They wasted not a minute, for every second was spent in mutual, lustful grati-fication, making up for the hours lost during their short separation which had caused them both to suffer greatly. They lingered in their room, dawdling on the bed all night and all day, lacking courage to get dressed entirely and go out. They dreaded the curiosity of the townspeople, who made mountains out of molehills. Lucien and Clarette were still burning with desire, always ready to join their bodies and taste fresh pleasures, unable to quench their voluptuous thirst in these torrents of caresses as if invisible flames were licking and burning their loins, goading them on to partake of the joys of carnal possession.

By no act of repentance, imprudent speech, or regretful utterance had either of them recalled their old disagreements, their momentary divorce, and the rancour and anguish which still scarred their being. The boy followed his mistress's example and held his tongue. They had not questioned each other, avoiding all dangerous and indiscreet explanations; intertwining exactly as if just returned from an adventurous and troublesome journey during which regular correspondence had been kept up, and the minutes counted until the happy hour of reuniting. They made no plans and did not trouble as yet about the morrow, letting themselves live, floating down the stream in soulful torpor and happy intoxication. To see and hear them, no one would ever have believed that they had been almost enemies for a short time; misunderstanding and evil memories separating them, forcing each to take a different road, like convicts escaping from a penal settlement.

Clarette, radiant, her soul singing, was glad to lend herself to Lucien's fancies, and even suggested new whims. She romped like a hoyden with the perverted youth who was neither changed nor sobered by uniform and discipline.

She played a subtle, close game, keeping her adversary

continually on the alert, committing not a fault and only lowering her guard so as to better parry and thrust, or lead up to a straight aim at the heart. During disjointed talk when they rested, she made him gossip about the tedious details and hard work of a soldier's life; the sadness he endured and the slight amount of pleasure he had perhaps experienced at feeling himself more manly while showing off on horseback in line with his comrades. His confiding chat amused her like a novel theatrical performance or a book enjoyed in private. She laughed till she cried, forcing him to swear, in imitation of the oldest soldiers; and repeat, in deep bass tones, fragments of military slang which she rehearsed with him like a schoolgirl learning a lesson. She rolled her "r's," accentuating syllables with the gruff accent of sergeants drilling, laying stress on obscene words and barrack-room blasphemous oaths.

All of sudden, as if in confusion, she pressed her coaxing lips on her lover's mouth.

"You ought to be ashamed of yourself, sir! Fancy a brave hussar teaching me such awful things!" she murmured, pouting ironically like a boarding-school miss.

She continued her playful fun, and dressed herself in Lucien's uniform, pulling on his heavy slacks and buttoning herself up tightly in his tunic. A cigarette between her lips, his cap cocked over one ear, her hands in the trouser pockets, the actress's bearing was so tempting, saucy, and lewdly bold that Lucien clapped his hands applauding her.

"Oh, wouldn't you please me if I were a woman!" he shouted to her.

"Attention! Dress by files! Right turn! Left wheel! Don't you know your right hand from your left, you idiot? What did they teach you in the brothel where you were brought up?" she exclaimed, not heeding him.

Although Lucien had only served three months in the army, he was already broken in, being full of respect for the gold braid on the sleeves of superior officers and trembling in front of those petty tyrants with whom he was in daily contact. He dreaded instinctively any wretched accident, rivality in love, or jealous revolt that might shatter his momentary tranquility. In that case, his lazy life devoid of care, especially since his mistress had come back to him, would be changed immediately. He would find himself struggling against a heap of mischief, watched, punished, in the black list, and reduced to getting rid of Andrée or of putting up with the continual wretchedness of a common creature hampering his betters in their plans and desires. He did all he could not to attract their attention. Clarette had not walked out with him in the streets. As she never looked closely into any bill, but paid at sight without complaining, her hotelkeeper fancied that she was a high-born dame carrying on some mysterious intrigue. He expected visitors continually coming and going—a source of profit—so he took heed not to blab or let the godsend be noised abroad. By the aid of a great effort, he never gossiped about the strange case of this pretty Parisian pet, so elegant and open-handed, who welcomed a common trooper at all hours of the day and night and whose bed, always in disorder, bore witness to unceasing orgies. So, for three weeks, the couple succeeded in remaining in hiding. Nobody knew of their existence and they were absolutely happy.

Upholsterers from Paris transformed the interior of the little house, draping the walls with ancient stuffs, adding cushions, vases, and bric-à-brac to the worm-eaten furniture that filled bedrooms and sitting-rooms. Clarette was stirred by fresh, unexpected excitement in this sort of clandestine house-furnishing with its atmosphere of danger. It afforded her much amusement, and she found pleasure in putting Lucien to the proof by telling him stories of imaginary visits. She did not complain of this secluded life and was not bored for an instant.

Sometimes, she dressed herself up like a nun, receiving her lover with a hood on her head and a knotted cord round her waist, scolding him because he endangered her hopes of salvation. With downcast eyes, and her little hands hidden in her black sleeves, she mumbled words that sounded like prayers.

She would force her boy to chase her from room to room until, out of breath, she let herself be seized, but struggled hard and Lucien had to violate her.

"Aren't you ashamed of yourself, sir, to assault a poor nun?" she exclaimed, flat on her back at last, on sofa or bed.

III

D ays and hours sped by and Clarette took no heed of time. She felt herself overwhelmed by vague and confused sentimentality; a sensation of delicious ease in her rustic surrounding. The cool breezes of autumn brought repose to her nervous system, driving away all mental irritation, as if she was half-asleep in a warm, perfumed bath. She imagined she was a little child once more, amidst trees and flowers, in the profound peace of fields and meadows. In Paris, her nerves were always astretch, her body aching with fever and fatigue, her brain in a whirl; at Saillans, the most trifling incident thrilled her with pleasure; all her senses, especially sight and hearing, seemed increased tenfold as if by some mysterious force. The change to sylvan scenes, the scents and sounds of the countryside made as much impression on her as if she had just left Paris for the first time in her life.

One afternoon, her hair flowing at liberty over her shoulders, her feet in slippers, in the adorable *négligé* of a handsome woman just out of bed and who, half-awake, has not even taken the trouble to tie the ribbons of her *surah* dressing-gown, the actress strolled in a shaded alley of her garden. Suddenly, bugle-blasts rent the air merrily. Urged on by the sight-seeing mania inherent in Parisian sirens, she was allured by the music and, instead of going indoors, she ran to the gate giving on the high road.

Lucien's regiment came trotting along, returning from some military training manoeuvres. Pleased at such unexpected amusement, delighted to see the soldiers, she stood looking attentively, holding on to the railings. As the troops clattered bravely and rapidly by, she was all eyes, searching vainly for her boy's slender, upright figure; her lips ready to greet him with a loving smile.

The Colonel, tall and thin, with an angular profile, pulled up and let his men go on while he stopped to light a cigar. Catching sight of Clarette, he gave a start of surprise, staring at her with the look of a man hesitating, cudgelling his brains to recollect where he had seen her face and when, and whether he knew her or not. Anyhow, there was nothing like being polite, so he risked a respectful military salute, lifting his hand with a broad flourish to his silver-braided cap.

In the evening, Andrée lost no time in telling her story to Lucien.

"Well, we're in a nice mess if that ladykiller takes a fancy to you!" he exclaimed, greatly annoyed.

IV

Colonel Daumont de Croisailles was forty-four years of age and had seen much service. He was a bachelor, determined to enjoy the tranquility of single-blessedness till the end of his days. His adoration of all women, brunettes, blondes, or auburn-haired angels, was so passionate that there was no danger of the gallant officer condemning himself to a life-sentence of love in company of a single specimen who was naturally bound to grow old. A great rake, but not wishing to compromise himself, do anything undignified, or become the talk of the town, he had hired a solitary little villa in the Eglisottes, an outlying district, near the river, in a quiet street of leafy avenues and gardens.

As he considered that there was no fun in the recriminations of jealous husbands, and the chattering and howling of women gathering in small mobs to dispute and weep; and as everything disagreeable incidents, and imprudent

217

occurrences arising from mistakes and appointments not kept should be foreseen in a life of libertine adventure—the Colonel's dwelling had three different doors. His discretion was sincere enough to stifle the scruples of the most timid charmer and he feared no rival in the incomparable art of varying masculine kisses and caresses. He knew how to toy with a woman's nerves, lull her conscience to sleep, and hold pampered pussies by their curiosity and the temptation of a darkened, scented room where the exquisite collation of the prologue and the entr'actes is already laid out.

Therefore, any man in the garrison—common private or swaggering officer—lucky enough to have started a love-affair or plucked a rare blossom, feared the lascivious old warrior like the devil, for he never failed to find out a weak spot enabling him to storm the fortress. In the pursuit of petticoats, his pay, allowances for expenses of representation, and his private income of fifteen thousand francs disappeared drop by drop like water from a cracked decanter. He was continually on the hunt, following women and nosing out intrigues with the keen scent of a private inquiry agent. There was no audacious move or clever trick that he did not know, thanks to his twenty years' experience—that of a man who had devoted himself to enjoying women without ever losing his head. At his age, he was able to boast without telling a lie that he could still keep his place in the line of march and never fall out till his billet was reached, without needing any great amount of music to encourage him to keep in step.

Among all the frisky matrons or sly young lasses who were ready to please a man, there were not half-a-dozen who could have asserted veraciously that they had not stayed a little late—if only once—in the Colonel's bower of bliss. They dared not swear that once there, their corset had not been thrown on an easy chair, or that when they crept sheepishly home they were not more full of deep thought than when they had gone to the assignation, feeling as they slipped quickly out of the backdoor like governesses having been granted a diploma after a long, severe final examination.

V

Probing his brain and exercising his excellent memory after the fairy-like apparition of Lucien's mistress behind her garden railings, M. de Croisailles found that he had recognised the celebrated, dashing comédienne, Andrée Clarette.

Whatever could this flighty beauty be doing on the quiet in the suburbs of Saillans? Who shared her mysterious seclusion—a vicious female friend or a lusty lover? The Colonel nearly lost his wits trying to work out the problem, neglecting his other adventures. He was knocked off his perch when he got to know that Clarette had suddenly rented her cottage for the trifle of two hundred louis, banishing herself so far from Paris with the sole idea of abandoning her well-known, beautiful boy to a common soldier she adored and who idolised her in return.

Nevertheless, he feigned ignorance, on the alert for the earliest opportunity enabling him, without being unjust, abusing his authority, or suppressing by a brutal stroke the obstacle in the way of the desire, to attempt an attack in which there would not be too much risk of defeat.

Lucien Hardanges put great faith in the recommendations with which he had been favoured on joining his regiment, and was somewhat of a malingerer, one of those ne'er-do-well slackers who are continually in hot water, getting out of the way when work has to be done and apparently treating orders and duties with contempt. He had often been punished, either for having been too late to respond to the evening roll-call, or for being absent from some inspection. He got into the habit of coaxing his brigadier and slipping out of barracks by climbing the wall at night. It was not long before a punctilious quarter-master denounced him, and M. de Croisailles took care to profit by the lucky hazard that gave him a full hand of trumps.

To all appearances, he had to be severe in spite of himself and make an example of Andrée Clarette's young lover on whom he inflicted a sentence of twenty days' confinement to barracks. As the reasons for the punishment were made out with great severity, the brigadier general added another fortnight.

VI

The lad counted the hours in the evil-smelling guard-room, where only a few sad and gloomy rays of light struggled through the closed windows. He champed his bit with his heart full of gall and his aching head fit to burst, as he cursed his sudden fit of ill-luck. To remain isolated, and not have to answer the importunate queries of comrades in the same plight as he was, he stretched himself out on his plank-bed, shut his eyes and feigned sleep. While the minutes seemed long and weary to him, his Colonel and a few officers—the libertines of the regiment always dangling after women whenever there seemed a chance of a new taste of carnal enjoyment—showed off on horseback every day in front of Clarette's garden-gate. It remained closed to them all, despite suppli-cating letters, generous promises, bold curiosity, high-stepping tricks of fine riding on the road, and inter-minable ambushing close to the ivy-covered railings.

Slipping a five-franc piece into the hand of one of the troopers on guard, Lucien was able to inform Andrée of his misfortune by sending her a pencilled note. He begged her to be patient and not forsake him, telling her his troubles and cursing the career of a trooper with words of hatred and loathing.

Clarette, gifted with more forethought and subtlety than a man, immediately divined the true cause of the punishment suddenly inflicted on her lover. She was exasperated and saddened at being deprived of his accustomed caresses and no longer seeing her boy who now formed part and parcel of her being. Utterly alone and mournful, burning with useless sensuous flames, she condemned the front of her dwelling giving on the road and remained in bed until late in the afternoon. She never showed herself on her balcony, nor in the alleys of linden trees; nor allowing the shutters to be opened and only taking exercise in the plantation at the back of the house, far from prying eyes.

She was unnerved at being thus besieged and imprisoned; tortured by being driven from the feast of love in the middle of the luscious banquet; just as they had both arranged their new life and upset so well the jealous plans of Marie-Rose. It was all Clarette could do to refrain from hurling a shower of stones and bawling insults at the daily procession of officers who hung round her gate like dogs after a bitch in heat. The Colonel, with the stripes denoting his rank, was the one she loathed the most. She was haunted by such a mad longing to mock at them and make them fully aware of her rancour, that now and again she felt inclined to pull up her skirts to the waist and, with a great sardonic laugh, display to their astonished eyes her naked posterior enframed in a window suddenly thrown open.

She would have given a great deal to set the conceited

cavalry officers at defiance by this show of vulgar, lewd irony and prove to the rutting idiots that they were wasting their time. She wanted them to know that she snapped her fingers at them and their trick-riding. Their offers and tenacious pursuit disgusted her and her delight would have been to spit out all her rage and spite and yell vile epithets through the railings as if in a street row. What delight to shriek out cutting truths, asking the old satyr of a Colonel if he took her for one of his provincial trollops; if he had the cheek to think she was going to take the trouble to warm up leavings; ask who had told him she was on sale or hire; and when he was going to make up his mind to turn tail and fall back on his base!

But she refrained reluctantly, remaining dumb and invisible, trying to tire them out by her indifference, fearful lest she might do harm to Lucien and expose him to reprisals. So that her boy should suffer less by their separation, the actress kept a long diary forming almost a daily gazette. Each day her manuscript provided him charitably with a shower of the manna of love; overwhelming him besides with consoling promises, helping him to endure the most severe ordeals.

Wicked dreams, impulsive rebellious ideas haunted her, prevented her from sleeping; incrusting themselves in her brain and hammering into her being like the sharp nails of Calvary. She thought of finishing her horrible existence by boldly running away with Lucien as soon as he regained his liberty and forcing him to tear off his hated uniform.

Marie-Rose reckoned upon breaking off her son's liaison and destroying his passion by making him a soldier. Was not this a reason—without counting all others—for Clarette, the enemy, to be haunted by the obsession of defying the law by leading Lucien on to take the last leap of despair, forcing him to flee, become a deserter, and induce him to commit a fault that would link them together more securely than any oaths of fidelity, fleshly attraction, or memories of delicious lust?

She then grew frightened of her own thoughts and tried not to ruminate in such insane fashion. She recoiled, hanging back as if facing a barrier masking some unknown abyss, while she tried to forget her troubles and drive these absurd, perilous projects from her mind.

VII

Lucien wrote to Clarette, sobbing while he scribbled.

I'm going mad through lack of liberty and being away from you, dearest. If I didn't get your kind letters, so loving, sweet, full of affection, and soothing, no power on earth could prevent me from joining you, defying odious discipline, and fleeing from these barracks where I'm locked up and kept for so many days in prison.

I kiss you over and over again. Think always of me—only of me. I dream of you all day and all night. My heart and my whole being are full of you. I adore you and when we meet again at last we'll double the ration of kisses and make up for all this time lost. That night, I want you to wear your chemise of Chantilly lace through which your flesh glistens so strangely;

227

and you'll perfume your golden hair with the clove-pink scent I like—won't you? Do you count the days as I do? Does this period of solitude seem long to you? Do you really regret me as much as you say? Do you really feel a longing for your Lulu—that real craving, you know, darling, which thrills one through and through and drives one crazy?

Another day he wrote as follows, on an old envelope:

I expect you'll laugh at me, my own. I killed time to-day by carving a monogram—the initials of our two names—in the wood of my plank bed. I ought to have added the traditional heart pierced with an arrow. I do wish you could get into this vile guard-room, if only for a minute or two, and read what the poor devils who have been punished left behind them. Their hopes, desires, and anguish are scribbled, scratched, and sketched all along the whitewashed walls and on the heavy beams polished and worn by the bodies of somnolent drunkards, sullen mutineers, and unlucky simpletons. There are multitudes of inscriptions: silly, furious, obscene, humorous. Some are fiery like the blaze of a house on fire. Others resound quite sweetly and prettily like the echo of a rustic hurdy-gurdy. Oh, idol of my heart, I love you so much that everything pertaining to love enchants me, excites my pity, and grants me dreams of ecstasy!

The inexorable slowness of each long day exasperated him and he rebelled against the life of passive obedience to which he was condemned. He bitterly cursed his mother and all others who had lured him into his present predicament, fooling him like a ten-year-old child to be got rid of by any perfidious wheedling tale. So he declared in another note, spotted with round stains by the tears that had fallen from his eyes like the big drops of a summer rainstorm. He continued thus:

> Understand well what I say, darling: I've had enough, enough of this filthy soldiering. My strength is exhausted; my patience worn out. I fear I may lose all self-control, begin to feel like a murderer, and drive both my fists into the beastly face of the quarter-master who treats us like brutes, laughs at us, and forgets us in the sun after hours of useless drilling. I'd like to tear my uniform to rags, run away and hide in a hole in the ground. Save me my darling; save us both since you love me and belong to me the same as I belong to you. I have confidence in you only. I can only count on your assistance and I'll obey you blindly. It's too bad to be so unhappy and be crushed by such sad trouble at my age.

The lad's exaggerated ideas found their echo in Clarette's overwrought brain. They responded to her secret thoughts, fanning them into flames like smouldering ashes rekindled by the fierce gust of a gale.

VIII

The big table of the club was piled with half-emptied glasses and the grey veins of the marble were covered by large yellow stains flecked by foaming bubbles.

Captain Cazergues was leaving the garrison and his brother-officers offered him a farewell bumper, to drink to his health and prosperity in the new post to which he was appointed. Ever since he had entered on a military career, he had never left his regiment and something seemed to snap in his being at the idea of abruptly leaving his comrades and not having on his collar the number to which he was accustomed. He felt it hard to begin life anew at his age and change his old habits. Deep emotion moved him gradually and he was unable to hide it. He wiped his forehead automatically and his wrinkles made deeper lines in his face and resembled scars. He tossed off one glass after another, as if he was trying to get drunk, and his little blinking eyes glanced uneasily from one officer to another, as he searched his memory.

The early gaiety of the evening cooled down, and noisy conversation became general. There was no more singing.

Making an effort to struggle against the grief that seemed on the point of overpowering him, Cazergues jumped up and with one bound stood erect on his chair.

"Now, then, you youngsters! Wake up!" he cried, turning to the sub-lieutenants with a gay, mocking gesture. "When I was your age I was a thousand times jollier than you! Waiter, more wine! Let it rain champagne! And let's have a roaring chorus—a real roar, by God!" He flourished his arms like a bandmaster. "One—two—three! Now, boys, all together!—like in the good old days!"

Enthroned in the seat of honour at the end of the room, Colonel Daumont de Croisailles was waiting until he should be called upon to propose the farewell toast, when the principal medical officer, Couramille, put a question to him.

"Is it true what they tell me about the soldier Hardanges having deserted?"

"Considering he hasn't answered to the roll for seventeen days, what are we to suppose?"

"And the wench from Paris?"

"Gone off with him."

"Damn scented skirts, say I! When a man gets petticoat-stuck, it's all over with him!"

The old doctor was about to set forth some of his misanthropical maxims and, according to his wont, thunder against the fair sex he hated and dreaded as much as new, unknown, mysterious maladies that baffle science.

"Hold your tongue, Couramille, and don't try to mask your batteries!" interrupted the Colonel, with mocking bluntness. "If women didn't exist, somebody would have to invent them. The dear creatures are the only things in this life that are true and amusing. Of course, I know they drive us crazy now and again, and the majority are not worth more than a vicious broken-down riding-school mare. Their most loving kisses have an after-taste of battles and lies, but love would be tedious and disgusting if it didn't bring suffering and if there wasn't something keen and cutting about it that sharpens the delight of its memory. In spite of myself, I envy this boy-trooper who ruins himself sooner than be separated from his mistress. He's in hiding with her, I'll swear. How the adorable enchantress must make him wallow in enjoyment and overwhelm him in sensual sport fit to send a chap into a lunatic asylum! Oh, doctor, you don't know what it is to be young!"

He twisted the points of his moustaches, gazing into vacancy, while the clouds of past erotic remembrances veiled his pupils. The medical officer, quite indifferent, smiling incredulously with the air of a man forced to listen to commonplace chatter, drummed with his fat fingers on the table in time to the chorus of the young officers.

The Colonel frowned suddenly, and turning away a little, took a sly peep at his watch. It was ten o'clock and he had an appointment that night with the pretty wife of a dealer in corn and oats who passed his life on the road visiting fairs for miles round.

M. Daumont de Croisailles rose to his feet and coughed noisily to clear his throat. There was dead silence at once and the officers, glass in hand, drew round him in a circle.

"Gentlemen, I have the honour to propose a toast. Let us drink to the health of our old comrade, Captain Cazergues, promoted to be Major in the Light Cavalry. He was one of the veterans of our fine regiment, where he served from early youth with bravery, loyalty, and abnegation which never failed in the hours of glory, nor during the painful ordeals of the terrible year of '70. We'll never forget him, and among us—as at a family table—there will always be room for good old Cazergues! Major, your very good health!"

There was a roar of applause. The old officer, with tears in his eyes, tried to stammer out a word or two, but could only mutter: "Oh, Colonel—Colonel—"

All the glasses were clinked together while the regimental buglers played in front of the open windows.

"Right about turn!" exclaimed M. de Croisailles. "We'll now leave the young'uns to enjoy themselves without us old fogies."

Followed by Couramille and the superior officers, he left the clubroom.

As soon as they were gone, the din started again like a flight of rockets. Each soldier sang in turn—and sometimes together—a music-hall echo, a ding-dong march, or a ballad of sickening sentimentality. The veterinary, an undersized, shortsighted fellow, gave out a few verses, unutterably indecent, with byplay to match.

"Oh, you smutty old surgeon!" gurgled Cazergues, chewing his moustache and his mouth watering.

When the song was finished, Lieutenant Roqueval, an old stager waiting to be added to the retired list, warbled a tender cavatina, dwelling on every note. He turned up his eyes till only the whites were visible, placed his hand on his heart, and with his last gasp of breath, tried to climb to a shrill falsetto and cracked up miserably amidst outbursts of merriment which resounded far into the quiet, deserted street.

A few sub-lieutenants had taken refuge on the club

balcony and they chatted as the smoke of their cigars mounted into the air in white spiral wreaths.

"It was bound to happen," one of them went on. "You don't suppose she came down here to this God-forsaken hole to enliven the garrison? Besides, we've all been equally stupid. Isn't it strange, how the unexpected appearance of a pretty woman knocks one all of a heap? Young Hardanges must have had a deuce and all of a time when they got to grips after he'd been forty days on the plank. Say what you like—it's damned fine to be loved by the gals!"

The lighted windows streaked the blackness of the night with luminous stripes; the dark blue sky was spangled with stars and the only sounds were the footsteps of belated idlers. The wind played with the blue flames of the bowls of punch that followed the libations of champagne. Straddling the chairs, knocking over all obstacles, overturning the tables where the glasses crashed on the ground with the tinkling clatter of broken crystal, the officers executed a burlesque cavalry charge, laughing, bawling, imitating trumpet calls, cheering, and their sabres clanging.

"Maybe it's a grand thing to have all the women at one's feet—but it may turn out to be rather a bore after all!" said one of the subalterns, shrugging his broad shoulders.

IX

Lucien finished his cigarette, strolling along the shady alley with a dawdling step, yawning and kicking at the pebbles. He was just out of bed and continuing an interrupted dream. He sat down on the parapet of the terrace, its white lines mirrored in the ripples of the lake. His arms and neck were bare; his chest well-defined in a jersey and, with his flannel cap, his hard muscles swelling at every movement he made, he might have been taken for an Oxford man in training. The weak, slender youth who formerly, by his effeminate grace, gave an epicene impression, had become a man. But the bar of boredom that wrinkled his brow already, the deep lassitude always lurking in his gloomy, worried glances, the bitter sneer that curled his lips, showed that he had lived his short series of years at double speed. His athletic shoulders and apparent strength hid the lamentable agony of a heart worn out by precocious disappointment, and the decomposition of a

brain slowly and surely corroded by an immense and insurmountable distaste of life. His body was young, proudly
displayed, full of the health and vigour of his twenty
summers; desirable, superb, redolent of the supreme
emanation of adolescence; defying the attacks of physical
fatigue and the brunt of the battles of Venus. His soul was at
bay, exhausted, panting, extinguished, inert, as if crushed
by some disaster.

One leg cocked over the other, his hands clasping his
knee, Lulu—as his mistress still called him, much to his
annoyance because the childish pet name seemed in his
opinion to be disgusting now, and out of date—stared at the
landscape without appreciating its beauty. He knew the
enchanting view by heart. He would have liked to knock it
to pieces and change it like an old stage set-scene that has
been shown too often.

In the distance, on the right, was the village of Ouchy
with the pointed roof of its old tower encircled by the palpi-
tation of the white wings of pigeons. There was the
landing-stage and its anchorage of pleasure-boats painted
in lively tints and their sails spreading. There could be seen
the venerable plane-trees of the Hôtel Beaurivage forming a
canopy of foliage over the roadway, dipping their slender
branches in the smooth waters of the lake. On the left, hills
rose one above the other, streaked with dark splashes of
colour that were pine forests, spotted here and there by
villages whose roofs glistened like silver mirrors. In the
extreme background, far away, among wild, fleeting mists,
notched peaks stood up; the sun sparkled on glaciers and
mountains of a soft, vague, bluish hue, looking like the
crumbling walls of fairy fortresses. Amidst all the summits,
the lake spread out and its currents marked sinuous tracks
on its pearly surface, tinted with gleams of emeralds and

opals in which the jagged outlines of the shore formed unfathomable abysses of shadow.

At this early morning hour, the view evoked the idea of a Garden of Eden, with the swans gliding slowly and majestically; seagulls whirling in the air, filling it with a fleeting snowfall of white feathers, and even the boats with their big sails resembled great birds hovering close to the water. The sky was radiant with marvellous light. Honeysuckle and roses interwoven scattered showers of perfumed petals on the terrace as if the choir-boys in a nuptial procession had just passed by, strewing flowers from their nosegays.

The clock at Ouchy struck half-past six in a silvery, trembling chime. Lucien stretched his limbs, yawned again and seemed to wake up suddenly.

"My God! I'm bored to death!" he moaned hoarsely.

He went and untied the rope by which a neat outrigger was made fast with a couple of other skiffs in a little anchorage at the end of the terrace. Three strokes of the oars and he was off, steering straight ahead with no object in view and whistling through his teeth two or three bars of the same melody over and over again.

Thus it was that the wretched, fettered young fellow tried to exhaust his strength, fatigue his frame, and interest himself in something that might kill time and help him to pass the long, slow, monotonous hours that were always the same; and so stifle regrets and sadness. He got away from himself, lost between sky and water, revelling in the enforced repose of the brain. The silence, only disturbed by transient meetings and rapid exchange of greetings shouted across the tiny waves; the measured splash of the oars, or the cry of a bird lulled him, nearly sent him to sleep, and enwrapped him in a dreamy atmosphere. He never rested a minute. He seemed trying furiously to break himself down and at times his muscles were so strained, and he got into such fits of passion that his boat creaked and sprang forward in a foaming furrow, while his hands became blue, swelling under the rush of blood. To row was his sole pleasure and all he had to change his thoughts.

When it was time to return and take his seat at table in front of Clarette, putting his head in the collar again, he often asked himself if it would not be better to kick a hole in the bottom of the boat, there and then, in the middle of the Lake of Geneva and let himself sink like a stone with the last thing that had amused him and helped him to drag out his life. He could go to his eternal sleep with his broken toy under the long, sweet, soft aquatic plants that were like women's tresses. But death frightened him, so feeling cowardly and with some unknown secret hope of escape at the back of his brain, he pulled steadily homewards, lashed his boat to its accustomed ring, and dropped his own anchor in his mistress's skirts—the haven where a kind of mysterious and implacable malaria undermined him. His thoughts always reverted to happy beings who were free, living according to their fancies and needs, able to travel towards unknown lands, or seek fresh joys and new horizons.

Twenty-five months of love passed with Clarette seemed to him like a maddening series of centuries. He knew the number of days to a minute, having so often gone over the reckoning and been disgusted with himself whenever he did so. The remembrance of lost delights and abolished ecstasies reopened his wound with a brutal shock and made it smart sill more as if suddenly torn by a sharp, poisoned claw. The perfectly felicity of olden days was so very far away. He had been wrecked in such tempests of disillusion that all was lost, crew and cargo. Although the escape from

Saillans in a mad fit of high fever dated but from yesterday, as it were, he felt as if it had taken place many years ago. In this guilty departure, he seemed to have been spirited away by Clarette, who left him no time to recover his senses, reflect, or get a clear idea of the consequences of the crime of desertion. She made him drunk with her kisses, drove him mad with the enjoyments of sensuality, bolting his body to her burning flesh, threatening to leave him and flee without him to the end of the world, never to set eyes on him again. Without a halt of even five minutes in Paris, she carried him like a bundle of stolen goods from one town to another until they reached Venice.

How far it seemed—alas!—that splendid, terrible flare of passion that had once again burnt them both to the marrow and heart. The tender sentiments of other days seemed far, far away!

Perhaps it was because the beginning had been too beautiful and intoxicating? Maybe they had both been wrong to revel too rapidly in overdoses of kisses, and exhaust at one gulp, as if tossing off a glass of champagne without taking breath, the whole amount of happiness that fate had in store for them? Perchance it had been imprudent to revive with so much frenzy the delights of early days, trying to live the first hours of love over again—dreaming of them, longing for them and trying hard to surpass them by inventing others that were sweeter, keener and more tender? Who could tell?

One thought that crushed his spirit and caused sharp, disappointing anguish was that after all it was his own fault —his very great fault—that things had turned out so badly, leaving him to struggle hemmed in on all sides and imprisoned. Had he not forged and riveted his shackles with his own hands? All he could imagine was that he must have suddenly gone mad. He recollected the most insignificant details of their flight. Running fast, one night, he reached their dwelling. When he had torn his mouth from that of Clarette and their thirst was quenched in a long, delirious caress, their lips were at last free and able to stammer out a few words and form disjointed sentences.

"Suppose we run away? What do you say?" he sobbed with feverish excitement and in a tone that begged the answer. "I'm dead done! I've had enough!"

His mistress, instead of holding him back, reasoning with him, soothing him, kissed him more lasciviously than ever, lead him into their bedroom and showed him the wardrobe empty and trunks all packed.

"Can't you see I'm ready?" she cried, enjoying his astonishment, throwing her arms about him and pressing her cheek to his face coaxingly. "Say the word, darling boy— and we're off!"

They laughed together long and merrily, shaking off all unpleasant thoughts by forming incoherent projects as if merely arranging some libertine adventure to fool a husband or a jealous lover, and not the crime of desertion wrecking and besmirching a man's career, driving him into exile or the penal servitude of punitive military service in French Africa, searing him with a brand of dishonour for the rest of his life. They appeared to be planning a surprise party or a practical joke, vastly diverted as they pictured the Colonel's disappointment and the sensation created by this secret tableau concluding the last act of the play. In their mutual madness, they imagined that they had never been so happy since the beginning of their liaison; never revelled in such unparalleled intoxication, or enjoyed the felicity of loving and being loved with greater intensity. They saw the future like the dawn of a divine day, irradiating the whole of the firmament with rosy gleams.

Their night was one long kiss, one cry of joy, one ecstasy, one great clasp, as they were coupled in the illusion of the same mirage and repeated the same words in their brief intervals of repose. Lucien's exuberant joy bubbled over like that of an escaped convict, having found shelter, unable to realise as yet that he is free, no longer in his dim cell, and that the glance of his eyes will never more be shattered against the high walls of the prison yard.

Free! Yet willingly, cheerfully, he had played the fool, hurrying to bend beneath the vilest yoke, yielding blindly to a woman much older than he; condemning himself to a life-sentence of imitation matrimony; sinking in quicksands up to his neck; debasing himself unutterably; renouncing everything—in fact, committing suicide, so to say. And why? For a mere hindrance in the course of their love; momentary separation; so as to be a soldier no longer and not work out the years of military service he owed to the State.

What was the thickness of the bandage that blindfolded him at what moment? What occult spell had bewitched and unbalanced him? What temptations had allured him, destroying his commonsense and his strength to such an extent that his irreparable act did not even cause him to hesitate, recoil, or allow him to remember the sinister penalties in the military code read out weekly in barracks? He had also forgotten comrades' warnings and his mother's good advice. What horrible influence had prevented him from seeing his mistake until it was too late to retrace his steps? Why do mortals never dream of the consequences of each departure from the straight path and of the slightest imprudence or fault? Why is some sudden vision of a bright or gloomy morrow never vouchsafed?

Clarette had left nothing to chance, and as they had no

debts, the rent of the villa having been paid in advance, they fled at dawn, tightly embraced in a travelling carriage drawn by a pair of galloping horses flogged hard by a postilion, just as if the lovers were acting in a comic opera. They drove on straight before them, having no fixed destination; so much so that, when they pulled up at a small railway station, Andrée asked:

"Where are we going, Lulu?"

"Wherever you like," he replied.

Little he recked whether he journeyed to the north or the south, so long as he was by the side of his mistress, offering him her lips when he wanted them, and overwhelming him unceasingly, no matter where they were, with sensual enjoyment and warm affection.

Thrilled by an exquisite sensation of danger and childish terror; laughing when they met suspicious strangers; behaving with useless bravado; revelling in depraved voluptuousness; they made long journeys. They shut themselves up in two-place compartments of sleeping-cars, or had railway carriages reserved so as to be always alone, adoring each other, exchanging caresses and joining their flesh as if they feared to be left to a moment's reflection that might deprive them of their intoxication or force them to think.

In this way, they reached the Italian frontier. Feeling themselves in safety at last, to the great hidden relief of Andrée, they flitted hither and thither, unable to make up their minds to settle in seclusion, living like migratory birds that at eventide, before roosting in field or forest, fly in wide circles high in the air, coming and going, gazing at the misty horizon, craning their necks and uttering hoarse cries.

The ardent pair stayed at hotels and remaining late in bed, missed train after train.

"Hide nothing from me, darling boy," queried Clarette

often, with apparent uneasiness. "Are you happy? Perhaps you regret our departure?"

With great sincerity, not yet having had time to regain his self-control or measure the depth of the abyss into which he had fallen; his eyes closed and brain dulled, the bewitched boy, unconscious of everything that was not the flesh and spirit of his mistress, was vexed by her doubting question.

"Haven't you confidence in me, dearest?" he interrupted with tears in his eyes.

"You crazy pet!" she went on sweetly. "It's because I adore you that I see danger in everything!"

Such "ineffable felicity" as their Italian servants called it, and careless mutual confidence was soon swept away, never to return.

It was in Venice, the city of love and dreams, where remembrance is ever on the watch to creep into wounded hearts, that the charm was broken. This was the first shock that started gaping cracks in the magic castle of affection and illusions. They lived unnoticed, far from everywhere, only halting in their exchange of hot kisses to be rowed in a gondola during the sweet hours of sunset, when lofty spires stood out in relief on a background of burnished gold; the frontage of palaces gleamed and the still waters of the canals rippled with strange light.

The couple experienced a marvellous revival of the fairy play that had run so many months at Mentone. It seemed as if they were continuing the same dream, interrupted by no breaking-off; darkened by no jealousy, nor hampered or wounded by any pain. Clarette gave herself up to this rising tide of sensuous enchantment, floating down the stream without thinking of anything. All her efforts tended solely to keep her lover's fervour at boiling point and never be the same, but always leading him to desire her. She tried her utmost to make his life delicious, peaceful, and charming, that he would never imagine anything could be better, or wish for any other affection, sensation, or adventure.

But soon, in their absolute isolation, terrible and insurmountable boredom—like a white ant gnawing, invading, ruining priceless wood carving—destroyed the delicate, subtle work of the mistress and gripped her stripling. Warned by Lucien's yawns, anxiety, and ill-tempered, sulky remarks, she followed up the secret labour and ceaseless advance, as if by a microscopical examination she would have been able to sound and inspect her lover's heart and brain from which love was leaking through gaping fissures. The woman and the lad began to lie to each other, venturing no longer to put questions or exchange clear views. They dragged at their chain and their fleshly joys were only artificial.

Of the two, he mastered himself the best, becoming cold and gradually drawing away from her with subdued irritation and sudden fits of bitterness. As he measured the extent of his fault and became suddenly more sensible under invisible influence, he found himself cornered in a miry blind alley, and got tired of perpetual sensual happiness, always the same. He was disgusted at being adored; the fever of lust, causing the blood to boil in his veins, searing the flesh and swelling the limbs with the rush of sap, had died away. Half-finished sentences issued from his lips. He fell asleep at Clarette's side; pondered during long, silent afternoons over absurd, fantastical schemes and worried continually about the consequences of his desertion.

When Clarette perceived his perturbed state, she put her arms round his neck coaxingly; tormenting him with her timid curiosity and murmured tearfully with tenderness as loving as it was maternal: "What are you thinking about, my own? Why do you stare into vacancy?" He replied in the harsh accents of a man tired out and annoyed at being awakened from deep, refreshing sleep: "What's that matter to you?"

He seized every opportunity to escape from the dwelling where he seemed to be stifling, and stroll alone round the town, ogling and following any woman who stirred up fleeting temptation or sudden desire in his flesh, leading him to forget his illicit union and his obligatory, glutted sensuality. He was excited by the elegant figures of young lady tourists who, guide-book in hand, admired the superb statue of Colleone; the Byzantine beauty of St. Mark; or the luminous orgy of colour of the Grand Canal. But lascivious feelings were also created by fair, unknown women looking exquisitely pretty under the shade of their light-hued parasols, or by handsome Venetian workgirls with great velvety eyes and auburn locks. These winsome lassies were always ready to return smile for smile as they lounged lazily in the sun on bridges and quays.

He passed entire days seated in a café, eagerly reading the Paris papers from title to the last advertisement, as if every article and news-item comforted him and carried him back to the scenes he was condemned never to see again, unless perhaps towards the end of his life. Criticisms of first-nights, smart and comic topical notes, distant rumours of the French capital noted like echoes of a symphony, leaderettes bringing into prominence in printed columns the daily happenings in literary and artistic circles, delighted him but not without torturing him with painful rancour and cruel fits of home-sickness. He never talked to his mistress about these impressions and made other excuses to explain his absences, dreading, most likely, that she too might fall a victim to the same contagion and want to return to France, thereby forsaking him.

Days followed days full of monotony, separating Clarette and Lucien more and more, extinguishing the flames that had been again kindled in their hearts and flesh.

Sometimes the actress succeeded in mastering his rebellious crises and regaining her despotic authority over his sensual, vacillating, weak disposition. In that case, she was rewarded by many a joyous truce and enjoyed transient hours of happiness without a cloud, which only caused a more bitter awaking, heavier and more gloomy relapses, and scenes of increased violent hatred, so much so that it seemed as if some hidden force was opposed to their mutual felicity. Both weighed their demonstrations of affection, concluding by finding them meritorious and praiseworthy, like alms bestowed on a beggar, or attention paid to an incurable invalid.

Nevertheless, they had reached no further than momentary sulky fits; prudent, hypocritical skirmishes and underlying quarrelling currents finishing in smiles when replies became cutting and politeness was on the point of being forgotten.

Some traveller doubtless recognised the pair, revealing their presence in Venice, raising many a laugh in Paris behind the scenes or in newspaper offices. Society journals narrated this finish to a scandal which had already created a great sensation, and recalled in tantalising, perfidious paragraphs the verdict of the court-martial when the son of Marie-Rose Hardanges was condemned in default, although granted extenuating circumstances—"nobody knew why." A smart writer outlawed him forever with one stroke of his facile pen and pilloried him brutally as a low-class bully exploiting a common prostitute.

Livid with rage, his cheeks burning as if he had been publicly slapped in the face, Lucien rushed back to the ancient palace where they lodged.

"Look at that—and that—read them all!" cried Lucien on the threshold of their bedroom, his fingers clutching convulsively a number of rumpled periodicals. "See how they cut me up because of you!"

"Oh, the beasts!" exclaimed the actress.

"Not at all. They're right," he interrupted in a rage. "I've no occupation. My mother sends me no money. Don't I live on you?"

"Don't say that, Lucien!" she gasped, stuttering, her frame shaken and quivering.

"I'll give you back your money. You know I've got some. I'll get out of your debt."

His fists clenched, Lucien Hardanges strode up and down the room, repulsing Clarette when she approached him, trying to pacify him with demonstrations of gentle affection. He raised his voice with harsh, jerky sobs; beating the air with his hands; starting and shuddering convulsively with all the movements and gestures of a madman in a fury, struggling in exasperation against a fixed idea and seemingly breaking his head against massive bars.

Andrée, in affright, with wild eyes, followed him in his demented, fierce pacing.

"Let me beg of you, Lulu, to be calm! Oh, do try and be quiet!" she implored again and again.

He pushed her away roughly. "It was bound to happen!" he replied insultingly in the harsh tones of an enemy resolved to spare no affronts. "Everything conspires to strike me now I'm down! You're old enough to be my mother and I'm your lover. You're rich and I'm broke. I'm despised, but what can I do?—what can I say in reply to their slating! As things are, who would consent to second me in a duel, risk his life against mine, or grant me reparation? Am I not disqualified, outlawed, liable to instant arrest if I cross the frontier? Shouldn't I be handcuffed and led back between two gendarmes to Saillans like a criminal?"

"Hold your tongue?" she murmured, not knowing what to say, feeling herself powerless and defeated in this unequal struggle; covering her ears with her hands, tortured by the distressing facts he enumerated and predicted in his cries of despair. She saw the downfall of her dream of love like a bright shooting-star disappearing in dark clouds. "Say no more—you break my heart!"

"The best thing for both of us is to put an end to our union and separate. It must happen sooner or later as this sort of thing always does, so what's the odds? We'll be off to Paris, each taking a different road. I'll give myself up decently to the military authorities without making paltry excuses, just as if I'd merely been too long on furlough. Mamma is certain to get me indulgently treated through the bigwigs she knows and then all the other people will perhaps leave me in peace!"

While he unrolled his plans for breaking with her, Clarette did not interrupt him. She recovered from the sudden shock, controlling her feelings coolly like a duellist after the first attack, disputing every inch of the ground, parrying each thrust; the sword-arm steadfast, close to the breast. She feigned absolute calm and profound lassitude; making a show of submission to fate and apparently tired of their tragic plight. Putting on a mask of indifference, hiding her grief, wishes, and hopes, she fell back listless in an armchair.

"Just as you like, dear!" she exclaimed, betraying no regrets or reproaches. "Perhaps, you're right—who can tell?"

Her torpor, the capitulation of a soul yielding weakly, with charity and docility, froze Lucien to the marrow. He was sobered at once as if a gust of icy wind had smarted his feverish, burning cheeks on leaving a tavern. Disconcerted and uneasy, he stopped speaking.

"When will it suit you best to be off?" she went on, laying stress on every syllable; "to-morrow, or the day after?"

"What do you care? We're not travelling together!" he bellowed, scowling, and in tones where there was an undercurrent of vexation at being so easily forsaken.

During the whole of dinnertime, a little later, both absent-minded, they only exchanged a few words. Lucien kept watching Clarette, looking at her with growing regret in his glances. He seemed to be contemplating some enchanting landscape that one is loath to leave because the best part of one's affection is centred therein. He turned over incoherent sentences in his mind, weighing up the serious resolution he had just made so suddenly. His courage forsook him. He began to think about the disagreeable results of his return and the mournful change of life, not forgetting the imprisonment awaiting him until he was arraigned before the military tribunal. Then there was the terrible term of penal servitude in the disciplinary regiments of the French colonies in Africa. He recollected stories he had been told of confinement in pits under a tropical sun and enforced tasks that madden and kill. Military law was inexorable and Marie-Rose, despite efforts, prayers, and favour, would never be able to preserve him from its rigour or obtain his pardon. Without the slightest transition, or having become hardened to future suffering by any painful apprenticeship, he would be forced to pass out of the warm boudoir where he lived in laziness, give up the luxurious ease of a travelling millionaire, say farewell to a happy existence merely ruffled by moral suffering joined to the anxiety of love and wounded pride, in order to lead a dog's life, herding with the sum of soldiery, vicious malefactors, miscreants regardless of law and gospel, huddled together under the eyes of sentinels with loaded rifles and fixed bayonets.

Andrée did not seem to notice Lucien's growing anguish. She pecked here and there at the dessert on table, and marked most attentively an international railway guide, placed by the side of her plate, as she took notes of departures and arrivals of trains and scribbled figures. She never turned a hair, playing the part of an unmoved woman like a most talented actress.

"So it's settled, eh? We go our separate ways. You leave me, Andrée?"

"Didn't we agree about it? You go one road and I another. You asked me to do so—didn't you?"

"Doesn't my determination touch you just a little? Have you no regret? You feel nothing, nothing, nothing!"

He emphasised the last words as if intoning some melancholy psalm. She leant forward on her elbows, her features undisturbed, her eyes staring fixedly as if all her former languor of lust had faded away entirely. She appeared to be listening automatically to some language with which she had been conversant a long while ago, but had now entirely forgotten.

"What would be the good of whining?" she returned. "It's no use crying over what's done with!"

"You don't love me any longer."

"I love you, Lucien, as much as you love me!"

He knelt humbly at her feet, clasped her hands in his, and covered them with devout kisses.

"Pardon me, darling! Forgive me, I pray you!" he stammered like a punished child promising to be good in future.

As in olden days, the bed crowned the triumphant victory of the mistress over her lover. Between the sheets, Clarette was once again the dominating empress, the dangerous sorceress whose lips distilled mysterious charm, whose body created demented lust. She knew how to excite Lucien's senses, bewildering him, depriving him of his mental balance, maddening him with scientific sensuality and prolonging the caresses he preferred. Being quite as salacious as he, and perhaps more depraved, she crushed him in her embraces, making up all her lost ground in one night. But that was the end, the final combats, nothing more than artificial successes, scarcely postponing the dénouement.

Leaving Venice in order to travel about, change the scene, and break the monotony of exile, the couple migrated to Lausanne on the Lake of Geneva. At the bottom of Andrée's heart, there lurked perchance some spark of hope or stubborn illusion maintaining a superstitious desire to have the enchantment of moving waters in every part of Europe where she halted with Lucien. He followed like a docile poodle, trotting behind his mistress and going wherever he was led. Discouraged, he reached the border-line of idiocy, having exhausted his moral strength in one useless fit of rebellion, the last spasm of honesty and vigour; letting himself be towed along like a floating log; resigned to his fate; content with creature comforts to play the part of a parasite vegetating in stagnation in the pay of a benefactress.

As it was impossible for him to modify his shady position, affront the misery awaiting him if he resolved to break with Clarette and give himself up to military justice, he

remained where he was, listless, flabby-minded, and placid
in the refuge where he found board and lodging. Soon
afterwards, he fell again deeper than ever into his old state
of malevolence with fits of disgust and overpowering sickening regret. He was heartily tired of his mistress, detesting
her and unjustly attributing his suffering and his downfall
to her. He felt cruel pleasure in torturing himself with ever-
increasing disillusion, depriving himself of love's delights
and destroying the last vestiges of the idolatry that had
bewitched him. He revelled in the signs of old age appearing in Andrée's features; watching for them, counting them
with the secret wicked joy of an enemy waiting to be
avenged for some shameful defeat. Their forced existence
in common exasperated him with gnawing, villainous fury.

It was terrible to go to bed night after night with a
woman no longer loved and for whom all desire had fled.
She took up too much room between the sheets and,
despite himself, he was continually obliged to come in
contact with her and allow her flesh to touch his body. He
had to submit to the touch of her hands, welcome her
kisses, go through the work of a lover willy-nilly, and
consummate the supreme sacrifice because the animal had
to answer Nature's call eventually. He got away from the
enforced spasm of salacity whenever he could manage it,
and passed nights in broken, fitful slumber when he
would have given much to slip under other coverlets and
stretch his limbs freely to enjoy the cool repose of a solitary couch.

Sometimes, when he slipped out of bed at the first crow
of the cocks in neighbouring farmyards, and deserted the
hated bedroom to fly to the lake and throw off all pollution
in the fresh, light morning air, he felt inclined to wring her
neck in his fingers that would close like a vise on her wind-

pipe and so be rid of her, even by committing murder; or crush her face and smother her between two pillows.

Horrified by his own thoughts, he rushed away, fleeing in anguish, to the tiny harbour where his boat was made fast, and broke himself down with fatigue until he had emptied his brain of such criminal idea.

Their nerves keyed up to breaking-point, their tempers soured, they started never-ending disputes for an ill-timed word, a doubtful allusion, or for nothing at all. Despite all his impudent and slimy mockery and the venomous remarks that went straight home to her heart like poisoned arrows, she always got the better of him, put up a valiant defence and reduced him to silence.

"All right then! Get out! Go right away from here, since you say you've no more love for me and you're bored to death. Go back to your regiment, my dear boy! I'm not holding you. I'll lend you the money to pay your fare over the frontier, if you like."

"You know damned well that I darent't do it!" he groaned in a rage, confessing his powerlessness. "You know you've got me tied to you, hand and foot!"

When Clarette debated with herself inwardly, listening to the beating of her heart, she felt beyond a doubt that the instrument she had once played on was out of tune and broken. All the notes were false and none of the old songs rang true. It was only pride and the tenacious, bitter resolve to have the best of the game till the end and not be left in the lurch by her lover, but to be the first to break away. When cured, she should feel inclined to take a rest and return to the exquisite indolence of a life of luxury diversified by unimportant liaisons like those of former days. She meant to suit her own convenience when the cup was full and brimmed over. At that moment, besides, the force of habit prevented her from ringing down the curtain on the play which had turned out a failure.

While the young fellow was rowing, the sun mounted slowly in the sky, lighting it up with a radiant golden torrent. The water at first carried along masses of glittering spangles, but it became like an oily expanse without a wrinkle. The heat increased. There was not a breath of air in the transparent atmosphere. All of a sudden, the bells of the hotels and that of the villa announced the hour of *déjeuner*, filling the silence of solitude with joyous, discordant chimes.

With sweeping strokes of his sculls, his athletic frame bending forward and backward in measured cadence, Lucien rowed to the terrace whose white lines streaked the lake as with a silken scarf loosely floating.

X

Marie-Rose was prostrated by Lucien's sudden desertion at his mistress's first call. His unexpected flight from France was the tragic ruin of all his mother's hopes. The mad revival of her boy's unfortunate connection just when she thought she had won the game and regained her ordinary equanimity, gradually getting over and forgetting rough shocks and cruel anxieties, caused her to glow with pride at the result and she began to enjoy life anew surrounded by old affections and renewed friendships.

With calculated reticence, half-truths, and gallant delicacy, General Rosarieulles brought her the bad news and read out a laconic telegram from Colonel Daumont de Croisailles. The wretched woman turned livid and, stunned as by a blow, staggered, struck wildly at the air with her clenched hands and rolled heavily in a swoon on one of the sofas in her drawing-room. To all appearances she had given up the ghost, but regaining her senses by dint of careful nursing, her brain still weak, she could not believe the truth of the lamentable disaster. It must be a pack of lies. How could her dear little lad have done such a dreadful thing, so quickly break his word and be false to every promise? Surely Clarette, in her raging lust, had never been so tenacious as to run after him in the ranks?

Marie-Rose, her eyes full of tears, choking with keen anguish, begged for minute details, muttering incoherently, and nodding her head like a patient in pain.

"Are you sure—quite sure, mind you—that he ran away?" she kept on repeating without a break. "It isn't a stupid joke, eh? You're not having a lark with me, are you?"

Greater torture than her first sufferings was the haunting thought that her son was a deserter, about to be judged in his absence and surely condemned. At any moment, a gendarme might seize him by the collar like a common criminal and force him into a prison cell. This idea threw her into fits of despair, when she fell on her sofa or bed, overpowered by profound grief, sobbing, accusing and upbraiding herself. It was she—his mother—who had pushed Lucien into the bewitching embrace of a woman hungering after the delights of lust. When the lad, confiding in maternal affection, had returned, seeking shelter and protection at her side and was under her influence, she allowed herself to be blinded by idiotic illusions. Then was the time to watch over him narrowly, save him from old and new temptations and cure him of his unwholesome, dangerous passion. She should have safeguarded him and defended him, keeping him tied to her apron-strings.

But she had listened to everybody's advice and enduced Lucien to enlist—a thing he would never have thought of—and depart for a distant garrison town. She had brought about the end of the tragedy. Struck down, crushed by the violence of the shock, frightened lest she increase the evil already consummated and took the wrong road again if she made the least move. Marie-Rose had lost all confidence in herself and dreaded acting imprudently, or making some great mistake if she mixed herself up in this horrible intrigue. She held back, imagining that she brought bad luck to her son, and had not tried to track the fugitives and see her son again if only for five minutes on the sly, to pour a little soothing balm on the wound of her broken heart; and once more go to war with her hated enemy.

She got into her head that she was shadowed by the police, followed in the street; that detectives dogged her steps if she went into a post-office. No doubt they reckoned on her usual frivolous and careless behavior to capture the guilty youngster and discover his hiding-place. Her letters, she thought, were opened; her walks and talks noted. She was the object of unceasing, secret spying. Her mania weakened her morally and physically; her mind became unbalanced; she grew listless and resembled a pretty marionette doll whose wires and strings being out of gear loses its attractiveness and lies flattened and ridiculous on the darkest shelf of a lumber-room. Nothing amused or delighted her. The ghost of any desire or curiosity was never awakened in her sorrowing soul. The joyous smile had fled from her drawn lips.

She locked herself up in her house, denied herself to most of her friends and received no visitors in her drawing-room—nor in her boudoir. Her former coquetry of dress and toilet arrangements left her. She no longer troubled about her frocks, living in voluntary seclusion, all alone, dragging her load of regret and affliction from room to room, while shivering in the solitude she dreaded. She trusted no one, carrying dozens of keys in her pocket, burning the most insignificant scraps of paper and replacing all the wooden shutters of the front of her house by the strongest iron railings.

"She must have led a nice kind of life to go off her head like this!" sneered her servants in the pantry, alluding to her among themselves as a madwoman.

Marie-Rose, the pet of the public, who had been applauded to the echo in bygone days when her voice filled every corner of a theatre with the melody of her trills sounding like the laugh of girls, never touched her piano, sang not a note, nor opened a score. All her contracts were annulled. She paid several heavy forfeits. What did she care about making money or being idolised by the playgoing public now that her life was wrecked and she had lost her little lad? It mattered nothing to her if she grew ugly and her hair turned white, announcing the end of a woman's career; silver threads that in former times, with mournful face, she used to tear out one by one. She did not even trouble when her name dropped "out of the bills," because each minute of existence brought an after-taste of gall to her lips, and she was forbidden to kiss and fondle the flesh of her flesh, the only being she loved and had ever loved in the whole course of her wretched life.

All the vampire scum of Bohemian Paris swooped down upon her: shady lawyers, usurers, Jews with jewellery on "appro.," dealers in modern antiques and secondhand clothing, and procuresses who swarm in the wake of a successful actress, on the alert to profit by weakness, ready to suck her blood, share her belongings when she is ruined, drive her on the streets, exploiting, gnawing and drawing her into their nets without the victim knowing what is done to her, like a fly caught by a spider. She was soon penniless and struggling in a sea of debt. Lacking expert counsel, signing legal documents with the rigid gestures and staring eyes of a sleepwalker in a dream, borrowing money at fabulous interest, mortgaging her house, getting rid of her magnificent objects of art, she experienced true misery of the kind that unseats the most robust and breaks the loins of the most courageous of mortals.

Even this downfall did not suffice to stir her from her sluggishness. It did not open her eyes, nor kindle a ray of intelligence. Her brain was cloudy, as if paralysed. She never thought of defence, nor called for help and try to save a trifle from the total wreck so as to buy a small annuity for her old age. She charged no one to go through her accounts, verify claims, and settle the amount of her indebtedness, strictly negotiating with those who clamoured the loudest and were most untractable, but submitted calmly to ungrateful destiny that robbed her of her fortune, comfort, and her home after having deprived her of Lucien.

Who would have assisted her and dragged her out of the abyss of distress where she struggled without calling anyone to her aid and where she awaited the end of her sufferings in a state of morbid stupor? For other footlight favourites who had never any luck and whose talent had not sufficed to ward off the brutal attacks of poverty, lagging behind on the road of life, broken down, incapable of earning their daily bread, nailed on a bed of pain, or condemned to an invalid's chair, driven from the stage through no fault of their own, friends got up a performance for their benefit.

But was there anything interesting or worthy of the public's pity in the case of Marie-Rose Hardanges? Had not millions run through her tiny, capricious hands; and had she not imprudently wasted a fortune that would have satisfied a king if his civil list had amounted to that figure? Her lucrative trip to Buenos Aires, chronicled in newspapers as something extraordinary, was but of yesterday. If the star of operetta had not retired from the stage in a fit of folly, prompted by some inexplicable whim of a pretty woman—at least, so did the world explain matters—she was so much in vogue, so charmingly alluring with her adorable features, great black eyes, fair flossy hair, voice as clear as crystal, that she might have signed ten contracts for one and at her own price.

It was not long before Marie-Rose was crushed by weighty, implacable oblivion where not a vestige of her defunct glory survived. Forgotten, her name was erased from every programme. She was buried like an idol cast from its pedestal and fallen into a hole.

Considering that she seemed delighted to withdraw from the world of pleasure and forsook all who had loved her and loved her still; that she had demolished with no sign of regret her oldest and most solid friendships; that she appeared to be following the example of Andrée Clarette, sacrificing in the same way her ease and happiness in favour of some vile scamp who excited her lust, fearing to show herself and be caught, thus revealing the secret depravity that goaded her on; the most dirty stories circulated explaining the sudden change in her way of living and her shamefaced, strange flight.

Unfortunate Marie-Rose never sought to contradict the rumours. She never laid bare the great open wound in her maternal heart; sought for no pity; never told the story of her deadly suffering and her distaste of life and amusement ever since a villainous strumpet had again robbed her of her son without leaving her the slightest chance of saving him—at least, so she thought, labouring under the anguish of her tragic affliction.

Besides, would it not have seemed incredible, "a corking good story," if it were told how Marie-Rose, "that flashy bit o' good," turning like a windmill at every joyous gust of wind, her giddy sails catching up all the butterflies of love; every fantastical scheme of lascivious roystering, love-songs, avowals of tender longing, and refined mocking humour, should try to play in real life the part of the sorrowing mother as portrayed in sensation dramas?

Her house, jewellery, bric-à-brac, horses, carriages, and peerless old lace brought under the hammer and sold for a song; her brain daily more dulled, becoming more gloomy and dazed by such a run of black ill-luck; after having gathered a few crumbs enabling her to vegetate in a humdrum way, being about as rich as the wife of a small clerk, she took refuge at Asnières with her pug-dogs, cats, and a parrot.

In her narrow ground-floor apartment of two rooms giving on an uncultivated garden patch, these animals—her sole companions—omitted such a rank stench that no servant consented to do her housework or remain more than a week in her service. Marie-Rose had only some odd pieces of furniture which in her best days she would not have taken the trouble to store in a garret of her beautiful house. She slept in a little brass bedstead which had been used by Lucien till he reached the age of fourteen. It was quite big and roomy enough for her and made her conjure up memories that carried her back to old times.

She recalled Lucien's childhood, the supreme happiness of her life. It seemed to her now very far away, like a fairy tale, or a delicious dream. What a funny little laughing, loving mite he was, as handsome as the infant Jesus in his cradle, when he gave her a noisy kiss with his moist, pulpy lips; warbling like a bird and stuttering out his first sentences that made one die of laughter!

By dint of evoking unceasingly these abolished joys that she alone mourned and regretted, the forsaken woman tortured and wore herself out, gradually becoming unable to sleep. The nights when she heard every hour strike; when her burning temples beat like the roll of a drum on her pillow, and when she fell a prey to sudden, frightful hallucinations, seemed slow death-agony and finished her off like an increase of torture.

The dying day, the slow approach of darkness, froze her whole being; weighing her down with unknown grievous pain like a warning of coming death. Her lamp and many candles remained alight, illuminating her room with artificial brilliancy until dawn when she could open her shutters. It was this that cost her the most money and she would have lived on bread and water sooner than be deprived of light.

Pinned to the dingy wall-paper and on her two mantelpieces were nothing else than portraits of Lucien: photographs, water-colours, unfinished pencil drawings, which she had saved from the wreck. The monotonous and perpetual contemplation of her son's likenesses hypnotised her. There was a photograph where for the fun of the thing he had posed at a country fair. He was swaggering, his head in the air, wearing his hussar uniform, his two hands resting on the hilt of his sabre. It was the very last she had of him and she hid it under her bolster at night; always carrying it in her bodice by day, as if fearing it might be stolen from her. She stared at it greedily, passionately, for hours and hours, feasting on this remembrance with the dilated, ecstatic eyes of a visionary haunted by mystic fervour and hoping to be lifted up to heaven. She spoilt the wretched twopenny tintype slowly, forcing it to fade gradually by her ceaseless kisses and the moisture of her breath.

She talked to it as if Lucien's portrait had become

endowed with life and hearing. She dreamt and spoke aloud without being asleep, murmuring many a long series of coaxing, motherly words; questioning and answering him as if her dearly-beloved son was seated by her bedside and they were continuing unending dialogue, exchanging confidences, making difficult confessions, but certain of indulgent forgiveness—the sort of conversation during which one opens the door, now and again, so as to make sure that no one is listening at the keyhole.

Marie-Rose exacted solemn promises, displaying her wounded heart like the beggar-woman who, to excite the pity of passers-by near a church door, tells the beads on her string of sorrows. She supplicated and promised, belittling herself with such heartbreaking accents of humiliation that anyone overhearing would have been thrilled in the inmost depths of the being. Between her sobs, she was shaken by jerky outbursts of convulsive laughter. She became over-excited, tossed to and fro, sat up in bed, stiffened and happy, singing scraps of songs from operettas at the top of her voice, as if at a concert, bowing to imaginary applause and ovations, vocalising with such strange intonations in the solemn silence of night that her frightened dogs howled as if their mistress was dead.

Getting worse and worse, Marie-Rose chose to imagine that Lucien was writing letters to her, under certain pre-arranged initials, to be fetched at the post-office to which she went fifteen times every day, reiterating the same request, her heart palpitating wildly. She used to get out of temper with the clerks, insulting them grossly and making use of obscene language until she was shoved into the street. She still laboured under the fixed idea that she was persecuted because of her son's desertion. His letters were intercepted and sent to the Minister of War.

She tried trickery, disguising herself, painting her face and altering her appearance by putting on strange, sordid apparel so as not to be recognised. She altered the tone of her voice in a simple-minded and silly way that would have moved a heart of stone. As she always had to return home empty-handed, for, of course, despite her fits of rage, cunning enquiries and prayers, no letter was forthcoming, although she was inwardly sure that her boy posted her one by every mail from some imaginary country, the wretched creature remained in anguish, trembling for the safety of the deserter, firmly believing that as a result of her frequent visits to post-offices and noisy quarrels, she had unwittingly denounced him and caused his arrest.

This was her last obsession, the second symptom of the madness that gripped her brain and gnawed at it like a rapacious vulture. It caused her to sicken at food. The torture of hunger added to the almost absolute deprivation of sleep was the end of all, and dealt the death-blow.

Like a gust of icy wind, it extinguished the last gleam of her intelligence which still flickered, feebly resembling the gleam of the little pink carnival candles that masked revellers try to put out, at Nice, on the night of Shrove Tuesday.

XI

Clarette was thoroughly tired of her liaison. She realised at last, in disgust, that she was wasting the last years of youthful womanhood in an absurd and stupid adventure. She regretted her quiet life of luxurious ease and good old Lévêque, easy-going and submissive. Lucien's mistress had even kind thoughts of Prince Tchernadieff whose calm, gentlemanly stupidity was amusing and soothing to her nerves.

More than once, Clarette was within an ace of bringing about the dénouement abruptly, by taking flight early in the morning, leaving the villa while her youngster was out rowing; and departing from Ouchy by the steamboat that zigzagged between the two shores of the Lake of Geneva. Many a time, her mind had been made up. She wrote a commonplace good-bye note, as frigid as a visiting-card with three words scribbled on it, and placed it, well displayed, on the chimney-piece. In this connection, she also turned things topsy-turvy by casting herself for the part generally played by a gallant lover, behaving honourably to the finish and making a last gift to the woman he discards: Clarette slipped a packet of banknotes into the envelope; enough for Lucien to live on during four or five months.

But it seemed as if some invincible force held the actress back. She hesitated to break the chain by a brutal blow and put off her departure from day to day. It must not be forgotten also that she still had occasional sensual cravings that drew her towards Lucien.

Although all their love was dead, they were both still ablaze with salacity, being in the throes of furious stupration that stirred them, as if tragically damned, to the uttermost depths of their physical organisation. They rushed to try all kinds of voluptuous enjoyment, exhausting themselves to the point of pain; causing them to shriek in the acuity of their erotic spasms. Afterwards, the reaction almost annihilated them and they remained limp and powerless, empty-headed, sprawling with outstretched limbs on the bed where pillows, sheets, and coverlets had been tossed hither and thither.

They seemed to have been fighting a battle where both adversaries were bound to be killed; their bodies being purposely exhausted as if trying to run a frightful race to reach a goal in the black regions of nothingness. Despite all their efforts, and fierce attacks, neither succeeded in conquering the other. So they continued their bitter and delicious duel. It might have been said that they were trying to murder each other, both calling on death to take them.

Their lips never met except in momentary skimming contact, but their bodies were lashed together, flesh cemented to flesh unceasingly, scarcely allowing a minute to pass during the few hours of the night without being dominated by bestial aberrations and running through the entire catalogue of long drawn-out, refined, meretricious manœuvres.

Lucien's muscles were wonderfully developed, hardened by the violent exercise he took every morning in the open air, expanding his lungs, increasing his strength tenfold and training his body until he was as fit as a boxer ready to step into the ring. He condescended, with a feeling of haughty, triumphant scorn, to let himself be used for the lewd combat of love, never weakening, nor succumbing beneath the ardour of his mistress's lascivious embraces. If Clarette abandoned her charms thus madly and debased herself in rutting debauchery to the extent of making herself ill, it was with the idea of glutting her sensual appetite all the more rapidly and finishing the salacious story.

Their mutual purgatorial existence became so gloomy, interspersed with such insane threats, bitter violence and murderous exchange of slaps, kicks, and blows that the actress, in alarm, had but one thought: to escape, regain her freedom, divert herself according to her fancy and only do in future what pleased her.

Decidedly there was but one course for her to take: close the account, throw off the yoke and wash out of her life these stained remains of love that soiled her flesh and barred her way. She meant to reappear behind the footlights, like a wayward runaway disembarking from some mysterious country. It would be delightful to keep open house at her Norman cottage of Deauville during the race-week and celebrate her return by a merry, sumptuous, magnificent garden-party which would serve to place her again in the front rank of fashion, and wipe away the effect—disastrous perhaps—of her last freakish flight in company with a young deserter.

She did not regret her experiment in the least, feeling herself still deliciously warmed, palpitating, and entirely satiated by the bath of luscious love in which her body and soul had tarried so long. Her lascivious enjoyments amply compensated bitter and carking care, the jealous rearguard of happiness. She had finished her education, learning much which she had not been taught hitherto, and she had been thrilled by infinite beatitude, over and over again; tasting what many women seek for in vain without ever attaining it, even unto the last days of declining beauty. She had endured the supreme ordeal without losing her heart or her wits. She had lived through it all and was alive and well, being weaned from sentimentality and ready to face, more selfishly than ever, the temptations, troubles, and adventures of an actress's career.

It did not strike her for an instant that it was a bad action to forsake her lover, ruthlessly and uselessly ruined by her so that she might enjoy the novelty of lewd gratification in the arms of a beautiful boy. She never grasped the fact that to quench her lecherous thirst, she had wrecked a lad's future and a mother's peace of mind, or that evil would come of it and Lucien suffer thereby.

The play had run long enough. The bill was changed and that was all. Why should a woman—and above all, a Parisian pet—complicate the daily round of her pranks of passion with vain consideration, stupid remorse, or sentimental, old-fashioned ideas? Had she not the right, when the ship was sinking, to free herself from bonds that hampered her movements and endangered her safety? Lucien, at his age, with the conceit and bold effrontery of his disposition, would doubtless wriggle out of his muddle and find another petticoat to hang on to.

One morning, after generously rewarding the complicity

of the servants hired by the week to work at the villa, Andrée Clarette quietly forsook her boy, shook off her shackles and went away without turning round or feeling the slightest emotion, being heartily sick of her illicit ties and in the greatest hurry to recover her liberty, lost by her own fault.

Mme. Lévêque was waiting for her mistress in Paris at the Gare de Lyon. The old housekeeper trembled with anxiety, unable to believe that her mistress's foolishness was finished and that dear Clarette was cured and had recovered from the effects of her disastrous caprice. When Mme. saw *Madame,* as pretty, nimble, and well-dressed as ever, spring lightly on to the platform, the worthy dame's eyelids swelled with tears and she threw out her arms widely with a gesture of maternal welcome.

"Ah, Madame!—there you are at last—none too soon!" she grumbled, trying to stifle her inward joy and speak harshly while the actress kissed her.

It was the close of a lovely day. The transparent atmosphere of the City of Light was tinted with mauve, pink, and grey. The sun was setting as if regretfully in the restful hum of the traffic of the town. The air was redolent with the indefinable and exciting odour peculiar to Paris—beloved of cities.

During the ride home at top speed in her victoria, Andrée smiled, feeling in her happiness as if growing stouter. She sank back against her cushion in a state of delicious torpor, reborn like a convalescent woman taking the air for the first time after a dangerous illness.

Lévêque suddenly woke her up with a start. "So it's settled—once for all?" asked the old lady with her ordinary good-natured vulgarity. "Have you had your fill of love?"

"Yes, my dear—a thousand times yes! I'll never be caught again, I swear it!"

The Masquerade Erotic Newsletter

From **Masquerade Books**, the World's Leading Publisher of Erotica, comes *The Masquerade Erotic Newsletter*—the best source for provocative, cutting-edge fiction, sizzling pictorials, scintillating and illuminating exposes of the sex industry, and probing reviews of the latest books and videos.

Featured writers and articles have included:

Lars Eighner • *Why I Write Gay Erotica*
Pat Califia • *Among Us, Against Us*
Felice Picano • *An Interview with Samuel R. Delany*
Samuel R. Delany • *The Mad Man* (excerpt)
Maxim Jakubowski • *Essex House: The Rise and Fall of Speculative Erotica*
Red Jordan Arobateau • *Reflections of a Lesbian Trick*
Aaron Travis • *Lust*
Nancy Ava Miller, M. Ed. • *Beyond Personal*
Tuppy Owens • *Female Erotica in Great Britain*
Trish Thomas • *From Dyke to Dude*
Barbara Nitke • *Resurrection*
and many more....

The newsletter has also featured stunning photo essays by such masters of fetish photography as **Robert Chouraqui, Eric Kroll, Richard Kern,** and **Trevor Watson.**

A one-year subscription (6 issues) to the *Newsletter* costs $30.00. Use the accompanying coupon to subscribe now—for an uninterrupted string of the most provocative of pleasures (as well as a special gift, offered to subscribers only!).

Free **GIFT**

PINK
CHAMPAGNE

SUSAN ANDERS

ROSEBUD BOOKS

THE ROSEBUD READER

Rosebud Books—the hottest-selling line of lesbian erotica available—here collects the very best of the best. Rosebud has contributed greatly to the burgeoning genre of lesbian erotica—to the point that authors like Lindsay Welsh, Aarona Griffin and Valentina Cilescu are among the hottest and most closely watched names in lesbian and gay publishing. Here are the finest moments from Rosebud's contemporary classics. $5.95/319-8

ELIZABETH OLIVER

PAGAN DREAMS

Cassidy and Samantha plan a vacation at a secluded bed-and-breakfast, hoping for a little personal time alone. Their hostess, however, has different plans. The lovers are plunged into a world of dungeons and pagan rites, as the merciless Anastasia steals Samantha for her own. B&B—B&D-style! $5.95/295-7

SUSAN ANDERS

PINK CHAMPAGNE

Tasty, torrid tales of butch/femme couplings—from a writer more than capable of describing the special fire ignited when opposites collide. Tough as nails or soft as silk, these women seek out their antitheses, intent on working out the details of their own personal theory of difference. $5.95/282-5

LAVENDER ROSE

Anonymous

A classic collection of lesbian literature: From the writings of Sappho, Queen of the island Lesbos, to the turn-of-the-century *Black Book of Lesbianism*; from *Tips to Maidens* to *Crimson Hairs*, a recent lesbian saga—here are the great but little-known lesbian writings and revelations. $4.95/208-6

EDITED BY LAURA ANTONIOU

LEATHERWOMEN II

A follow-up volume to the popular and controversial *Leatherwomen*. Laura Antoniou turns an editor's discerning eye to the writing of women on the edge—resulting in a collection sure to ignite libidinal flames. Leave taboos behind—because these Leatherwomen know no limits.... $4.95/229-9

LEATHERWOMEN

These fantasies, from the pens of new or emerging authors, break every rule imposed on women's fantasies. The hottest stories from some of today's newest and most outrageous writers make this an unforgettable exploration of the female libido. $4.95/3095-4

LESLIE CAMERON

THE WHISPER OF FANS

"Just looking into her eyes, she felt that she knew a lot about this woman. She could see strength, boldness, a fresh sense of aliveness that rocked her to the core. In turn she felt open, revealed under the woman's gaze—all her secrets already told. No need of shame or artifice...." $5.95/259-0

AARONA GRIFFIN

PASSAGE AND OTHER STORIES

An S/M romance. Lovely Nina is frightened by her lesbian passions until she finds herself infatuated with a woman she spots at a local café. One night Nina follows her and finds herself enmeshed in an endless maze leading to a mysterious world where women test the edges of sexuality and power. $4.95/3057-1

ROSEBUD BOOKS

VALENTINA CILESCU

THE ROSEBUD SUTRA

"*Women are hardly ever known in their true light, though they may love others, or become indifferent towards them, may give them delight, or abandon them, or may extract from them all the wealth that they possess.*" So says *The Rosebud Sutra*—a volume promising women's inner secrets. One woman learns to use these secrets in a quest for pleasure with a succession of lady loves.... $4.95/242-6

THE HAVEN

The shocking story of a dangerous woman on the run—and the innocents she takes with her on a trip to Hell. J craves domination, and her perverse appetites lead her to the Haven: the isolated sanctuary Ros and Annie call home. Soon J forces her way into the couple's world, bringing unspeakable lust and cruelty into their lives. The Dominatrix Who Came to Dinner! $4.95/165-9

MISTRESS MINE

Sophia Cranleigh sits in prison, accused of authoring the "obscene" *Mistress Mine*. For Sophia has led no ordinary life, but has slaved and suffered—deliciously—under the hand of the notorious Mistress Malin. How long had she languished under the dominance of this incredible beauty? $4.95/109-8

LINDSAY WELSH

PROVINCETOWN SUMMER

This completely original collection is devoted exclusively to white-hot desire between women. From the casual encounters of women on the prowl to the enduring erotic bonds between old lovers, the women of *Provincetown Summer* will set your senses on fire! A nationally best-selling title. $5.95/362-7

NECESSARY EVIL

What's a girl to do? When her Mistress proves too systematic, too by-the-book, one lovely submissive takes the ultimate chance—choosing and creating a Mistress who'll fulfill her heart's desire. Little did she know how difficult it would be—and, in the end, rewarding.... $5.95/277-9

A VICTORIAN ROMANCE

Lust-letters from the road. A young Englishwoman realizes her dream—a trip abroad under the guidance of her eccentric maiden aunt. Soon the young but blossoming Elaine comes to discover her own sexual talents, as a hot-blooded Parisian named Madelaine takes her Sapphic education in hand. $5.95/365-1

A CIRCLE OF FRIENDS

The author of the nationally best-selling *Provincetown Summer* returns with the story of a remarkable group of women. Slowly, the women pair off to explore all the possibilities of lesbian passion, until finally it seems that there is nothing—and no one—they have not dabbled in. $4.95/250-7

PRIVATE LESSONS

A high voltage tale of life at The Whitfield Academy for Young Women—where cruel headmistress Devon Whitfield presides over the in-depth education of only the most talented and delicious of maidens. Elizabeth Dunn arrives at the Academy, where it becomes clear that she has much to learn—to the delight of Devon Whitfield and her randy staff of Mistresses! $4.95/116-0

BAD HABITS

What does one do with a poorly trained slave? Break her of her bad habits, of course! The story of te ultimate finishing school, *Bad Habits* was an immediate favorite with women nationwide. "Talk about passing the wet test!... If you like hot, lesbian erotica, run—don't walk...and pick up a copy of *Bad Habits.*"—*Lambda Book Report* $4.95/3068-7

ROSEBUD BOOKS

ANNABELLE BARKER
MOROCCO

A luscious young woman stands to inherit a fortune—if she can only withstand the ministrations of her cruel guardian until her twentieth birthday. With two months left, Lila makes a bold bid for freedom, only to find that liberty has its own excruciating and delicious price.... $4.95/148-9

A.L. REINE
DISTANT LOVE & OTHER STORIES

A book of seductive tales. In the title story, Leah Michaels and her lover Ranelle have had four years of blissful, smoldering passion together. One night, when Ranelle is out of town, Leah records an audio "Valentine," a cassette filled with erotic reminiscences.... $4.95/3056-3

RHINOCEROS BOOKS

GARY BOWEN
DIARY OF A VAMPIRE

"Gifted with a darkly sensual vision and a fresh voice, [Bowen] is a writer to watch out for."
        —Cecilia Tan

The chilling, arousing, and ultimately moving memoirs of an undead—but all too human—soul. Johnson's Rafael, a red-blooded male with an insatiable hunger for same, is the perfect antidote to the effete malcontents haunting bookstores today. *Diary of a Vampire* marks the emergence of a bold and brilliant vision, firmly rooted in past *and* present. $6.95/331-7

ANONYMOUS
FLESHLY ATTRACTIONS

Lucien Hardanges was the son of the wantonly beautiful actress, Marie-Rose Hardanges. When she decides to let a "friend" introduce her son to the pleasures of love, Marie-Rose could not have foretold the erotic excesses that would eventually lead to her own ruin and that of her cherished son. A Victorian rarity, intact! $6.95/299-X

EDITED BY LAURA ANTONIOU
SOME WOMEN

Over forty essays written by women actively involved in consensual dominance and submission. Professional mistresses, lifestyle leatherdykes, whipmakers, titleholders—women from every conceivable walk of life lay bare their true feelings about about issues as explosive as feminism, abuse, pleasures and public image. $6.95/300-7

BY HER SUBDUED

Stories of women who get what they want. The tales in this collection all involve women in control—of their lives, their loves, their men. So much in control, in fact, that they can remorselessly break rules to become the powerful goddesses of the men who sacrifice all to worship at their feet. $6.95/281-7

JEAN STINE
SEASON OF THE WITCH

"A future in which it is technically possible to transfer the total mind... of a rapist killer into the brain dead but physically living body of his female victim. Remarkable for intense psychological technique. There is eroticism but it is necessary to mark the differences between the sexes and the subtle altering of a man into a woman."   *—The Science Fiction Critic* $6.95/268-X

SOME WOMEN

EDITED BY
LAURA ANTONIOU

INTRODUCTION
BY PAT CALIFIA

RHINOCEROS BOOKS

JOHN WARREN
THE LOVING DOMINANT
Everything you need to know about an infamous sexual variation—and an unspoken type of love. Mentor—a longtime player in the dominance/submission scene—guides readers through this world and reveals the too-often hidden basis of the D/S relationship: care, trust and love. $6.95/**218-3**

GRANT ANTREWS
SUBMISSIONS
Once again, Antrews portrays the very special elements of the dominant/submissive relationship…with restraint—this time with the story of a lonely man, a winning lottery ticket, and a demanding dominatrix. One of erotica's most discerning writers. $6.95/**207-8**

MY DARLING DOMINATRIX
When a man and a woman fall in love it's supposed to be simple, uncomplicated, easy—unless that woman happens to be a dominatrix. Curiosity gives way to unblushing desire in this story of one man's awakening to the joys to be experienced as the willing slave of a powerful woman. A touching volume, devoid of sleaze or shame. $6.95/**3055-5**

LAURA ANTONIOU WRITING AS "SARA ADAMSON"
THE TRAINER
The long-awaited conclusion of Adamson's stunning Marketplace Trilogy! The ultimate underground sexual realm includes not only willing slaves, but the exquisite trainers who take submissives firmly in hand. And it is now the time for these mentors to divulge their own secrets—the desires that led them to become the ultimate figures of authority. Only Sara Adamson could conjure so bewitching a portrait of punishing pleasure. $6.95/**249-3**

THE SLAVE
The second volume in the "Marketplace" trilogy. *The Slave* covers the experience of one exceptionally talented submissive who longs to join the ranks of those who have proven themselves worthy of entry into the Marketplace. But the price, while delicious, is staggeringly high…. Adamson's plot thickens, as her trilogy moves to a conclusion in the forthcoming *The Trainer*. $6.95/**173-X**

THE MARKETPLACE
"Merchandise does not come easily to the Marketplace…. They haunt the clubs and the organizations…. Some of them are so ripe that they intimidate the poseurs, the weekend sadists and the furtive dilettantes who are so endemic to that world. And they never stop asking where we may be found…." $6.95/**3096-2**

THE CATALYST
After viewing a controversial, explicitly kinky film full of images of bondage and submission, several audience members find themselves deeply moved by the erotic suggestions they've seen on the screen. "Sara Adamson"'s sensational debut volume! $5.95/**328-7**

DAVID AARON CLARK
SISTER RADIANCE
From the author of the acclaimed *The Wet Forever*, comes a chronicle of obsession, rife with Clark's trademark vivisections of contemporary desires, sacred and profane. The vicissitudes of lust and romance are examined against a backdrop of urban decay and shallow fashionability in this testament to the allure—and inevitability—of the forbidden. $6.95/**215-9**

RHINOCEROS BOOKS

THE WET FOREVER

The story of Janus and Madchen, a small-time hood and a beautiful sex work-er, *The Wet Forever* examines themes of loyalty, sacrifice, redemption and obsession amidst Manhattan's sex parlors and underground S/M clubs. Its combination of sex and suspense led Terence Sellers to proclaim it "evoca-tive and poetic." $6.95/117-9

ALICE JOANOU

BLACK TONGUE

"Joanou has created a series of sumptuous, brooding, dark visions of sexual obsession and is undoubtedly a name to look out for in the future." —*Redeemer*

Another seductive book of dreams from the author of the acclaimed *Tourniquet*. Exploring lust at its most florid and unsparing, *Black Tongue* is a trove of baroque fantasies—each redolent of the forbidden and inexpressible. Joanou creates some of erotica's most unforgettable characters. $6.95/258-2

TOURNIQUET

A heady collection of stories and effusions from the pen of one our most daz-zling young writers. Strange tales abound, from the story of the mysterious and cruel Cybele, to an encounter with the sadistic entertainment of a bizarre after-hours cafe. A sumptuous feast for all the senses.. $6.95/3060-1

CANNIBAL FLOWER

"She is waiting in her darkened bedroom, as she has waited throughout histo-ry, to seduce the men who are foolish enough to be blinded by her irresistible charms....She is the goddess of sexuality, and *Cannibal Flower* is her haunt-ing siren song."—Michael Perkins $4.95/72-6

MICHAEL PERKINS

EVIL COMPANIONS

Set in New York City during the tumultuous waning years of the Sixties, *Evil Companions* has been hailed as "a frightening classic." A young couple explores the nether reaches of the erotic unconscious in a shocking confronta-tion with the extremes of passion. With a new introduction by science fiction legend Samuel R. Delany. $6.95/3067-9

AN ANTHOLOGY OF CLASSIC ANONYMOUS EROTIC WRITING

Michael Perkins, acclaimed authority on erotic literature, has collected the very best passages from the world's erotic writing—especially for Rhino*cer*os readers. "Anonymous" is one of the most infamous bylines in publishing his-tory—and these steamy excerpts show why! $6.95/140-3

THE SECRET RECORD: Modern Erotic Literature

Michael Perkins, a renowned author and critic of sexually explicit fic-tion, surveys the field with authority and unique insight. Updated and revised to include the latest trends, tastes, and developments in this misunderstood and maligned genre. An important volume for every erot-ic reader and fan of high quality adult fiction. $6.95/3039-3

HELEN HENLEY

ENTER WITH TRUMPETS

Helen Henley was told that woman just don't write about sex—much less the taboos she was so interested in exploring. So Henley did it alone, flying in the face of "tradition" by producing *Enter With Trumpets*, a touching tale of arousal and devotion in one couple's kinky relationship. $6.95/197-7

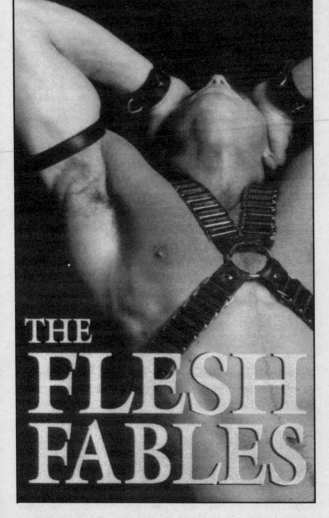

THE FLESH FABLES

RHINOCEROS BOOKS

PHILIP JOSÉ FARMER

FLESH

Space Commander Stagg explored the galaxies for 800 years, and could only hope that he would be welcomed home by an adoring—or at least *appreciative*—public. Upon his return, the hero Stagg is made the centerpiece of an incredible public ritual—one that will repeatedly take him to the heights of ecstasy, and inexorably drag him toward the depths of hell. $6.95/303-1

A FEAST UNKNOWN

"Sprawling, brawling, shocking, suspenseful, hilarious..."—Theodore Sturgeon
Farmer's supreme anti-hero returns. *A Feast Unknown* begins in 1968, with Lord Grandrith's stunning statement: "I was conceived and born in 1888." Slowly, Lord Grandrith—armed with the belief that he is the son of Jack the Ripper—tells the story of his remarkable and unbridled life. Beginning with his discovery of the secret of immortality, Grandrith's tale proves him no raving lunatic—but something far more bizarre.... $6.95/276-0

THE IMAGE OF THE BEAST

Herald Childe has seen Hell, glimpsed its horror in an act of sexual mutilation. Childe must now find and destroy an inhuman predator through the streets of a polluted and decadent Los Angeles of the future. One clue after another leads Childe to an inescapable realization about the nature of sex and evil.... $6.95/166-7

SAMUEL R. DELANY

EQUINOX

The *Scorpion* has sailed the seas in a quest for every possible pleasure. Her crew is a collection of the young, the twisted, the insatiable. A drifter comes into their midst, and is taken on a fantastic journey to the darkest, most dangerous sexual extremes—until he is finally a victim to their boundless appetites. $6.95/157-8

ANDREI CODRESCU

THE REPENTANCE OF LORRAINE

"One of our most prodigiously talented and magical writers."

—NYT Book Review

An aspiring writer, a professor's wife, a secretary, gold anklets, Maoists, Roman harlots—and more—swirl through this spicy tale of a harried quest for a mythic artifact. Written when the author was a young man, this lusty yarn was inspired by the heady—and hot—days and nights of the Sixties. $6.95/329-5

DAVID MELTZER

ORF

He is the ultimate musician-hero—the idol of thousands, the fevered dream of many more. And like many musicians before him, he is misunderstood, misused—and totally out of control. Every last drop of feeling is squeezed from a modern-day troubadour and his lady love. $6.95/110-1

LEOPOLD VON SACHER-MASOCH

VENUS IN FURS

This classic 19th century novel is the first uncompromising exploration of the dominant/submissive relationship in literature. The alliance of Severin and Wanda epitomizes Sacher-Masoch's dark obsession with a cruel, controlling goddess and the urges that drive the man held in her thrall. The letters exchanged between Sacher-Masoch and an aspiring writer he sought as the avatar of his forbidden desires—are also included. $6.95/3089-X

RHINOCEROS BOOKS

SOPHIE GALLEYMORE BIRD

MANEATER

Through a bizarre act of creation, a man attains the "perfect" lover—by all appearances a beautiful, sensuous woman but in reality something far darker. Once brought to life she will accept no mate, seeking instead the prey that will sate her hunger for vengeance. A biting take on the war of the sexes, this debut goes for the jugular of the "perfect woman" myth. $6.95/103-9

TUPPY OWENS

SENSATIONS

A piece of porn history. Tuppy Owens tells the unexpurgated story of the making of *Sensations*—the first big-budget sex flick. Originally commissioned to appear in book form after the release of the film in 1975, *Sensations* is finally released under Masquerade's stylish Rhino*ceros* imprint. $6.95/3081-4

DANIEL VIAN

ILLUSIONS

Two disturbing tales of danger and desire in Berlin on the eve of WWII. From private homes to lurid cafés to decaying streets, passion is explored, exposed, and placed in stark contrast to the brutal violence of the time. A singularly arousing volume. $6.95/3074-1

PERSUASIONS

"The stockings are drawn tight by the suspender belt, tight enough to be stretched to the limit just above the middle part of her thighs..." A double novel, including the classics *Adagio* and *Gabriela and the General*, this volume traces desire around the globe. International lust! $6.95/183-7

LIESEL KULIG

LOVE IN WARTIME

An uncompromising look at the politics, perils and pleasures of sexual power. Madeleine knew that the handsome SS officer was a dangerous man. But she was just a cabaret singer in Nazi-occupied Paris, trying to survive in a perilous time. When Josef fell in love with her, he discovered that a beautiful and amoral woman can sometimes be wildly dangerous. $6.95/3044-X

MASQUERADE BOOKS

The Marquis de Sade's JULIETTE   *David Aaron Clark*

The Marquis de Sade's infamous Juliette returns—and at the hand of David Aaron Clark, she emerges as the most powerful, perverse and destructive nightstalker modern New York will ever know. Under this domina's tutelage, two women come to know torture's bizarre attractions, as they grapple with the price of Juliette's promise of immortality.

Praise for Dave Clark:

"David Aaron Clark has delved into one of the most sensationalistically taboo aspects of eros, sadomasochism, and produced a novel of unmistakable literary imagination and artistic value."   —Carlo McCormick, *Paper* $5.95/240-X

THE PARLOR   *N.T. Morley*

It was a rainy New Year's Day when Kathryn entered bondage. Lovely Kathryn gives in to the ultimate temptation. The mysterious John and Sarah ask her to be their slave—an idea that turns Kathryn on so much that she can't refuse! But who are these two mysterious strangers? Little by little, Kathryn comes to know the inner secrets of her stunning keepers. $5.95/291-4

MASQUERADE BOOKS

NADIA   *Anonymous*

"Nadia married General the Count Gregorio Stenoff—a gentleman of noble pedigree it is true, but one of the most reckless dissipated rascals in Russia..." Follow the delicious but neglected Nadia as she works to wring every drop of pleasure out of life—despite an unhappy marriage. A classic title providing a peek into the secret sexual lives of another time and place. $5.95/267-1

THE STORY OF A VICTORIAN MAID   *Nigel McParr*

What were the Victorians really like? Chances are, no one believes they were as stuffy as their Queen, but who would have imagined such unbridled libertines! One maid is followed from exploit to smutty exploit! $5.95/241-8

CARRIE'S STORY   *Molly Weatherfield*

"I had been Jonathan's slave for about a year when he told me he wanted to sell me at an auction. I wasn't in any condition to respond when he told me this..." Desire and depravity run rampant in this story of uncompromising mastery and irrevocable submission. $5.95/228-0

CHARLY'S GAME   *Bren Flemming*

Charly's a no-nonsense private detective facing the fight of her life. A rich woman's gullible daughter has run off with one of the toughest leather dykes in town—and Charly's hired to lure the girl back. One by one, wise and wicked women ensnare one another in their lusty nets! $4.95/221-3

ANDREA AT THE CENTER   *J.P. Kansas*

Kidnapped! Lithe and lovely young Andrea is, without warning, whisked away to a distant retreat. Gradually, she is introduced to the ways of the Center, and soon becomes quite friendly with its other inhabitants—all of whom are learning to abandon all restraint in their pursuit of the deepest sexual satisfaction. $5.95/324-4

ASK ISADORA   *Isadora Alman*

An essential volume, collecting six years' worth of Isadora Alman's syndicated columns on sex and relationships. Alman's been called a "hip Dr. Ruth," and a "sexy Dear Abby," based upon the wit and pertinence of her advice. Today's world is more perplexing than ever—and Isadora Alman is just the expert to help untangle the most personal of knots. $4.95/61-0

THE SLAVES OF SHOANNA   *Mercedes Kelly*

Shoanna, the cruel and magnificent, takes four maidens under her wing—and teaches them the ins and outs of pleasure and discipline. Trained in every imaginable perversion, from simple fleshly joys to advanced techniques, these students go to the head of the class! $4.95/164-0

LOVE & SURRENDER   *Marlene Darcy*

"Madeline saw Harry looking at her legs and she blushed as she remembered what he wanted to do.... She casually pulled the skirt of her dress back to uncover her knees and the lower part of her thighs. What did he want now? Did he want more? She tugged at her skirt again, pulled it back far enough so almost all of her thighs were exposed...." $4.95/3082-2

THE COMPLETE *PLAYGIRL* FANTASIES   *Editors of* Playgirl

The best women's fantasies are collected here, fresh from the pages of *Playgirl*. These knockouts from the infamous "Reader's Fantasy Forum" prove, once again, that truth can indeed be hotter, wilder, and *better* than fiction. $4.95/3075-X

STASI SLUT   *Anthony Bobarzynski*

Need we say more? Adina lives in East Germany, far from the sexually liberated, uninhibited debauchery of the West. She meets a group of ruthless and corrupt STASI agents who use her as a pawn in their political chess game as well as for their own perverse gratification— until she uses her talents and attractions in a final bid for total freedom! $4.95/3050-4

MASQUERADE

ANDREA AT THE CENTER

J. P. KANSAS

$4.95 • MASQUERADE BOOKS

MASQUERADE BOOKS

BLUE TANGO
Hilary Manning

Ripe and tempting Julie is haunted by the sounds of extraordinary passion beyond her bedroom wall. Alone, she fantasizes about taking part in the amorous dramas of her hosts, Claire and Edward. When she finds a way to watch the nightly debauch, her curiosity turns to full-blown lust! $4.95/3037-7

LOUISE BELHAVEL

FRAGRANT ABUSES

The saga of Clara and Iris continues as the now-experienced girls enjoy themselves with a new circle of worldly friends whose imaginations match their own. Polymorphous perversity follows the lusty ladies around the globe!
$4.95/88-2

DEPRAVED ANGELS

The final installment in the incredible adventures of Clara and Iris. Together with their friends, lovers, and worldly acquaintances, Clara and Iris explore the frontiers of depravity at home and abroad. $4.95/92-0

TITIAN BERESFORD

CINDERELLA

Beresford triumphs again with this intoxicating tale, filled with castle dungeons and tightly corseted ladies-in-waiting, naughty viscounts and impossibly cruel masturbatrixes—nearly every conceivable method of erotic torture is explored and described in lush, vivid detail. $4.95/305-8

JUDITH BOSTON

Young Edward would have been lucky to get the stodgy old companion he thought his parents had hired for him. Instead, an exquisite woman arrives at his door, and Edward finds his compulsively lewd behavior never goes unpunished by the unflinchingly severe Judith Boston! $4.95/273-6

NINA FOXTON

An aristocrat finds herself bored by amusements for "ladies of good breeding." Instead of taking tea with proper gentlemen, Nina invents a contraption to "milk" them of their most private essences. Her frisky plan guarantees that no man ever says "No" to Nina! $4.95/145-4

A TITIAN BERESFORD READER

A captivating collection! Beresford's fanciful settings and outrageous fetishism have established his reputation as one of modern erotica's most imaginative and spirited writers. Wild dominatrixes, deliciously perverse masochists, and mesmerizing detail are the hallmarks of the Beresford tale—and can be encountered her in abundance. $4.95/114-4

CHINA BLUE

KUNG FU NUNS

"When I could stand the pleasure no longer, she lifted me out of the chair and sat me down on top of the table. She then lifted her skirt. The sight of her perfect legs clad in white stockings and a petite garter belt further mesmerized me. I lean particularly towards white garter belts." The infamous China Blue returns!
$4.95/3031-8

HARRIET DAIMLER

DARLING • INNOCENCE

In *Darling*, a virgin is raped by a mugger. Driven by her urge for revenge, she searches New York in a furious sexual hunt that leads to rape and murder. In *Innocence*, a young invalid determines to experience sex through her voluptuous nurse. Two critically acclaimed novels explode in one quality volume!
$4.95/3047-4

DEPRAVED ANGELS
"How exciting. What do you want her to do next?"
$4.95 (CANADA $5.95) • MASQUERADE BOOKS
ANONYMOUS

MASQUERADE BOOKS

AKBAR DEL PIOMBO

SKIRTS

Randy Mr. Edward Champdick enters high society—and a whole lot more—in his quest for ultimate satisfaction. For it seems that once Mr. Champdick rises to the occasion, nothing can bring him down. Rampant ravishment follows this libertine wherever he goes! $4.95/115-2

DUKE COSIMO

A kinky romp played out against the boudoirs, bathrooms and ballrooms of the European nobility, who seem to do nothing all day except each other. The lifestyles of the rich and licentious are revealed in all their glory. Lust-styles of the rich and infamous! $4.95/3052-0

A CRUMBLING FAÇADE

The return of that incorrigible rogue, Henry Pike, who continues his pursuit of sex, fair or otherwise, in the most elegant homes of the most debauched aristocrats. No one can resist the irrepressible Pike! $4.95/3043-1

PAULA

"How bad do you want me?" she asked, her voice husky, breathy. I shrank back, for my desire for her was swelling to unspeakable proportions. "Turn around," she said, and I obeyed....This canny seductress tests the mettle of every man who comes under her spell—and every man does! $4.95/3036-9

ROBERT DESMOND

PROFESSIONAL CHARMER

A gigolo lives a parasitical life of luxury by providing his sexual services to the rich and bored. Traveling in the most exclusive circles, this gun-for-hire will gratify the lewdest and most vulgar sexual cravings! This dedicated pro leaves no one unsatisfied. $4.95/3003-2

THE SWEETEST FRUIT

Connie is determined to seduce and destroy Father Chadcroft. She corrupts the unsuspecting priest into forsaking all that he holds sacred, destroys his parish, and slyly manipulates him with her smoldering looks and hypnotic aura. $4.95/95-5

MICHAEL DRAX

SILK AND STEEL

"He stood tall and strong in the shadows of her room… Akemi knew what he was there for. He let his robe fall to the floor. She could offer no resistance as the shadowy figure knelt before her, gazing down upon her. Why would she resist? This was what she wanted all along…." $4.95/3032-6

OBSESSIONS

Victoria is determined to become a model by sexually ensnaring the powerful people who control the fashion industry: Paige, who finds herself compelled to watch Victoria's conquests; and Pietro and Alex, who take turns and then join in for a sizzling threesome. $4.95/3012-1

LIZBETH DUSSEAU

TRINKETS

"Her bottom danced on the air, pert and fully round. It would take punishment well, he thought." A luscious woman submits to an artist's every whim—becoming the sexual trinket he had always desired. $5.95/246-9

THE APPLICANT

"Adventuresome young woman who enjoys being submissive sought by married couple in early forties. Expect no limits." Hilary answers an ad, hoping to find someone who can meet her needs. Beautiful Liza turns out to be a flawless mistress; with her husband Oliver, she trains Hilary to be submissive. $4.95/306-6

MASQUERADE BOOKS

SPANISH HOLIDAY

She didn't know what to make of Sam Jacobs. He was undoubtedly the most remarkable man she'd ever met.... Lauren didn't mean to fall in love with the enigmatic Sam, but a once-in-a-lifetime European vacation gives her all the evidence she needs that this hot man might be the one for her.... A tale of boundless romance and insatiable desires, this is one holiday that may never end!

$4.95/185-3

CAROLINE'S CONTRACT

After a long life of repression, Caroline goes out on a limb. On the advice of a friend, she meets with the dark and alluring Max Burton—a man more than willing to indulge her deepest fantasies of domination and discipline. Caroline soon learns to love the ministrations of Max—and agrees to a very *special* arrangement....

$4.95/122-5

MEMBER OF THE CLUB

"I wondered what would excite me.... And deep down inside, I had the most submissive thoughts: I imagined myself … under the grip of men I hardly knew. If there were a club to join, it could take my deepest dreams and make them real. My only question was how far I'd really go?" A woman finally goes all the way in a quest to satisfy her hungers, joining a club where she *really* pays her dues—with any one of the many men who desire her!

$4.95/3079-2

SARA H. FRENCH

MASTER OF TIMBERLAND

"Welcome to Timberland Resort," he began. "We are delighted that you have come to serve us. And…be assured that we will require service of you in the strictest sense. Our discipline is the most demanding in the world. You will be trained here by the best. And now your new Masters will make their choices." A tale of sexual slavery at the ultimate paradise resort—and one of our best-sellers.

$5.95/327-9

RETURN TO TIMBERLAND

Pack your bags—it's time for a trip back to Timberland, the world's most frenzied sexual resort! Prepare for a vacation filled with delicious decadence, as each and every visitor is serviced by unimaginably talented submissives. The nubile maidens of Timberland are determined to make this the raunchiest camp-out ever!

$5.95/257-4

SARAH JACKSON

SANCTUARY

Tales from the Middle Ages. *Sanctuary* explores both the unspeakable debauchery of court life and the unimaginable privations of monastic solitude, leading the voracious and the virtuous on a collision course that brings history to throbbing life. Bored royals and yearning clerics light fires sure to bring light to the darkest of ages.

$5.95/318-X

HELOISE

A panoply of sensual tales harkening back to the golden age of Victorian erotica. Desire is examined in all its intricacy, as fantasies are explored and urges explode. Innocence meets experience time and again.

$4.95/3073-3

JOYCELYN JOYCE

PRIVATE LIVES

The illicit affairs and lecherous habits of the illustrious make for a sizzling tale of French erotic life. A wealthy widow has a craving for a young busboy; he's sleeping with a rich businessman's wife; her husband is minding his sex business elsewhere!

$4.95/309-0

MASQUERADE BOOKS

CANDY LIPS

The high-powered world of publishing serves as the backdrop for one woman's pursuit of sexual satisfaction. From a fiery femme fatale to a voracious Valentino, she takes her pleasure where she can find it. Luckily for her, it's most often found between the legs of the most licentious lovers! A dazzling woman's climb up the corporate ladder of Lust Inc.! $4.95/182-9

KIM'S PASSION

The life of a beautiful English seductress. Kim leaves India for London, where she quickly takes upon herself the task of bedding every woman in sight! One by one, the lovely Kim's conquests accumulate, until she finds herself in the arms of gentry and commoners alike. $4.95/162-4

CAROUSEL

A young American woman leaves her husband when she discovers he is having an affair with their maid. She then becomes the sexual plaything of various Parisian voluptuaries. Wild sex, low morals, and ultimate decadence in the flamboyant years before the European collapse. $4.95/3051-2

SABINE

There is no one who can refuse her once she casts her spell; no lover can do anything less than give up his whole life for her. Great men and empires fall at her feet; but she is haughty, distracted, impervious. It is the eve of WW II, and Sabine must find a new lover equal to her talents. $4.95/3046-6

THE WILD HEART

A luxury hotel is the setting for this artful web of sex, desire, and love. A newlywed sees sex as a duty, while her hungry husband tries to awaken her to its tender joys. A Parisian entertains wealthy guests for the love of money. Each episode provides a new variation in this lusty Grand Hotel! $4.95/3007-5

JADE EAST

Laura, passive and passionate, follows her husband Emilio to Hong Kong. He gives her to Wu Li, a connoisseur of sexual perversions, who passes her on to Madeleine, a flamboyant lesbian. Madeleine's friends make Laura the centerpiece in Hong Kong's infamous underground orgies. Steamy slaves for sale! $4.95/60-2

RAWHIDE LUST

Diana Beaumont, the young wife of a U.S. Marshal, is kidnapped as an act of vengeance against her husband. Jack Beaumont sets out on a long journey to get his wife back, but finally catches up with her trail only to learn that she's been sold into white slavery in Mexico. $4.95/55-6

THE JAZZ AGE

The time: the Roaring Twenties. A young attorney becomes suspicious of his mistress while his wife has an fling with a lesbian lover. *The Jazz Age* is a romp of erotic realism from the heyday of the speakeasy. $4.95/48-3

AMARANTHA KNIGHT

THE DARKER PASSIONS:
THE FALL OF THE HOUSE OF USHER

The Master and Mistress of the house of Usher indulge in every form of decadence, and are intent on initiating their guests into the many pleasures to be found in utter submission. But something is not quite right in the House of Usher, and the foundation of its dynasty begins to crack.... $5.95/313-9

THE DARKER PASSIONS: *FRANKENSTEIN*

What if you could create a living, breathing human? What shocking acts could it be taught to perform, to desire, to love? Find out what pleasures await those who play God.... $5.95/248-5

Masquerade Books

RAWHIDE LUST

The marshal blazed a trail across the Wild West
to rescue his wife from the sex-starved desperados
who had snatched her

ANONYMOUS

MASQUERADE BOOKS

THE DARKER PASSIONS: *DR. JEKYLL AND MR. HYDE*

It is an old story, one of incredible, frightening transformations achieved through mysterious experiments. Now, Amarantha Knight explores the steamy possibilities of a tale where no one is quite who—or what—they seem. Victorian bedrooms explode with hidden demons. $4.95/**227-2**

THE DARKER PASSIONS: *DRACULA*

"Well-written and imaginative, Amarantha Knight gives fresh impetus to this myth, taking us through the sexual and sadistic scenes with details that keep us reading.... This author shows superb control. A classic in itself has been added to the shelves."
                                                    —Divinity $5.95/**326-0**

ALIZARIN LAKE

THE EROTIC ADVENTURES OF HARRY TEMPLE

Harry Temple's memoirs chronicle his amorous adventures from his initiation at the hands of insatiable sirens, through his stay at a house of hot repute, to his encounters with a chastity-belted nympho—and many other exuberant and over-stimulated partners. $4.95/**127-6**

EROTOMANIA

The bible of female sexual perversion! It's all here, everything you ever wanted to know about kinky women past and present. From simple nymphomania to the most outrageous fetishism, all secrets are revealed in this look into the forbidden rooms of feminine desire. $4.95/**128-4**

AN ALIZARIN LAKE READER

A selection of wicked musings from the pen of Masquerade's perennially popular author. It's all here: *Business as Usual, The Erotic Adventures of Harry Temple, Festival of Venus,* the mysterious *Instruments of the Passion,* the devilish *Miss High Heels*—and more. $4.95/**106-3**

MISS HIGH HEELS

It was a delightful punishment few men dared to dream of. Who could have predicted how far it would go? Forced by his sisters to dress and behave like a proper lady, Dennis finds he enjoys life as Denise much more! Crossdressed fetishism run amuck! $4.95/**3066-0**

THE INSTRUMENTS OF THE PASSION

All that remains is the diary of a young initiate, detailing the twisted rituals of a mysterious cult institution known only as "Rossiter." Behind sinister walls, a beautiful young woman performs an unending drama of pain and humiliation. Will she ever have her fill of utter degradation? $4.95/**3010-5**

FESTIVAL OF VENUS

Brigeen Mooney fled her home in the west of Ireland to avoid being forced into a nunnery. But the refuge she found in the city turned out to be dedicated to a very different religion. The women she met there belonged to the Old Religion, devoted to the ways of sex and sacrifices. $4.95/**37-8**

PAUL LITTLE

THE PRISONER

Judge Black has built a secret room below a penitentiary, where he sentences the prisoners to hours of exhibition and torment while his friends watch. Judge Black's House of Corrections is equipped with one purpose in mind: to administer his own brand of rough justice! $5.95/**330-9**

TUTORED IN LUST

This tale of the initiation and instruction of a carnal college co-ed and her fellow students unlocks the sex secrets of the classroom. Books take a back seat to secret societies and their bizarre ceremonies in this story of students with an unquenchable thirst for knowledge! $4.95/**78-5**

MASQUERADE BOOKS

DANGEROUS LESSONS

A compendium of corporeal punishment from the twisted mind of bestselling Paul Little. Incredibly arousing morsels abound: *Tears of the Inquisition, Lust of the Cossacks, Poor Darlings, Captive Maidens, Slave Island,* even the scandalous *The Metamorphosis of Lisette Joyaux*. $4.95/32-7

THE LUSTFUL TURK

The majestic ruler of Algiers and a modest English virgin face off—to their mutual delight. Emily Bartow is initially horrified by the unrelenting sexual tortures to be endured under the powerful Turk's hand. But soon she comes to crave her debasement—no matter what the cost! $4.95/163-2

TEARS OF THE INQUISITION

The incomparable Paul Little delivers a staggering account of pleasure and punishment. *"There was a tickling inside her as her nervous system reminded her she was ready for sex. But before her was...the Inquisitor!"* $4.95/146-2

DOUBLE NOVEL

Two of Paul Little's bestselling novels in one spellbinding volume! *The Metamorphosis of Lisette Joyaux* tells the story of an innocent young woman initiated into a new world of lesbian lusts. *The Story of Monique* reveals the sexual rituals that beckon the ripe and willing Monique. $4.95/86-6

CHINESE JUSTICE AND OTHER STORIES

Chinese Justice is already a classic—the story of the excruciating pleasures and delicious punishments inflicted on foreigners under the tyrannical leaders of the Boxer Rebellion. One by one, each foreign woman is brought before the authorities and grilled. Scandalous tortures are inflicted upon the helpless females by their relentless, merciless captors. $4.95/153-5

SLAVES OF CAMEROON

This sordid tale is about the women who were used by German officers for salacious profit. These women were forced to become whores for the German army in this African colony. The most perverse forms of erotic gratification are depicted in this unsavory tale of women exploited in every way possible. One of Paul Little's most infamous titles. $4.95/3026-1

ALL THE WAY

Two excruciating novels from Paul Little in one hot volume! *Going All the Way* features an unhappy man who tries to purge himself of the memory of his lover with a series of quirky and uninhibited women. *Pushover* tells the story of a serial spanker and his celebrated exploits in California. $4.95/3023-7

CAPTIVE MAIDENS

Three beautiful young women find themselves powerless against the wealthy, debauched landowners of 1824 England. They are banished to a sexual slave colony where they are corrupted into participation in every imaginable perversion. $4.95/3014-8

SLAVE ISLAND

A leisure cruise is waylaid, finding itself in the domain of Lord Henry Philbrock, a sadistic genius, who has built a hidden paradise where captive females are forced into slavery. The ship's passengers are kidnapped and spirited to his island prison, where the women are trained to accommodate the most bizarre sexual cravings of the rich, the famous, the pampered and the perverted. Slutty slaves degraded! $4.95/3006-7

MARY LOVE

THE BEST OF MARY LOVE

Mary Love leaves no coupling untried and no extreme unexplored in these scandalous selections from *Mastering Mary Sue, Ecstasy on Fire, Vice Park Place, Wanda,* and *Naughtier at Night*. $4.95/3099-7

erotic
PLAYGIRL
r o m a n c e

WOMEN AT WORK

$4.95 (CANADA $5.95) • MASQUERADE BOOKS

CHARLOTTE ROSE

MASQUERADE BOOKS

ECSTASY ON FIRE

The inexperienced young Steven is initiated into the intense, throbbing pleasures of manhood by the worldly Melissa Staunton, a well-qualified teacher of the sensual arts. Soon he's in a position—or two—to give lessons of his own! Innocence and experience in an erotic explosion! $4.95/3080-6

NAUGHTIER AT NIGHT

"He wanted to seize her. Her buttocks under the tight suede material were absolutely succulent—carved and molded. What on earth had he done to deserve a morsel of a girl like this?" $4.95/3030-X

RACHEL PEREZ

ODD WOMEN

These women are lots of things: sexy, smart, innocent, tough—some even say odd. But who cares, when their combined ass-ettes are so sweet! There's not a moral in sight as an assortment of Sapphic sirens proves once and for all that comely ladies come best in pairs. $4.95/123-3

AFFINITIES

"Kelsy had a liking for cool upper-class blondes, the long-legged girls from Lake Forest and Winnetka who came into the city to cruise the lesbian bars on Halsted, looking for breathless ecstasies. Kelsy thought of them as icebergs that needed melting, these girls with a quiet demeanor and so much under the surface...." A scorching tale of lesbian libidos unleashed, from an uncommonly vivid writer. $4.95/113-6

CHARLOTTE ROSE

A DANGEROUS DAY

A new volume from the best-selling author who brought you the sensational *Women at Work* and *The Doctor Is In*. And if you thought the high-powered entanglements of her previous books were risky, wait until Rose takes you on a journey through the thrills of one dangerous day! $5.95/293-0

THE DOCTOR IS IN

"Finally, a book of erotic writing by a woman who isn't afraid to get down—and with deliciously lavish details that open out floodgates of lust and desire. Read it alone ... or with somebody you really like!"

—*Candida Royal*

From the author of the acclaimed *Women at Work* comes a delectable trio of fantasies inspired by one of life's most intimate relationships. Charlotte Rose once again writes about women's forbidden desires, this time from the patient's point of view. $4.95/195-0

WOMEN AT WORK

Hot, uninhibited stories devoted to the working woman! From a lonesome cowgirl to a supercharged public relations exec, these uncontrollable women know how to let off steam after a tough day on the job. A wildly popular and critically acclaimed title, that includes "A Cowgirl's Passion," ranked #1 on Dr. Ruth's list of favorite erotic stories for women! $4.95/3088-1

SYDNEY ST. JAMES

RIVE GAUCHE

Decadence and debauchery among the doomed artists in the Latin Quarter, Paris circa 1920. Expatriate bohemians couple with abandon—before eventually abandoning their ambitions amidst the intoxicating temptations waiting to be indulged in every bedroom. Finally, "creative impulse" takes on a whole new meaning—as each lusty eccentric feels an impulse to create as many steamy sexual thrills as possible! $5.95/317-1

MASQUERADE BOOKS

THE HIGHWAYWOMAN

A young filmmaker making a documentary about the life of the notorious English highwaywoman, Bess Ambrose, becomes obsessed with her mysterious subject. It seems that Bess touched more than hearts—and plundered the treasures of every man and maiden she met on the way. $4.95/174-8

GARDEN OF DELIGHT

A vivid account of sexual awakening that follows an innocent but insatiably curious young woman's journey from the furtive, forbidden joys of dormitory life to the unabashed carnality of the wild world. Pretty Pauline blossoms with each new experiment in the sensual arts. $4.95/3058-X

ALEXANDER TROCCHI

THONGS

"...In Spain, life is cheap, from that glittering tragedy in the bullring to the quick thrust of the stiletto in a narrow street in a Barcelona slum. No, this death would not have called for further comment had it not been for one striking fact. The naked woman had met her end in a way he had never seen before—a way that had enormous sexual significance. My God, she had been..." $4.95/217-5

HELEN AND DESIRE

Helen Seferis' flight from the oppressive village of her birth became a sexual tour of a harsh world. From brothels in Sydney to harems in Algiers, Helen chronicles her adventures fully in her diary. Each encounter is examined in the scorching and uncensored diary of the sensual Helen! $4.95/3093-8

THE CARNAL DAYS OF HELEN SEFERIS

Private Investigator Anthony Harvest is assigned to save Helen Seferis, a beautiful Australian who has been abducted. Following clues in Helen's explicit diary of adventures, he Helen, the ultimate sexual prize. $4.95/3086-5

WHITE THIGHS

A fantasy of obsession from a modern erotic master. This is the story of Saul and his sexual fixation on the beautiful, tormented Anna. Their scorching passion leads to murder and madness every time they submit to their lusty needs. Saul must possess Anna again and again. $4.95/3009-1

SCHOOL FOR SIN

When Peggy leaves her country home behind for the bright lights of Dublin, her sensuous nature leads to her seduction by a stranger. He recruits her into a training school where no one knows what awaits them at graduation, but each student is sure to be well schooled in sex! $4.95/ 89-0

MY LIFE AND LOVES (THE 'LOST' VOLUME)

What happens when you try to fake a sequel to the most scandalous autobiography of the 20th century? If the "forgers" are two of the most important figures in modern erotica, you get a masterpiece, and THIS IS IT! One of the most thrilling forgeries in literature. $4.95/52-1

MARCUS VAN HELLER

TERROR

Another shocking exploration of lust by the author of the ever-popular *Adam & Eve*. Set in Paris during the Algerian War, *Terror* explores the place of sexual passion in a world drunk on violence. *Terror* reveals the legendary Van Heller at the top of his game. $5.95/247-7

KIDNAP

Private Investigator Harding is called in to investigate a mysterious kidnapping case involving the rich and powerful. Along the way he has the pleasure of "interrogating" an exotic dancer named Jeanne and a beautiful English reporter, as he finds himself enmeshed in the crime underworld. $4.95/90-4

THONGS

ALEXANDER TROCCHI

MASQUERADE BOOKS

LUSCIDIA WALLACE

KATY'S AWAKENING

Katy thinks she's been rescued after a terrible car wreck. Little does she suspect that she's been ensnared by a ring of swingers whose tastes run to domination and unimaginably depraved sex parties. With no means of escape, Katy becomes the newest initiate into this sick private club—much to her pleasure! $4.95/308-2

FOR SALE BY OWNER

Susie was overwhelmed by the lavishness of the yacht, the glamour of the guests. But she didn't know the plans they had for her. Sexual torture, training and sale into slavery! $4.95/3064-4

THE ICE MAIDEN

Edward Canton has ruthlessly seized everything he wants in life, with one exception: Rebecca Esterbrook. Frustrated by his inability to seduce her with money, he kidnaps her and whisks her away to his remote island compound, where she learns to shed her "inhibitions." Soon, Rebecca emerges as a writhing, red-hot love slave! $4.95/3001-6

DON WINSLOW

THE MANY PLEASURES OF IRONWOOD

Meet Charli, Robin, Kitteridge, Nikki, Annie, Diane and Meredith—seven lovely young women who are employed by The Ironwood Sportsmen's club for the entertainment of gentlemen. A small and exclusive club with seven carefully selected sexual connoisseurs, Ironwood is dedicated to the relentless pursuit of sensual pleasure. $5.95/310-4

CLAIRE'S GIRLS

You knew when she walked by that she was something special. She was one of Claire's girls, a woman carefully dressed and groomed to fill a role, to capture a look, to fit an image crafted by the sophisticated proprietress of an exclusive escort agency. High-class whores blow the roof off! $4.95/108-X

GLORIA'S INDISCRETION

"He looked up at her. Gloria stood passively, her hands loosely at her sides, her eyes still closed, a dreamy expression on her face ... She sensed his hungry eyes on her, could almost feel his burning gaze on her body...." $4.95/3094-6

THE MASQUERADE READERS

THE COMPLETE EROTIC READER

The very best in erotic writing together in a wicked collection sure to stimulate even the most jaded and "sophisticated" palates. $4.95/3063-6

THE VELVET TONGUE

An orgy of oral gratification! *The Velvet Tongue* celebrates the most mouthwatering, lip-smacking, tongue-twisting action. A feast of fellatio and *soixante-neuf* awaits readers of excellent taste at this steamy suck-fest. $4.95/3029-6

A MASQUERADE READER

Strict lessons are learned at the hand of *The English Governess*. Scandalous confessions are found in *The Diary of an Angel*, and the story of a woman whose desires drove her to the ultimate sacrifice in *Thongs* completes the collection. $4.95/84-X

THE CLASSIC COLLECTION

SCHOOL DAYS IN PARIS

A delicious duo of erotic awakenings. The rapturous chronicles of a well-spent youth! Few Universities provide the profound and pleasurable lessons one learns in after-hours study—particularly if one is young and bursting with promise, and lucky enough to have Paris as a playground. A stimulating look at the breathless pursuits of young adulthood. $5.95/325-2

KATE
PERCIVAL

ANONYMOUS

MICHAEL LASSELL

the hard way

RICHARD KASAK BOOKS

EURUDICE

F/32

F/32 has been called "the most controversial and dangerous novel ever written by a woman." With the story of Ela (whose name is a pseudonym for orgasm), Eurudice won the National Fiction competition sponsored by Fiction Collective Two and Illinois State University. A funny, disturbing quest for unity, *F/32* prompted Frederic Tuten to proclaim "almost any page ... redeems us from the anemic writing and banalities we have endured in the past decade of bloodless fiction." $11.95/350-3

LARRY TOWNSEND

ASK LARRY

Twelve years of Masterful advice from Larry Townsend (*Run, Little Leatherboy, Chains*), the leatherman's long-time confidant and adviser. Starting just before the onslaught of AIDS, Townsend wrote the "Leather Notebook" column for *Drummer* magazine, tackling subjects from sexual technique to safer sex, whips to welts, Daddies to dog collars. Now, with *Ask Larry*, readers can avail themselves of Townsend's collected wisdom as well as the author's contemporary commentary—a careful consideration of the way life has changed in the AIDS era, and the specific ways in which the disease has altered perceptions of once-simple problems. $12.95/289-2

RUSS KICK

OUTPOSTS:
A Catalog of Rare and Disturbing Alternative Information

A huge, authoritative guide to some of the most offbeat and bizarre publications available today! Rather than simply summarize the plethora of controversial opinions crowding the American scene, Russ Kick has tracked down the real McCoy and compiled over five hundred reviews of work penned by political extremists, conspiracy theorists, hallucinogenic pathfinders, sexual explorers, religious iconoclasts and social malcontents. Better yet, each review is followed by ordering information for the many readers sure to want these remarkable publications for themselves. $18.95/0202-8

WILLIAM CARNEY

THE REAL THING

Carney gives us a good look at the mores and lifestyle of the first generation of gay leathermen. A chilling mystery/romance novel as well. —Pat Califia

With a new Introduction by Michael Bronski. Out of print for years, *The Real Thing* has long served as a touchstone in any consideration of gay "edge fiction." First published in 1968, this uncompromising story of New York leathermen received instant acclaim.. Out of print for years, *The Real Thing* returns from exile, ready to thrill a new generation—and reacquaint itself with its original audience. $10.95/280-9

MICHAEL LASSELL

THE HARD WAY

Lassell is a master of the necessary word. In an age of tepid and whining verse, his bawdy and bittersweet songs are like a plunge in cold champagne. —Paul Monette

The first collection of renowned gay writer Michael Lassell's poetry, fiction and essays. Widely anthologized and a staple of gay literary and entertainment publications nationwide, Lassell is regarded as one of the most distinctive talents of his generation. As much a chronicle of post-Stonewall gay life as a compendium of a remarkable writer's work. $12.95/231-0

RICHARD KASAK BOOKS

LOOKING FOR MR. PRESTON

Edited by Laura Antoniou, *Looking for Mr. Preston* includes work by **Lars Eighner, Pat Califia, Michael Bronski, Felice Picano, Joan Nestle, Larry Townsend, Sasha Alyson, Andrew Holleran, Michael Lowenthal,** and others who contributed interviews, essays and personal reminiscences of John Preston—a man whose career spanned the industry from the early pages of the *Advocate* to various national bestseller lists. Preston was the author of over twenty books, including *Franny, the Queen of Provincetown,* and *Mr. Benson.* He also edited the noted *Flesh and the Word* erotic anthologies, *Personal Dispatches: Writers Confront AIDS,* and *Hometowns,.* More importantly, Preston became a personal inspiration, friend and mentor to many of today's gay and lesbian authors and editors. Ten percent of the proceeds from sale of the book will go to the AIDS Project of Southern Maine, for which Preston had served as President of the Board. $23.95/288-4

AMARANTHA KNIGHT, EDITOR

LOVE BITES

A volume of tales dedicated to legend's sexiest demon—the Vampire. Amarantha Knight, herself an author who has delved into vampire lore, has gathered the very best writers in the field to produce a collection of uncommon, and chilling, allure. Including such names as Ron Dee, Nancy A. Collins, Nancy Kilpatrick, Lois Tilton and David Aaron Clark, *Love Bites* is not only the finest collection of erotic horror available—but a virtual who's who of promising new talent. $12.95/234-5

MICHAEL LOWENTHAL, EDITOR

THE BEST OF THE BADBOYS

A collection of the best of Masquerade Books' phenomenally popular Badboy line of gay erotic writing. Badboy 's sizable roster includes many names that are legendary in gay circles. The very best of the leading Badboys is collected here, in this testament to the artistry that has catapulted these "outlaw" authors to bestselling status. John Preston, Aaron Travis, Larry Townsend, John Rowberry, Clay Caldwell and Lars Eighner are here represented by their most provocative writing. Michael Lowenthal both edited this remarkable collection and provides the Introduction. $12.95/233-7

GUILLERMO BOSCH

RAIN

An adult fairy tale, *Rain* takes place in a time when the mysteries of Eros are played out against a background of uncommon deprivation. The tale begins on the 1,537th day of drought—when one man comes to know the true depths of thirst. In a quest to sate his hunger for some knowledge of the wide world, he is taken through a series of extraordinary, unearthly encounters that promise to change not only his life, but the course of civilization around him. A remarkable debut novel. $12.95/232-9

LUCY TAYLOR

UNNATURAL ACTS

"A topnotch collection..." —Science Fiction Chronicle

A remarkable debut volume from a provocative writer. *Unnatural Acts* plunges deep into the dark side of the psyche, far past all pleasantries and prohibitions, and brings to life a disturbing vision of erotic horror. Unrelenting angels and hungry gods play with souls and bodies in Taylor's murky cosmos: where heaven and hell are merely differences of perspective; where redemption and damnation lie behind the same shocking acts. $12.95/181-0

RICHARD KASAK BOOKS

SAMUEL R. DELANY

THE MOTION OF LIGHT IN WATER

"A very moving, intensely fascinating literary biography from an extraordinary writer. Thoroughly admirable candor and luminous stylistic precision; the artist as a young man and a memorable picture of an age."
—William Gibson

The first unexpurgated American edition of award-winning author Samuel R. Delany's riveting autobiography covers the early years of one of science fiction's most important voices. Delany paints a vivid and compelling picture of New York's East Village in the early '60s—a time of unprecedented social transformation. Startling and revealing, *The Motion of Light in Water* traces the roots of one of America's most innovative writers. $12.95/133-0

THE MAD MAN

For his thesis, graduate student John Marr researches the life and work of the brilliant Timothy Hasler: a philosopher whose career was cut tragically short over a decade earlier. Marr encounters numerous obstacles, as other researchers turn up evidence of Hasler's personal life that is deemed simply too unpleasant. Marr soon begins to believe that Hasler's death might hold some key to his own life as a gay man in the age of AIDS.

This new novel by Samuel R. Delany not only expands the parameters of what he has given us in the past, but fuses together two seemingly disparate genres of writing and comes up with something which is not comparable to any existing text of which I am aware.... What Delany has done here is take the ideas of Marquis de Sade one step further, by filtering extreme and obsessive sexual behavior through the sieve of post-modern experience....
—*Lambda Book Report*

Reads like a pornographic reflection of Peter Ackroyd's Chatterton *or A.S. Byatt's* Possession.... *Delany develops an insightful dichotomy between [his protagonist]'s two worlds: the one of cerebral philosophy and dry academia, the other of heedless, 'impersonal' obsessive sexual extremism. When these worlds finally collide ... the novel achieves a surprisingly satisfying resolution....* —*Publishers Weekly* $23.95/193-4

KATHLEEN K.

SWEET TALKERS

Here, for the first time, is the story behind the provocative advertisements and 970 prefixes. Kathleen K. opens up her diary for a rare peek at the day-to-day life of a phone sex operator—and reveals a number of secrets and surprises. Because far from being a sleazy, underground scam, the service Kathleen provides often speaks to the lives of its customers with a directness and compassion they receive nowhere else. $12.95/192-6

ROBERT PATRICK

TEMPLE SLAVE

...you must read this book. It draws such a tragic, and, in a way, noble portrait of Mr. Buono: It leads the reader, almost against his will, into a deep sympathy with this strange man who tried to comfort, to encourage and to feed both the worthy and the worthless... It is impossible not to mourn for this man—impossible not to praise this book.

—Quentin Crisp

This is nothing less than the secret history of the most theatrical of theaters, the most bohemian of Americans and the most knowing of queens. Patrick writes with a lush and witty abandon, as if this departure from the crafting of plays has energized him. Temple Slave *is also one of the best ways to learn what it was like to be fabulous, gay, theatrical and loved in a time at once more and less dangerous to gay life than our own.* —*Genre*

Temple Slave *tells the story of the Espresso Buono—the archetypal alternative performance space—and the talents who called it home.* $12.95/191-8

MELTDOWN!

EDITED BY CARO SOLES

**AN ANTHOLOGY OF EROTIC
SCIENCE FICTION AND DARK
FANTASY FOR GAY MEN**

RICHARD KASAK BOOKS

DAVID MELTZER
THE AGENCY TRILOGY

...'The Agency' is clearly Meltzer's paradigm of society; a mindless machine of which we are all 'agents' including those whom the machine supposedly serves.... —Norman Spinrad

With the Essex House edition of *The Agency* in 1968, the highly regarded poet David Meltzer took America on a trip into a hell of unbridled sexuality. The story of a supersecret, Orwellian sexual network, *The Agency* explored issues of erotic dominance and submission with an immediacy and frankness previously unheard of in American literature, as well as presented a vision of an America consumed and dehumanized by a lust for power. $12.95/216-7

SKIN TWO
THE BEST OF *SKIN TWO* Edited by Tim Woodward

For over a decade, *Skin Two* has served the international fetish community as a groundbreaking journal from the crossroads of sexuality, fashion, and art, *Skin Two* specializes in provocative, challenging essays by the finest writers working in the "radical sex" scene. Collected here are the articles and interviews that established the magazine's reputation. Including interviews with cult figures Tim Burton, Clive Barker and Jean Paul Gaultier. $12.95/130-6

CARO SOLES
MELTDOWN!
An Anthology of Erotic Science Fiction and Dark Fantasy for Gay Men

Editor Caro Soles has put together one of the most explosive, mind-bending collections of gay erotic writing ever published. *Meltdown!* contains the very best examples of this increasingly popular sub-genre: stories meant to shock and delight, to send a shiver down the spine and start a fire down below. An extraordinary volume, *Meltdown!* presents both new voices and provocative pieces by world-famous writers Edmund White and Samuel R. Delany.

$12.95/203-5

BIZARRE SEX
BIZARRE SEX AND OTHER CRIMES OF PASSION
Edited by Stan Tal

Stan Tal, editor of *Bizarre Sex*, Canada's boldest fiction publication, has culled the very best stories that have crossed his desk—and now unleashes them on the reading public in *Bizarre Sex and Other Crimes of Passion*. Over twenty small masterpieces of erotic shock make this one of the year's most unexpectedly alluring anthologies. Including such masters of erotic horror and fantasy as Edward Lee, Lucy Taylor and Nancy Kilpatrick, *Bizarre Sex and Other Crimes of Passion*, is a treasure-trove of arousing chills. $12.95/213-2

PAT CALIFIA
SENSUOUS MAGIC

A new classic, destined to grace the shelves of anyone interested in contemporary sexuality.

Sensuous Magic is clear, succinct and engaging even for the reader for whom S/M isn't the sexual behavior of choice.... Califia's prose is soothing, informative and non-judgmental—she both instructs her reader and explores the territory for them.... When she is writing about the dynamics of sex and the technical aspects of it, Califia is the Dr. Ruth of the alternative sexuality set.... —Lambda Book Report

Don't take a dangerous trip into the unknown—buy this book and know where you're going!—SKIN TWO $12.95/131-4

HUSTLING

A Gentleman's Guide to the Fine Art of Homosexual Prostitution

JOHN PRESTON

THE
JOY
SPOT

A RICHARD KASAK BOOK

MARCO VASSI

THE STONED APOCALYPSE

" *...Marco Vassi is our champion sexual energist.*"—VLS

During his lifetime, Marco Vassi was hailed as America's premier erotic writer and most worthy successor to Henry Miller. His work was praised by writers as diverse as Gore Vidal and Norman Mailer, and his reputation was worldwide. *The Stoned Apocalypse* is Vassi's autobiography, financed by his other ground-breaking erotic writing. $12.95/132-2

A DRIVING PASSION

While the late Marco Vassi was primarily known and respected as a novelist, he was also an effective and compelling speaker. *A Driving Passion* collects the wit and insight Vassi brought to his infamously revealing lectures, and distills the philosophy—including the concept of Metasex—that made him an underground sensation. An essential volume. $12.95/134-9

THE EROTIC COMEDIES

A collection of stories from America's premier erotic philosopher. Marco Vassi was a dedicated iconoclast, and *The Erotic Comedies* marked a high point in his literary career. Scathing and humorous, these stories reflect Vassi's belief in the power and primacy of Eros in American life, as well as his commitment to the elimination of personal repression through carnal indulgence. $12.95/136-5

THE SALINE SOLUTION

During the Sexual Revolution, Marco Vassi established himself as an intrepid explorer of an uncharted sexual landscape. During this time he also distinguished himself as a novelist, producing *The Saline Solution* to great acclaim. With the story of one couple's brief affair and the events that lead them to desperately reassess their lives, Vassi examines the dangers of intimacy in an age of freedom. $12.95/180-2

CHEA VILLANUEVA

JESSIE'S SONG

"*It conjures up the strobe-light confusion and excitement of urban dyke life, moving fast and all over the place, from NYC to Tucson to Miami to the Philippines; and from true love to wild orgies to swearing eternal celibacy and back. Told in letters, mainly about the wandering heart (and tongue) of writer and free spirit Pearly Does; written mainly by Mae-Mae Might, a sharp, down-to-earth but innocent-hearted Black Femme. Read about these dykes and you'll love them.*" —Rebecca Ripley

A rich collection of lesbian writing from this uncompromising author. Based largely upon her own experience, Villanueva's work is remarkable for its frankness, and delightful in its iconoclasm. Widely published in the alternative press, Villanueva is a writer to watch. Toeing no line, *Jessie's Song* is certain to redefine all notions of "mainstream" lesbian writing, and provide a reading experience quite unlike any other this year. $9.95/235-3

SHAR REDNOUR, EDITOR

VIRGIN TERRITORY

An anthology of writing about the most important moments of life. Tales of first-time sensual experiences, from the pens of some of America's most uninhibited literary women. No taboo is unbroken as these women tell the whole truth and nothing but, about their lives as sexual women in modern times.

Included in this daring volume are such cult favorites as Susie Bright, Shannon Bell, Bayla Travis, Carol Queen, Lisa Palac and others. They leave no act undescribed, and prove once and for all that "beginner's luck" is the very best kind to have! $12.95/238-8

TAILPIPE
TRUCKER

CLAY CALDWELL

BADBOY BOOKS

THE JOY SPOT *Phil Andros*

"Andros gives to the gay mind what Tom of Finland gives the gay eye—this is archetypal stuff. There's none better."   —*John F. Karr*, Manifest Reader

A classic from one of the founding fathers of gay porn. *The Joy Spot* looks at some of Andros' favorite types—cops, servicemen, truck drivers—and the sleaze they love. Nothing's too rough, and these men are always ready. So get ready to give it up—or have it taken by force! $5.95/**301-5**

THE ROPE ABOVE, THE BED BELOW *Jason Fury*

The irresistible Jason Fury returns! Once again, our built, blond hero finds himself in the oddest—and most compromising—positions imaginable. And his combination of heat and heart has made him one of gay erotica's most distinctive voices. $4.95/**269-8**

SUBMISSION HOLDS *Key Lincoln*

A bright talent unleashes his first collection of gay erotica. From tough to tender, the men between these covers stop at nothing to get what they want. These sweat-soaked tales show just how bad boys can get.... $4.95/**266-3**

SKIN DEEP *Bob Vickery*

Skin Deep contains so many varied beauties no one will go away unsatisfied. From Daddy's Boys to horny go-go studs, no tantalizing morsel of manflesh is overlooked—or left unexplored! Beauty may be only skin deep, but a handful of beautiful skin is a tempting proposition. $4.95/**265-5**

ANIMAL HANDLERS *Jay Shaffer*

Another volume from a master of scorching fiction. In Shaffer's world, each and every man finally succumbs to the animal urges deep inside. And if there's any creature that promises a wild time, it's a beast who's been caged for far too long.... $4.95/**264-7**

RAHM *Tom Bacchus*

A volume spanning the many ages of hardcore queer lust—from Creation to the modern day. The overheated imagination of Tom Bacchus brings to life an extraordinary assortment of characters, from the Father of Us All to the cowpoke next door, the early gay literati to rude, queercore mosh rats. No one is better than Bacchus at staking out sexual territory with a swagger and a sly grin. $5.95/**315-5**

REVOLT OF THE NAKED *D. V. Sadero*

In a distant galaxy, there are two classes of humans: Freemen and Nakeds. Freemen are full citizens in this system, which allows for the buying and selling of Nakeds at whim. Nakeds live only to serve their Masters, and obey every sexual order with haste and devotion. Until the day of revolution—when an army of sex toys rises in anger.... By the author of *In the Alley*. $4.95/**261-2**

WHiPs *Victor Terry*

Connoisseurs of gay writing have known Victor Terry's work for some time. With *WHiPs*, Terry joins Badboy's roster at last. Cruising for a hot man? You'd better be, because one way or another, these WHiPs—officers of the Wyoming Highway Patrol—are gonna pull you over for a little impromptu interrogation.... $4.95/**254-X**

PRISONERS OF TORQUEMADA *Torsten Barring*

The infamously unsparing Torsten Barring (*The Switch, Peter Thornwell, Shadowman*) weighs in with another volume sure to push you over the edge. How cruel *is* the "therapy" practiced at Casa Torquemada? Rest assured that Barring is just the writer to evoke such steamy malevolence. $4.95/**252-3**

BADBOY BOOKS

SORRY I ASKED *Dave Kinnick*

Up close and very personal! Unexpurgated interviews with gay porn's rank and file. Haven't you wondered what it's like to be in porn pictures? Kinnick, video reviewer for *Advocate Men*, gets personal with the guys behind (and under) the "stars," and reveals the dirt and details of the porn business.

$4.95/3090-3

THE SEXPERT *Edited by Pat Califia*

For many years now, the sophisticated gay man has known that he can turn to one authority for answers to virtually any question on the subject of man-to-man intimacy and sexual performance. Straight from the pages of *Advocate Men* comes The Sexpert! From penis size to toy care, bar behavior to AIDS awareness, The Sexpert responds to real concerns with uncanny wisdom and a razor wit.

$4.95/3034-2

DEREK ADAMS

MY DOUBLE LIFE

Every man leads a double life, dividing his hours between the mundanities of the day and the outrageous pursuits of the night. In this, his second collection of stories, the author of *Boy Toy* and creator of sexy P.I. Miles Diamond shines a little light on what men do when no one's looking. Derek Adams proves, once again, that he's the ultimate chronicler of our wicked ways. $5.95/314-7

BOY TOY

Poor Brendan Callan—sent to the Brentwood Academy against his will, he soon finds himself the guinea pig of a crazed geneticist. Brendan becomes irresistibly alluring—a talent designed for endless pleasure, but coveted by others with the most unsavory motives.

$4.95/260-4

CLAY CALDWELL

STUD SHORTS

"If anything, Caldwell's charm is more powerful, his nostalgia more poignant, the horniness he captures more sweetly, achingly acute than ever."
—Aaron Travis

A new collection of this legendary writer's latest sex-fiction. With his customary candor, Caldwell tells all about cops, cadets, truckers, farmboys (and many more) in these dirty jewels. $5.95/320-1

QUEERS LIKE US

A very special delivery from one of gay erotica's premier talents. For years the name Clay Caldwell has been synonymous with the hottest, most finely crafted gay tales available. *Queers Like Us* is one of his best: the story of a randy mailman's trek through a landscape of willing, available studs. $4.95/262-0

CLAY CALDWELL/LARS EIGHNER

QSFX2

A volume of the wickedest, wildest, other-worldliest yarns from two master storytellers. Caldwell and Eighner take a trip to the furthest reaches of the sexual imagination, sending back stories proving that as much as things change, one thing will always remain the same.... $5.95/278-7

LARS EIGHNER

WHISPERED IN THE DARK

Hailed by critics, Lars Eighner continues to produce gay fiction whose quality rivals the best in the genre. *Whispered in the Dark* demonstrates Eighner's unique combination of strengths: poetic descriptive power, an unfailing ear for dialogue, and a finely tuned feeling for the nuances of male passion.

$5.95/286-8

BADBOY BOOKS

AMERICAN PRELUDE

Praised by the *New York Times*, Eighner is widely recognized as one of our best, most exciting gay writers. What the *Times* won't admit, however, is that he is also one of gay erotica's true masters. Scalding heat blends with wry emotion in this red-blooded bedside volume. $4.95/170-5

LARRY TOWNSEND

BEWARE THE GOD WHO SMILES

A torrid time-travel tale from one of gay erotica's most notorious writers. Two lusty young Americans are transported to ancient Egypt—where they are embroiled in regional warfare and taken as slaves by marauding barbarians. The key to escape from this brutal bondage lies in their own rampant libidos, and urges as old as time itself. $5.95/321-X

RUN, LITTLE LEATHER BOY

The classic story of one man's sexual awakening. A chronic underachiever, Wayne seems to be going nowhere. When he is sent abroad, Wayne soon finds himself bored with the everyday and increasingly drawn to the masculine intensity of a dark sexual underground. Back in print to inspire a new generation, *Run, Little Leather Boy* is a favorite with gay readers. $4.95/143-8

SEXUAL ADV. OF SHERLOCK HOLMES

What Conan Doyle didn't know about the legendary sleuth. Holmes's most satisfying adventures, from the unexpurgated memoirs of the faithful Mr. Watson. "A Study in Scarlet" is transformed to expose Mrs. Hudson as a man in drag, the Diogenes Club as an S/M arena, and clues only Sherlock Holmes could piece together. $4.95/3097-0

AARON TRAVIS

BIG SHOTS

Two fierce tales in one electrifying volume. In *Beirut*, Travis tells the story of ultimate military power and erotic subjugation; *Kip*, Travis' hypersexed and sinister take on film noir, appears in unexpurgated form for the first time—including the final, overwhelming chapter. One of the rawest titles we've ever published. $4.95/112-8

SLAVES OF THE EMPIRE

"[A] wonderful mythic tale. Set against the backdrop of the exotic and powerful Roman Empire, this wonderfully written novel explores the timeless questions of light and dark in male sexuality. Travis has shown himself expert in manipulating the most primal themes and images. The locale may be the ancient world, but these are the slaves and masters of our time...." —John Preston $4.95/3054-7

JOHN PRESTON

TALES FROM THE DARK LORD

Twelve stunning works from the man called "the Dark Lord of gay erotica." The ritual of lust and surrender is explored in all its manifestations in this triumph of authority and vision from the Dark Lord! One of our most popular collections. $5.95/323-6

MR. BENSON

A classic novel from a time when there was no limit to what a man could dream of doing. Jamie is led down the path of erotic enlightenment by the magnificent Mr. Benson, learning to accept cruelty as love, anguish as affection, and this man as his master. $4.95/3041-5

HARD CANDY

SKYDIVING ON CHRISTOPHER STREET *Stan Leventhal*
"Positively addictive."   —Dennis Cooper
Aside from a hateful job, a hateful apartment, a hateful world and an increasingly hateful lover, life seems, well, *all right* for the protagonist of Stan Leventhal's latest novel, *Skydiving on Christopher Street*. Having already lost most of his friends to AIDS, how could things get any worse? But things soon do, and he's forced to endure much more....   **$6.95/287-6**

THE GAUDY IMAGE *William Talsman*
"To read **The Gaudy Image** now is not simply to enjoy a great novel or an artifact of gay history, it is to see first-hand the very issues of identity and positionality with which gay men and gay culture were struggling in the decades before Stonewall. For what Talsman is dealing with...is the very question of how we conceive ourselves gay."—from the Introduction by Michael Bronski
$6.95/263-9

GAY COSMOS *Lars Eighner*
A thought-provoking volume from widely acclaimed author Lars Eighner. Eighner has distinguished himself as not only one of America's most accomplished new voices, but a solid-seller—his erotic titles alone have become bestsellers and classics of the genre. Eighner describes *Gay Cosmos* as being a volume of "essays on the place, meaning, and purpose of homosexuality in the Universe, and gay sexuality on human societies." A title sure to appeal not only to Eighner's gay fans, but the many converts who first encountered his moving nonfiction work.   **$6.95/236-1**

FELICE PICANO

AMBI*DEXTROUS*
The touching and funny memories of childhood—as only Felice Picano could tell them. **Ambi*dextrous*** tells the story of Picano's youth in the suburbs of New York during the '50's. Beginning at age eleven, Picano's "memoir in the form of a novel" tells all: home life, school face-offs, the ingenuous sophistications of his first sexual steps. In three years' time, he's had his first gay fling—and is on his way to becoming the writer about whom the *L.A. Herald Examiner* said "[he] can run the length of experience from the lyrical to the lewd without missing a beat."   **$6.95/275-2**

MEN WHO LOVED ME
In 1966, at the tender-but-bored age of twenty-two, Felice Picano abandoned New York, determined to find true love in Europe. Almost immediately, he encounters Djanko—an exquisite prodigal who sweeps Felice off his feet with the endless string of extravagant parties, glamorous clubs and glittering premieres that made up Rome's *dolce vita*. When the older (slightly) and wiser (vastly) Picano returns to New York at last, he plunges into the city's thriving gay community—experiencing the frenzy and heartbreak that came to define Greenwich Village society in the 1970s. Lush and warm, *Men Who Loved Me* is a matchless portrait of an unforgettable decade.   **$6.95/274-4**